ALSO BY KEN WELLS

Meely LaBauve

JUNIOR'S LEG

JUNIOR'S LEG

a novel

Ken Wells

random house · new york

Copyright © 2001 by Ken Wells

All rights reserved under International and Pan-American Copyright Conventions. Published in the United States by Random House, Inc., New York, and simultaneously in Canada by Random House of Canada Limited, Toronto.

RANDOM HOUSE and colophon are registered trademarks of Random House, Inc.

Library of Congress Cataloging-in-Publication Data
Wells, Ken.
Junior's leg: a novel / Ken Wells.
p. cm.
ISBN 0-375-50526-1 (alk. paper)
1. Organized crime—Fiction.   2. Louisiana—Fiction.   3. Amputees—Fiction.   4. Cajuns—Fiction.   I. Title.
PS3573.E4923 J8 2001
813'.54—dc21   2001019393

Random House website address: www.atrandom.com
Printed in the United States of America on acid-free paper
2   4   6   8   9   7   5   3
First Edition

BOOK DESIGN BY DEBORAH KERNER-DANCING BEARS DESIGN

TO MY DAD, WILLIAM REXFORD WELLS

DECEMBER 3, 1920–JULY 17, 2000

AS A MARINE, HUSBAND, AND FATHER,

SEMPER FI

Acknowledgments

To the Cranks, notably Carrie Dolan, Bill Grueskin, Dan Kelly, and Charlie McCoy, for their unalloyed camaraderie, helpful good humor, and support over many a moon; to Lorraine at Ridgewood Station, angel of caffeinated mercy; to Kim Strassel of *The Wall Street Journal* for a creative suggestion delivered in the elevator one day; to the careful early readers of this work, notably Becky Quick and Elizabeth Seay of the *WSJ* and Mary Patterson out in Houston, Texas, for their sage input and encouragement; to T. Lyons in Houma, Louisiana, who knows his muscle cars; to my roux of Louisiana friends—Al Delahaye at Nicholls State University, Judy and Donald Landry and Jerry and Shannon Hermann of Houma, Steve and Cherry Fisher May and Del and Anita Leggett of Lafayette—for their ongoing generous favors to this writer and his work; to Delbert, in particular, for sharing his keen knowledge of the Oil Patch; to the Wells brothers—Bill, Persh, Chris, and Bob—who help me keep one foot in the bayou and my mind in the swamps; to my agents, Joe Regal and Timothy Seldes at Russell & Volkening, who encouraged the leap of faith necessary to tackle Junior; to the magnificent Lee Boudreaux at Random House—a better book editor is not to be found, anywhere; to my daughters, Sara and Becca, who remind me what fun this all is, and to my wife, Lisa, for her smart and unflagging support and encouragement over many a moon.

Author's Note

The Cajun accent is an American peculiarity; Cajuns don't sound like the French speaking English, nor do they borrow much from the Southern drawl, though they are fond of Southern idioms. Many Cajuns also like to mix Cajun French expressions into their English sentences. In *Junior's Leg,* I've made an effort to bring readers the flavor of Cajun dialect under the theory that it would be impossible to write about Cajuns any other way. And, with readers in mind, I've also included, at the end of this book, a glossary and pronunciation guide of Cajun terms and surnames.

—K.W.

JUNIOR'S LEG

1

I seen her comin' up the steps. It was about dark, though, hell—night, day, it's all the same to me.

For all I knew, she could have been a ghost or a robber.

Ghost or robber, I just laid there on the sofa watchin' her come. Either one could cut my sorry throat and what could I do about it?

Shuh, nuttin'.

If she's gonna cut my throat, I hope she's got a sharp knife.

I'm drunk, or close to it. I am what I am. What I always am—*goddam Junior Guidry.*

And anyway, the door ain't locked. Nobody comes out here to this miserable godforsaken place. Ain't nuttin' out here but me and the swamp and nootra-rats and mosquitoes and a few damn ole hoot owls.

Before I pawned my 12-gauge, I shot me a few of them noisy bastids. You'd think they'd learn, but they don't.

The ole crook who put in these lots and sold me this wreck of a trailer calls this place Hackberry Bend Acres. But the ole Cajuns call this place *Mauvais Bois*—the bad woods—and I know why. This bit of high ground I'm on ain't nuttin' but a finger in the eye of the Great Catahoula Swamp. Get a hurricane blowin' through here and this trailer will be a submarine headin' for the Gulf of Mexico and I'll be up to my ass in water moccasins. Hell, there's probably a dozen of 'em crawlin' around under this trailer right now.

When the girl come in the door, it squeaked on rusty hinges. She didn't knock. She just come in, slow and sneaky like a dog that's been shot at a few times. She looked pale as the belly of a *sac-à-lait*. She had a small suitcase in her hand.

I looked around, not really able to move my head 'cause I had the spins perty bad. I thought about throwin' my leg at her. I looked around for it and I thought I saw it in a heap in the corner wit' the rest of the garbage—in between my busted-up hip boots and that greasy spare carburetor for my truck and a coupla cans of motor oil that have leaked all over that stack of *Playboy* magazines my podnah Roddy give me.

That oil has totally ruined Miss July's knockers, which is a shame 'cause she had some good ones, lemme tell ya.

I ain't worn my leg in a while. Hoppin's okay when you get used to it and you ain't got far to go.

Hell, I've even crawled a few places when I was too drunk to stand.

If I coulda got to my leg, I'da damned well tried to bean her wit' it. I used to be a good ballplayer. I could hit a ball to Kingdom Come and throw a strike to home plate from deep center field.

There was a bottle on the floor just below me and I coulda

tried to cold-cock her with that. But it still had whiskey in it. I didn't know when Roddy might be back wit' more.

He's a flaky bastid, Roddy is.

Anyways, I wadn't gonna waste good liquor on a damn ghost. Or a robber neither.

What the hell do I care about a robber? I'm so friggin' broke, even the mice and roaches that crawl around my kitchen have gone on the Relief. Them mice I can live wit'. Them roaches bug me.

Everything shorts out in this ratty trailer. One time I got so mad at them roaches that I smeared the bare bulb of my kitchen light with peanut butter. I waited about an hour and then I come in and threw the switch. That bulb popped and fussed and I electrocuted about twenty of them bastids—they fell to the floor like rain.

The girl come in and looked around. She slumped down in a corner over by my leg where it was already dark. She slumped down there and disappeared in the dark, though I heard her cryin'. I said get the hell out of my house. Get the hell out, damn you!

She stopped cryin'. For all I know, she stopped breathin' and I wouldn'ta cared whether she did or didn't.

The trailer got quiet.

I reached down for my bottle and I took me a big swallow. The whiskey rolled down my chin and onto my chest.

I took me another. A good one, this time.

The whiskey rolled down my throat and into my belly like a hot diesel chuggin' for New Awlins. I wiped my mouth and closed my eyes. The spins stopped and dark come down all around me.

Them hoot owls started up just to aggravate me and them crickets put up a racket in the *roseaus* and some big ole bullfrog started barkin' out across the swamp. But I didn't pay 'em no mind.

I closed my eyes tighter and headed on down to hell.

2

I dream about it all the time.

Time to go to work, Junior. Get off the damn boat, son. Go on. Go on. The crane's all fucked up so we ain't goin' up in the basket. We goin' up the ladder.

Go on, damn you! Get your sorry ass up there on that rig!

Oh, to hell wit' you, Armentau. It's damn rough out there. Must be pitchin' six foot.

Shuh, what, you chicken, Junior? Man, why the hell they send crybabies out to do men's work? Ehn, can you tell me that?

Armentau gives me one of them looks, the kind he knows I hate.

I say Armentau, you flea-dick, get off my ass. I got a hangover bigger than the Fourth of July, cain't you see that? If you're so hot to get up on that rig, then go on. Go on, I dare you.

I hate the skinny li'l prick. He's liable to stick a knife in my back one day. There's a few people who might be glad he done it, too.

Armentau slides past me and says pussy boy just loud enough so he knows I heard it. He gives me a shoulder, then steps out the hatch of the crewboat into the rain. It's blowin' out there like a doggone hurricane.

The rain's comin' in sideways—rain that could take the hide off a dog.

There's a long iron ladder that goes up to the landin' platform on the rig. Armentau wobbles like a drunk out on the deck but the skipper guns the engine and eases the boat forward and damn if Armentau don't make the ladder in three or four big steps. He climbs up on the rig proud as some monkey at the Audubon Zoo, which is just what he looks like. The skipper guns the boat in reverse and we go slidin' backward up a big swell so we don't bash the platform. That sumbitch is ninety-five foot of hard steel risin' above the Gulf.

I feel so doggone bad. My head's got a gator clamped to it. There's a sack of crawfish that have got loose and are crawlin' around in my gut, havin' supper.

I don't even 'member las' night. Well, not after the sixteenth beer.

But that bastid Armentau pisses me off. I'm gonna make it up on the rig and kick that greasy sumbitch into the Gulf. When he hollers for a life ring, I'm gonna throw a pipe wrench down there.

Grab *that,* Armentau!

I feel the boat slip into forward again for another pass at the ladder. I barge out.

The first step ain't right.

The boat pitches up on a wave like a spooked mule and I'm flung sideways. I bang into the deck rail and almost go over the side. Every bit of air's been popped out of my lungs. I spin around and grab for iron but the rail's as slippery as fried *boudin*. I'm knocked backwards and then the boat dances out from under me and I spin around again just in time to see the ladder.

I'm goin' into that sucker like a linebacker headfirst and I put out my hands to break the fall.

I slam into the ladder and I know I've busted my left wrist good but I grab on to a rung wit' my right hand and I'm on the damn thing, even if it weren't perty. I steady myself and reach up for the next rung.

I don't even see the boat pitchin' my way on a big swell.

I've got my right leg up on the next rung but the crewboat pitches forward and bashes into the ladder and there's a sound like the devil sawin' on a tin roof.

The bow catches my left leg and I hear every damn bone crack.

I know my knee's been crushed, like a bull redfish crushes a blue crab before it swallows it whole.

The crewboat pitches down and rises up again and I think the monster is just gonna wipe me off the ladder like a mosquito slapped off the wall. But it misses me the second time and scrapes up against a fender of the rig and I'm hangin' there by one arm like a baboon and some bastid is yellin' and the boat roars and finally backs away.

A cloud of diesel comes blowin' in my face.

It's a damn good thing I'm strong as I am.

I'm hangin' on and I'm lookin' down at the water. I see somethin' floatin' down there.

The Gulf is as rough and gray as the sky and then it's gray and red. There's a firehose sprayin' red and then I goddam *do* know what I see down there.

It's my leg.

Some sumbitch has got me by the wrist, by my bad one, and I'm risin' slow as the day moon and what's left of my leg is gushin' like an oil well that's blown its choke. And I realize I don't feel a single friggin' thing. I cain't figger it out. I can suddenly see everything that's happened to me—it's all bein' played back like some movie up at the Bijou in Ville Canard. It's like I've been picked up and thrown onto the screen. I ain't scared. I ain't worried. I'm just watchin' my leg fall into the drink.

Then I realize it's Armentau who's helped pull me up and I can smell the salty Gulf and a whiff of diesel and the oily metal catwalk and the stale cigarettes on Armentau's breath and the shrimp gumbo he ate for supper last night. I gotta look into his ugly face and even that hard sumbitch's got fear in his eyes.

I'm lookin' at him and he's lookin' down past me.

And he says Junior, a shark just come up and ate your leg.

3

I wake up in a cold sweat. I don't know how long I've been sleepin'. Sometimes it feels like years.

I've been down there in my dreams chasin' Armentau around wit' a hatchet. I ain't caught him yet but I hope I will one night.

I wish I could dream about nooky instead of ugly-ass Armentau. He looks like one of them oyster fish the trawlers dredge up from the bottom of Bayou Go-to-Hell—I'm not lyin'.

It's light in the trailer, enough so that maybe it's afternoon.

I come up slow and I'd forgot about the woman and, what the hell, I thought she was prob'ly a dream. But there she is, starin' at me, her face up close. She smells like dried sweat but she's got the sweet breath of a girl.

She's starin' at me and she is a damned freaky site. She is the color of fish bones and her hair is white—or closer to silver—and it's pulled back and tied up in a mop on top of her head. She's got the long, pale neck of a *gros bec*. Her face is freckled as a bird dog.

There ain't a line on it, though she has a nasty purple bruise on her right cheek. She could be a child or a woman—she looks like both.

She's wearin' a blue dress wit' buttons up the front. She ain't got no eyebrows that I can see or else they're so white they're invisible. She's got the scared eyes of a rabbit after you've wrassled it out the cage and are about to break its neck.

Them rabbits always know when they're about to become *sauce piquante.*

The first thing I think is that she must be some *traiteur* sent to put the *gris-gris* on my ass. Maybe the LaBauves, them trouble-makin' *sabine* bastids, sent her!

For some reason, I find this damn funny. I don't know why them slippery sumbitches are still a burr up my butt. I ain't even seen that squirrelly-ass Meely LaBauve in ten, twelve years.

I wanna yell at her or take a swing at her but I know it's hopeless. There's somethin' strange about the way I wake up these days. I feel like a big redfish tryin' to swim to the surface. I see some minnow up there swimmin' slow against the sun and he's mine for the takin'. But hard as I swim I cain't ever get to the top in time.

The doc, last time I went, said it was my liver. He said Junior, you only thirty years old but you got the liver of a hundred-year-old man. You better straighten up or you'll be gone in a few years.

I said well, Doc, that might be true but I got the dick of a five-year-old mule to make up for it, and I laughed even if he didn't.

I see the ghost is holdin' somethin' in her hands.

She says I fixed you some coffee, mister.

I wonder where the hell she found coffee in this house.

I also wonder if I got a voice. I do, but it takes me a while to find it.

I say I don't want no coffee. What the hell you doin' in my house?

She don't answer. She just looks at me with them freaky rabbit eyes.

She says you want some breakfast?

I don't eat breakfast.

Why not?

'Cause I drink it. Ha, ha! I drink my sumbitchin' breakfast!

I reach for my bottle but it ain't there.

I say where is it?

I threw it out.

Goddam you! Who the hell—

Somehow she sees I cain't move yet. She puts a hand over my mouth to shush me. She puts her other hand on my forehead.

Her hands are cool as November rain.

She says mister, you smell bad. Have you messed yourself?

I wish I had my gun so I could shoot her between the eyes.

She says how come you live like this? Don't you have anybody who cares about you?

I find my right hand and I swat at her. It's a pitiful swat I got to admit. She don't just look like a damn rabbit. She's quick as one, too.

She ducks under my swing and grabs me by the wrist.

Her eyes have got narrow and she says don't try to hit me, mister. It's not right. I was just asking you a question. I'm sorry if I came in without permission but I thought this trailer was empty and there's nothing I would do to hurt you. I was just asking you 'cause I know about some hard things. I know one of the hard things is that it's hard to live without the love you need.

Even in my state I realize I haven't heard such bullshit since catechism class in the fift' grade. I say what are you, some kinda religious freak? You one of them Jehovah's Witnesses comin' here to give me a Bible? Last one I got I used for toilet paper! How'd you sumbitches find me way out here in the swamp, ehn?

She looks at me and her eyes have got suddenly soft. She says I'm not anything at all but a child of God. And so are you.

I say lady, would you bring me my hip boots from over there? The shit's gettin' deep in here. You gotta be one of those nosy damned Holy Rollers or whatever they call 'em. Now get the hell out of my house before I sic my mean ole Catahoula Cur dog on you. He'll pull you right out of this trailer and drown you like a rat in the bayou, I guarantee. I feed him baby alligators for breakfast.

She stares at me for a long while, then says if there's a dog living here, I sure don't smell him and he sure didn't bark when I came in.

This does stump me for a second.

Then she bends down and pins my arms down under her and pulls close. And I can smell her, sweat and skin and breath, and I realize this is the closest I've been to a woman in a long, long while.

It might be the one thing I miss.

She keeps my arms pinned down under her and says in a soft voice, mister, I would leave but I've got nowhere to go.

I laid up in the hospital for ninety-seven days after the accident.

When they brought me in to Ville Canard on the Big Tex chopper, people said I'd lost so much blood that there were dead people in Myo Chauvin's funeral home who looked suntanned next to me.

Brady Boudreaux, the mud engineer on the rig, rode wit' me and it's a good thing, too. We were practically flyin' through a hurricane and at one point we hit an air pocket and for about ten seconds the chopper was flyin' upside down. Good thing I was strapped to a gurney 'cause when the chopper flipped over, the gurney was flung against the ceilin' and the only reason I didn't bash my brains out is 'cause poor ole Brady was the cushion I landed on.

The only reason he didn't have his brains knocked out is that he was still wearin' his hard hat. That poor sumbitch said he felt like he'd been sucker-punched by Sonny Liston. He was knocked out for about three minutes and his hard hat had a dent in it so big you could eat gumbo out of it.

Lucky he come to when he did 'cause my tourniquet had slipped off and I was spoutin' blood again like a hog stuck for the *cochon de lait*. Brady got it tied on again but by that time that poor bastid looked like he'd been scuba divin' in the blood tank at Autin's Slaughter House, I'm not lyin'.

People think I'm a jerk but I did buy Brady and his wife a damn nice ribeye dinner at the Oaks after I got out the hospital and got all my money. The pilot of the chopper, too, though I forget his name.

Anyway, by the time they got me to hospital they figgered I was a goner. Momma come by wit' my li'l sister Irene, though Daddy was drunk someplace as usual and they couldn't find him for two days. He never did come to the hospital but once the whole time I was there. He never has forgiven me for kickin' his ass all those years ago. Well, it was either his ass or mine.

They brought some ole priest from the rectory in town to give me the las' rites 'cause they figgered I wouldn't make it till Father Giroir, the Catahoula Bayou priest, could come. But I knew that was b.s. I knew I wadn't gonna die, otherwise I might've taken the las' rites serious. Momma had put the Cat'lic Church on me when I was young and it's just like a tattoo, you cain't never totally erase it.

Hell, right then and there I didn't feel all that bad, though late that night I landed hard and there wadn't enough morphine in South Loosiana to kill the pain that wrapped itself 'round my ass. My leg was in the belly of a shark someplace but doggone if it didn't feel like it was still there and bein' chewed on slow by a six-pack of gators.

The docs later said Junior, you were in shock and people in shock sometimes don't feel their pain right away.

Shock or not, I tried to tell Father not to waste his water.

He said Joseph Guidry, do you now renounce Satan and all his followers?

I wouldn't answer.

He said Joseph Guidry, are you sorry for your sins?

I wouldn't answer.

He said Joseph Guidry, do you take Jesus Christ as your savior?

I wadn't gonna answer that one, neither.

But the priest wouldn't go away and kept sprinklin' me wit' holy water and layin' some of that Latin mumbo-jumbo on me and though I couldn't feel my leg one bit, the drip of that water down my forehead really bugged me. Bugged me!

I was so aggravated that finally I said Father, if you can find me a beer and a ride to the Hollywood Bayou Go-Go Bar, I'll say okay to each and every one of them questions. I mean it.

Momma and Irene were so *honte,* they ran out the room.

Anyway, the priest didn't waste no more holy water on ole Junior.

When I refused to die, they took me to the operatin' room and spent seven hours sewin' up my stump four inches above my knee. They pumped a bargeful of blood into me. And I laid there for two weeks in intensive care while they stuck me wit' morphine and I moaned and screamed and threatened to kill every damn body who done this to me, especially that flea-dick Armentau.

Hell, I think for a while they thought I *was* the devil. They had me strapped to the bed and still them nurses wouldn't come in my room wit'out some orderly to hold my head down so I couldn't spit at 'em or try to bite 'em. I kept tryin' to ride them ole boys so one of 'em would be stupid enough to untie my straps and we could fight man to man. I figgered even one-legged and shot full of dope, I could handle two or three of them soft bastids. I wanted me some blood.

I mean, what kind of man is an orderly, anyways? Hell, I'd starve before I'd empty somebody's bedpan or change some geezer's diapers.

But one of them orderlies, a fat-ass guy named Gaudet, sent the nurses out one night and leaned over me and said Junior, you're a big, ugly mad dog and I'd like to give you the satisfaction you want but I cain't 'cause the hospital would fire me for beatin' up a helpless gimp like you. But mad dogs oughta be put down and I know about some stuff locked up in the nurses' closet down the hall. If I jab your sorry ass in the middle of the night wit' a needle full of that shit, you'll be dead in three minutes, and no-body will know what I done. Not a soul.

I looked at him hard and I figgered he was bullshittin' me 'cause I've come up against the murderin' kind and he didn't look the part. But just in case, I shut my mouth and stopped spittin' at or tryin' to bite the nurses. It's one thing to be mean but, like I al-ways say, ole Junior's momma drowned all the dumb ones. But I put Gaudet on the list of people whose asses I was gonna kick big time after I got out the hospital.

After a while, the pain turned and my stump started to heal and they put me in a regular room and come around talkin' about therapy and stuff. They fitted me wit' a wooden leg and made me walk on it and I surprised them all by practically runnin' on that sumbitch the second day out.

Shuh, I tole them nurses I was ready to get the hell out of the hospital and go zydeco dancin' and did they wanna come? C'mon, girls, *laissez les bon temps rouler!*

By then, though, most of them nurses were scared of me and I guess I couldn't blame 'em. But there was this one li'l gal, Vera Verret, who come late to my case and had missed my devil state, and she thought ole Junior here was a doggone comedian, and good-lookin', too, which I damn shore used to be. She worked the late shift and she'd come in nights and, man, that girl was a flirt.

They'd cut my morphine down low by this time but I still got a nice li'l buzz out of it and I hadn't had no nooky since God first made the *choupique* and that Vera had a fine behind, lemme tell you. She'd come in and flirt and I'd flirt back and one night she come in and shut the door and pulled the curtain way around my bed and said Junior, I gotta give you your treatments, boy.

Then she took out a tube of somethin' or other—KY Jell-O I think it was called—and smeared a big gob of it on her right hand and reached right up under my hospital gown and grabbed me you-know-where and said Junior, now you tell Nurse Vera if this starts to hurt.

Doggone!

I said come close, darlin', and she did and she even put one foot up on my bed and I reached over and lifted her nurse's skirt and that girl had left her draws someplace. That girl was so wet I thought I might catch me a catfish in there—serious!

But she stepped away and said Junior, no noise and no penetration but you can play with my clitoris.

Hell, to be honest, I wadn't totally shore what a clitoris was since nobody I know ever called it that. But by that time I was like a drillin' bit that had hit pay dirt and I blew about the third time she went up and down.

Me and ole Vera had a good thang goin' on—good!—but one

night she started to go all soft on me and ax me had I ever been in love and had I ever considered marriage. That kind of junk.

She was fine and sweet and smart, too; plus them nurses make doggone good money. If I'da married that girl, I coulda been fixed up real good—shuh, maybe I would'na had to work at all, even if I hadn't gotten rich off my leg.

But I'd already had me two wives and I wadn't even sure I was divorced from the second one. So I tole her that and she got all *boude'd* and said that was sad 'cause people thought I was a bad person but she knew I really wadn't and I deserved somebody special to look after me. But she was a good Cat'lic and she could never marry a divorced man and would I think about tryin' to get an annulment?

Lawd. I hated to tell the girl, but what I knew of the Cat'lic Church, most rich people have a hard time gettin' one annulment. No way was a backslidin' rig hand like me gonna get two.

I said baby, there's somethin' I think about all the time, too, but it ain't no annulment, and I pulled her close and I run my hand up her skirt and went right for the money 'cause by this time I damn well knew what a clitoris was. She said don't, Junior, I'm serious, and tried to push me away but I pulled her down on my bed and wrassled up her skirt and started kissin' her on the neck and was in the process of shuckin' my hospital gown when she walloped me.

That girl punched like a roughneck!

Anyway, I let her go 'cause I ain't never been so hard up that I had to force a woman to give me some. Plus I was afraid she'd scream and then that big-ass Gaudet would come in here and try to stick a needle full of poison in my butt. She got up in a huff and straightened her nurse's outfit and stormed out wit'out sayin' one single word and when she slammed the door as hard as she did, I knew she was never comin' back.

I was right 'cause the next night there was a different nurse, a sour hag named Thelma, who tole me Vera had got herself transferred to the baby ward.

Now, ole Junior here has done some stupid things in his life but I gotta say that one ranks right up there wit' the real big-time boners 'cause I knew none of them other nurses was gonna come in every night and grease my gator. Hell, it turned out I still had twenty-one days to go in the hospital and I bet I broke the world record for jackin' off in a hospital bed.

That was about my only satisfaction, 'cept knowin' that fat-ass Gaudet had to change the sheets.

Anyway, I finally got out the hospital and was feelin' perty doggone good. Momma wanted to take me home but, hell, since Daddy had mostly ignored me the whole time I was in the hospital, I wadn't gonna have nuttin' to do wit' him.

I had my own li'l rent shack on the edge of town 'cause I already had to give one house and a real nice double-wide trailer to my two ex-wives. But I didn't wanna go home—hell, no. I was dyin' for a damn beer and I also didn't want nobody to think that Junior Guidry, just 'cause he'd got a peg leg, had turned into a pussy boy.

So the first thing I did was go to Oncale's Dime Store on Ville Canard Square and bought a pair of scissors and chopped my left blue-jean leg off so my peg leg would show through. Then I headed for the Alibi, a bar an easy walk from the square. I went in and sat at the bar and ordered a beer and then another and then another.

Perty soon, some ole boys come in who I could tell had

just come from seven days workin' offshore. They musta been diesel mechanics 'cause they smelled like they'd been swimmin' in motor oil and they were whoopin' it up and lookin' at the barmaids like they might try to hop 'em before they even had their first beer. I'd already talked to one of them barmaids—Wanda somebody or other—and I could tell they'd be wastin' their time wit' her.

They got three kinds of barmaids in the world—them that'll do you for money, them that'll do you 'cause they think you might be their ticket out the rathole they workin' in, and them that wouldn't do you for all the money in the world.

My second wife, Alma, she was the second kind. Shuh, I got her out of the bar, awright, but her problem was that she thought marryin' me would get *me* out of the bar, too.

Ole Wanda here was the last kind, even though she was a damn fine-lookin' girl. Damn fine.

Anyway, them ole boys come in and scooched up to the bar next to me and perty soon one of them looks at me and looks at my leg and says doggone, podnah, what the hell happened to your leg?

He wadn't sayin' it bad, I knew that. But I had a point to make so I said what the hell is it to you what happened to my leg? Why don't you be a good girl and mind your own business, ehn?

He says hey, look podnah, I ain't tryin' to make trouble. You look like maybe you've had some bad luck and could use a beer.

I said well, I can buy my own damn beer and I want you to stop starin' at my leg like you some dog plannin' to hump it.

That's all it took.

That sumbitch come off the bar stool after me but I'd practiced this in the hospital.

I whupped off my leg and I took him down with a backhanded swing—caught him right across the throat and knocked his wind out. That leg's tapered just like a bat.

Hell, them other ole boys were about to pile on, and there were about six of 'em, so that woulda been my ass. But the bar owner, Joe Prosperie, come outta the back quick as a chicken and jumped over the bar and in between us wit' a blackjack. He let me put my leg back on and then grabbed me by the scruff of my shirt and threw me out in the street. I did fall on my ass but I picked myself up quick.

Joe yelled get the hell out of here, goddam Junior Guidry!

And I yelled back that's right, y'all remember that! I might be a one-legged gimp but I'm still goddam Junior Guidry!

I figgered them ole boys would spread the word—Junior Guidry is still goddam Junior Guidry. He goddam is.

Tell you what, it worked.

For a while.

5

I can hear the ghost rattlin' around the kitchen. I don't know what the hell she's doin'.

Don't ax me about time. Shuh, I live in the damn Twilight Zone. Most times I don't know today from yesterday. Me and my big brother Beau go rabbit huntin' and then next thing I know I realize Beau's been dead for fifteen years. I 'member seein' his body on the side of the road, blood runnin' out his right ear. He'd rolled that truck so hard he'd been thrown out on the highway.

Took three of his good podnahs wit' 'im.

He was drunk when he done it.

He didn't look bad, really, 'cept for the blood comin' out his ear. Or until you rolled him over and saw how the back of his head was bashed in.

I was comin' back from rabbit huntin', walkin' down the road, and there he was. I didn't see the truck till after I saw him. It had flipped so many times it was flat as a stingeree. Them other boys were mashed inside.

He'd knocked up Marie Ardoin and they married 'em some-how, before the funeral. Shuh, Beau—he might be the only guy I know who spent his weddin' night in a coffin. Marie had a miscar-riage and later married a man who moved her off to Baton Rouge and she ain't never been back. I don't think Momma ever got over either one of them things.

Sometimes I'm about to bust ass on that damn Meely LaBauve and I wake up from a dream. Pisses me off when that happens.

The ghost comes in wit' a plate of toast. I see it before I smell it but when I smell it I realize how my nose has gone to sleep, too. It's toast and butter done in a cast-iron skillet, the way Momma did it.

I say I already tole you I don't want no breakfast.

She says that was yesterday.

This does throw me a bit.

I say well, I still don't want it, so get it out of here.

She says you have to eat.

I say are you my momma?

She says no, but I know you must have a mother and she'd want you to eat.

I say well, it's true Momma used to ride my ass about every-thing but you don't know nuttin' 'cause Momma's gone.

Her big rabbit eyes blink and go moist. She don't say nuttin'.

Cat got your tongue? I ax.

She don't answer that, neither.

I say where'd you get some bread?

She says I bought it.

Where?

At that store way up at the end of this road across the highway.

Elmore's?

Yes, I think that's what it was called.

How'd you get there?

Borrowed your truck.

How'd you find the keys?

They were in the ignition.

You drive a stick shift?

Yes, I do.

You were able to start that damn ole Plymit?

I guess I was. I drove it to the store. You could use points and plugs.

I look at her careful. I say that truck needs more than that since it's about the last Plymit truck they made. But I guess you ain't totally wort'less.

She stands there lookin' down at me.

I look at her good. She definitely could be one of them goody-goody types. I'm just waitin' for her to pull out that Bible and start tellin' me how fast I'm goin' to hell. Shuh, she can save her breath.

That's the one thing I already know.

I say how'd you know how to get to Elmore's?

I passed it on the way in.

And how'd you get all the way out here in the first place?

I walked, she says.

Walked? Bullshit. Ain't nobody walks all the way out here. It's close to six miles to the main road.

She says well, I hitched a ride out of Ville Canard to the turnoff and then I walked. I napped in the canefield and then, as it started to get dark, I walked on. Like I said before, I thought this trailer was abandoned.

Where were you goin'?

I wasn't sure.

You runnin' from the law? You rob a bank? Steal from the poor box at your church?

Her eyes go narrow again and I think I see some color in her cheeks.

I say well, hey, listen, it don't matter to me if you killed the Pope. You just welcome to keep on walkin'. If you turn left out my screen door and walk down to the end of this li'l road you'll be up to your ass in the Catahoula Swamp. Watch for them cotton-mouths. Oh, and them gators—they got some out there bigger than you and me put together.

She blinks them big rabbit eyes but she don't answer me.

It's nice and light in the trailer now and I see her good now. She looks different—her hair is down around her shoulders. It's as shiny as a new stainless-steel bolt. She's got on the same dress she had when she come in. That bruise on her cheek has faded some.

She's not built bad—long-legged but a bit skinny for the way I usually like my women though I know a lotta hardlegs who like them skinny women. She's tall, maybe five foot nine. She seems to have some perky tits. If she put on some lipstick and wore a decent dress, she might look awright.

I say how long you been here?

She says two days.

Where'd you sleep?

The first night over in that corner. Last night in that bed in that room.

That's my bed, you know.

I thought it was.

Ain't no sheets on that bed.

I found some and washed them.

I say well, then that's where I'm sleepin' tonight.

She says you should sleep in a proper bed.

I say I like it right here on this sofa. But if you wanna sleep in that bed wit' me, that'd be okay. I could use some nooky—that's about the one thing you might have that I need. In fack, if you give ole Junior here some nooky or even just a blowjob I might let you stay three or four nights. Rent free.

She stares right through me like she didn't hear.

Nobody says nuttin' for a while.

Then she says what happened to your leg?

I say a shark bit me. I bit the bastid back, though. Out there in the Gulf someplace is a shark wit' an artificial fin.

She says you talk a lot in your sleep.

Well, don't listen.

Who's Armontur or Armature or something like that? He must've done something bad to you the way you grumble about him all the time.

I say it ain't none of your business who Armentau is. So what else did I say?

She shrugs. You talk a lot of nonsense. You talk like some of those old people in the nursing homes who are going demented.

I look her over. She clearly don't know I'm goddam Junior Guidry. I'm gonna have to teach her.

I say well, I don't talk more nonsense than that God crap you talk.

She says you cry, too.

Bullshit.

Well, it's true. Are you sad, mister? Are you sad about your leg? You cried last night for an hour.

I shake my head. I say don't start wit' crap like that.

Well, you're living rough out here. This place is filthy. Don't you care anymore?

I've about heard enough. She might just make me mad enough to get off my ass and slug her.

I try sittin' up but the spins catch me about halfway and I slump back.

She puts the toast down on that rickety table I've got and reaches down around me and pulls.

C'mon, I'll help you up.

She does it quick and I'm sittin' up and the room spins, then stops. Even that li'l bit of movin' leaves me out of breath. I'm sweatin' like a whore in church.

I wait till I get my wind then say the only reason I want up is to get you out. I mean it. Go and leave me alone.

She looks at me like she's tryin' to decide somethin'. She says I bought some groceries.

Where'd you get the money?

It was my own. Don't worry, mister, I wouldn't steal from you.

I laugh at this. Lady, you looked around this house? If you lookin' to steal, you come to the wrong place. Anyway, take your groceries and go.

I'm making a gumbo, she says.

I'm amazed I cain't smell it. Momma used to make chicken gumbo wit' *andouille* and it smelled good from a mile down the road.

I tell her I don't want no gumbo, though I wonder if that's totally true.

She says all you had in your cupboard was potted meat and tins of Three Little Pigs sausages. You can't live on that, mister.

Well, I didn't say I was livin' on it. You think anybody would come out here to this hellhole to *live*?

Her rabbit eyes blink and go moist again.

She says I gave you a bath last night and got you into some pajamas I found. I'm sorry, but I couldn't stand the way you smelled. You've obviously lost a lot of weight but you probably had a beer belly anyway. You've got a long way to go, though, if you're planning to starve yourself to death.

I look down and damn if I ain't in some friggin' pajamas.

She says that's what I do—well, used to do. I looked after old people too frail to look after themselves.

And what? You carried me into the bathtub and I didn't even know it? Shuh—more crap.

She says it's something they taught us to do in training. I came in and found you half awake and helped you up and got you most of the way to the bathroom before you conked out on me. I propped you up against the wall like a mop and ran the tub and got you in.

I lift my right arm and smell my armpit.

It smells like Old Spice.

This just ain't gonna do, this woman bargin' in here and givin' me shit like this. I gotta think about what would really piss her off.

I got it.

I say did you wash my pecker?

She looks away.

I say well, I hope I didn't get a hard-on 'cause there've been quite a few girls who got scared when they saw that thing get up on its hind legs.

I think I see another bit of red in them *sac-à-lait* cheeks of her.

She looks at me and I figger she's gonna clobber me. I hope she tries.

Instead, she shrugs. She says mister, I know how to bathe an invalid and no, I didn't notice anything unusual. Anyway, we're taught in training not to pay attention to things like that. It's not important.

Oh, I see. You're one of them lily-white Cat'lic girls too good for people like me.

She gets a curious look in her eyes and says I am far from lily-white and the rest of it is just silly because I don't even know you. But it might be true that I could never think too highly of any man who eats Three Little Pigs sausages from a can. With his fingers.

That's it—I feel goddam Junior Guidry get up on his hind legs.

I say how do you know I do that?

She says because you throw all your cans in the sink and you didn't have a knife or fork or spoon in this house that wasn't covered with slime or mold. You're lucky you haven't given yourself ptomaine poison the way you live.

I yell listen, you ugly mullet-belly freak! You cain't come sneakin' in my house and treat me like some gimp and then insalt me like I'm some kind of retard. I am goddam Junior Guidry and if I had my strengt' I would kick you out right now! And if I really needed some nooky, wouldn't be nuttin' to stop me from takin' what I want! Nuttin', you hear me?

She turns from me and I'm so boilin' mad that I manage to lean forward and grab her elbow and spin her around.

I fall back on the sofa but I done what I needed to do 'cause I see she's got tears in her eyes.

She's got tears runnin' down her cheeks and she's sputterin'.

She says you could try that, mister, but why would you want to do that? What good is it to take such a thing if it is not given freely? What would it earn you except what a dog earns in the yard, and the hatred of the person you've done it to?

I can hardly stand to listen to her. I just want her out.

She turns her back and I hear them sobs I heard the night she come in and I see her tremblin' and I figger I at least have finally got her out of my hair.

And then she stops herself and she turns to me and there's fire in them watery rabbit eyes.

Oh, yeah, there's fire and she points a long white finger at me and says you could try to do that mister, you could. But the last man who tried to do that to me, well, do you know what I did?

I killed him.

6

Did I tell you about my lawsuit?

Oh, I sued them sumbitches, awright.

My insurance company made nice and paid for my hospital. But the first thing I did after I kicked that ole boy's ass at the Alibi was go to New Awlins and get me a Jew lawyer, ole Sydney Shainburg, somebody that my podnah Chug Eschete tole me about. He said Junior, don't go messin' 'round wit' these local lawyers—*crapuleux*. Hire Syd! Everybody knows them Jews are the smartest doggone people in the world.

Me, I wouldn't know a Jew from gypsy, but old Syd had made Eschete rich. Eschete drove a cement truck and had backed it up one day to pour a swimmin' pool for some millionaire redneck from Texas who had moved to Ville Canard to run a drillin' company. Ole Eschete was down in the hole when his moron helper hit the wrong lever and buried him in about six feet of cement. He had a collapsed lung and two broke legs plus some problem wit' his brain.

Syd sued 'em hard 'cause he proved the helper was a mental retard on dope. He won big time. Eschete got so much money that people say he not only bought a Cadillac but he got a gold-plated toilet put in his trailer—serious!

Anyway, ole Syd—he talks wit' words longer than Patin's pirogue. The man don't take no shit, neither. But he ain't like me, puttin' up his dukes every time he gets pissed off. He just takes out some of them big words and cuts people up like he had a knife.

Me and Syd, we went after everybody up one side and down the other. Big Tex, the company that was drillin' the well. The crewboat company, the rig owner, Gros Bec Drilling and Workover, the roustabout outfit I worked for, the insurance companies.

Hell, I even tried to get Syd to sue that damn Armentau. He even looked into it. It was Armentau that had helped pull me up on the rig after the boat bashed me but then the coward run away and hid in the bathroom up on the drillin' deck, cryin' and shakin' like a spanked puppy. If Brady Boudreaux hadn't come down from the drillin' platform and tied a tourniquet on my stump and then radioed for the helicopter, they might as well've fed the rest of me to the fish. But Syd found out that Armentau owed so much money to the loan sharks in Yankee City that the sumbitch could shit ten-carat diamonds for five years and still not get out of debt.

We sued the rest of 'em, though, 'cause Syd found out that there were tropical storm warnings that mornin' and the boat had been tole to turn around and bring us back to the dock 'cause it was too dangerous to unload. Plus, you usually get a lift up on the rig in a big personnel basket, but the crane that lifts the basket was broke down. We shoulda never been usin' the ladder. But the tool pusher on the rig—he's the one that runs the drillin' crew—and the crewboat captain were ole podnahs, and a coupla hard-asses to boot. So we were goin' to work one way or another 'cause the captain had promised to get his podnah off the rig so they could go redfishin' together. Plus the crew out there was already a week overdue goin' home and them boys were hornier than a three-legged bull tryin' to hop a red-hot cow. They were about to throw the tool pusher off the rig if he didn't get 'em to shore.

Hell, I don't necessarily blame 'em. Offshore is bust-ass work, seven days a week, twelve hours a day. You're either hot and dirty or cold and dirty. And you've got to watch yourself every minute 'cause some dumbass above you could drop a pipe wrench on your head or some engineer has figgered wrong and the well decides to spit the drill bit and send it flyin' up your ass. It's true they feed you good and you sleep like the dead, but after a week of that, you're damn ready to get off that rig. I must know at least six, seven guys who work offshore who got a toe or finger missin'. Shuh, they the lucky ones. About four years ago, a whole doggone drillin' rig toppled over in a storm over off Caillou Island and every one of them sumbitches aboard drowned. I'd drunk beer wit' a couple of them ole boys.

And that ain't the half of it. Most of them married guys who work seven-and-seven out on the rigs have got divorced 'cause they're gone so much their wives get lonely and decide they need a lot more than carpet cleaner from the Fuller Brush man.

I know one ole boy whose wife run off wit' the Avon *lady*—serious!

Anyway, when we found out they had ignored them small-craft warnings, the whole mess of 'em caved in like a muskrat mound under a bull gator. They paid me two hundred thousand dollars, plus all the medical bills I would ever run up plus all the wooden legs I'd ever need, not to mention a job for life pushin' a pencil at my company, Gros Bec Drilling.

Syd took one-third of the money but, shuh, I still come away with awmost one hundred and fifty thousand dollars. I felt like I had more money than Rockefeller!

After I got my check, I called and offered to buy Syd some deluxe pussy at the Hollywood Bayou Go-Go Bar. Syd laughed and said he was a family man and already spent plenty time in Ville Canard. He said I should take that money and spend it on some worthy cause. So, shuh, I went out and bought me some nooky instead!

Anyway, I felt rich as Rockefeller and, man, I tried to live like ole Rockefeller, too. I ditched my rust-bucket Chevy pickup and bought me a brand-new '72 Corvette and I give up my li'l rent shack and moved into some fancy-ass new apartment complex in a subdivision where they were building big ole houses for rich oil-field people who've been movin' down here like red aints. All them apartments were built to look like castles. I didn't even ax what the rent was—I just moved in.

King Junior!

I wrapped that 'Vette around a tree one night about four months later drivin' shit-blind drunk down the Bourg–Catahoula Highway. I crawled away wit' nuttin' but a hickey on my head though I did screw up my leg perty bad. After I bailed myself outta jail for DWI, 'cause Daddy wouldn't do it, I went to New Awlins and found this place that only sold fast cars and I picked up a canary-yellow Plymit Superbird, a 1969 but in cherry condition. It had an eight-cylinder, 440-cubic-inch engine and one of them doggone airplane spoilers on the trunk and that sumbitch, even if it did have a four-speed automatic, ran like a scalded dog and could make a hundred miles an hour in a quarter-mile.

I run that one in the bayou about six months later when I fell asleep comin' back from an all-night poker game at the Go-Go Bar. I drove that thing down like a submarine into about ten foot of muddy water but somehow managed to kick clear, though I still don't remember how.

Somehow I'd crawled outta that bayou and I woke up on the bank covered wit' mud and eelgrass, and Roddy Bergeron, who I went to school wit' down Catahoula Bayou, was shinin' a flashlight in my face. He'd actually finished high school and become a sheriff's deputy, though he's still crooked as a broke-back chicken snake.

He said goddam, Junior, is that you?

I said who the hell does it look like, Roddy?

He said you look like the damn Creature from the Black Lagoon. I have to admit I laughed my ass off over that one 'cause we'd gone to the Bijou Theater in town and seen that movie together when we were kids.

He didn't take me in for reckless drivin' 'cause we're podnahs, though he coulda. Good thing, too. I'd got two or three speedin' tickets after I totaled the 'Vette and I hadn't paid any of 'em.

They eventually got my ass for that, too.

No, hell, he didn't run me in. Instead, Roddy took a good look at me and said Junior, podnah, you're hurt. Look at you, you done broke your leg. We better get you to the emergency room quick. You must be in pain, bro!

I looked down and realized that it was my wooden leg he was talkin' about—that thing had more cracks in it than Grandma's face. Chips were fallin' out of it like bad plaster.

Roddy turned on his siren and police light and we took off down the Catahoula Bayou Road in his police car, drivin' about ninety miles an hour runnin' everybody off the road till we got to the turnoff for Sevin's Roadside.

It's a broke-down beer joint stuck off a li'l slough comin' off of Catahoula Bayou. It used to have a few slot machines, though when, so-said, Boog Sevin, the owner, stopped payin' bribes to Sheriff Go-Boy Geaux, the deputies come and dumped 'em in the bayou. There's an ole boy who fishes goggle-eye back here and says he's lost ten or fifteen Beetle Spins gettin' hung up on those slot machines.

We went haulin' ass down that bumpy road a mile or two to Sevin's and did a police turn right into the back shell parkin' lot, scatterin' clamshells every which way. Ole Sevin hisself come out to see what the hell was goin' on. Roddy said Boog, police emergency, Junior here needs somethin' for his broke leg. Make it a bottle of Ole Crow. Then Roddy spoke some shit on the police radio tellin' the sheriff's office he was busy investigatin' some crime. Boog brought out that bottle and we drunk whiskey and took out a Q-beam he had rigged up wit' the car and sat on the hood and shined nootras in the slough and took turns shootin' at 'em with his .38.

Hell, there were so many damn nootras out there that it sounded like World War III, though perty soon we were so drunk we couldn'a hit a Brahma bull at twenty feet.

At some point, Roddy pointed that gun at me, which I didn't think was funny.

He said I'm gonna make you dance, podnah, just like in them cowboy movies.

I said I'm too drunk to dance.

He said well, I guess I'm gonna have to shoot you in the leg.

He done it, too. Blew a big-ass hole right in my cracked peg leg.

I said aw, Roddy, what the hell you doin', man?

He said it was ruint anyway, Junior!

At some point, we passed out and woke up layin' on the hood of the car in the pourin' rain. It was mornin' and I felt like God was steppin' on my head.

The insurance paid off on the Superbird 'cause they could never charge me wit' nuttin' and I got me a big-ass Oldsmobile, one of them 98s, 'cause I figgered the way I was drivin' I needed a li'l more car 'tween me and them trees and ditches and bayous. I started hangin' out at the Go-Go Bar regular and I bought enough beer for my podnahs to sink a two-ton oil barge. Ole Junior here was one pop'lar sumbitch, lemme tell you that!

They had some fine-lookin' gals who danced there and you'd slip a dollar in their G-strings and they'd shake them titties in your face and if it was late enough, for five dollars, or maybe it was ten or twenty, dependin' on the girl, you could cop a perty good feel. One night I got real drunk and said to hell wit' a feel and hired two of them gals and they got hold of a case of tequila and, man oh man, we shacked up in some cheap motel outside of Ville Canard on the Yankee City Road. They invited a coupla their friends to come over and one of 'em brought over some cocaine or some kinda dope that you stick up your nose and I got more nooky in one night than some men get all year.

Shuh, I believe for one night I got more pussy than Frank Sinatra!

We just kept partyin' and I woke up about three days later and my wallet and keys and the 98 were gone.

So was my Rolex with the twelve diamonds on it. So was my nootra-skin coat, my custom-made twenty-four-carat-gold gator chain, and my three-hundred-dollar lizard-skin cowboy boots.

Hell, they'd even stole my damn leg!

They found the Olds burnt to a shell about a month later at the bottom of a canyon way the hell out in Texas someplace. Them whores were long gone by then and, far as I know, they never caught 'em.

If I ever catch 'em, I know where I'm gonna put my new wooden leg.

Anyway, I bought me another Olds just like the one I had, though I was kinda out of commission for a coupla weeks 'cause the company that made my leg up in Tennessee somewhere had been blowed over by a tornado and they had to go out for about two weeks pickin' up legs all over creation till they found my size.

I practically started livin' at the Go-Go Bar and they was runnin' a blackjack game in the back room and I started playin' and that sumbitch turned out to be rigged as a TV wrasslin' match. They'd let me win a few hands early on and I'd be up a few hundred dollars and get cocky and they'd deal them stacked cards and perty soon I'da done dumped a thousand damn dollars down the drain. I sat there for a whole week like that one time, just throwin' money away like a cow pissin' on a blacktop road.

One night when I wadn't there the state troopers raided the place—shuh, everybody knew that the sheriff and his boys were on the take and wouldn't touch it—and they busted the whole thievin' gang of 'em. But by the time ole Junior here had caught on, I was down maybe thirty, forty thousand damn dollars—hell, maybe more. I'd lost track.

I called my lawyer, Syd, to come sue them bastids, too, but after he looked into it Syd said Junior, you're out of luck, son. There are about two hundred men just like you who have been cheated but whatever money the bar had, they've buried it so deep that you might as well try to ride a drill bit down to hell to find it. Besides, the man who runs the place, the one they call Rocko Marchante, is up to his ass in the New Orleans Mafia— trust me, Junior, you don't want to end up on the wrong side of those guys. I represented one of the Mafia's goons in a divorce matter sometime back and, I have to tell you, he was an animal. Plus, the way I hear it, Rocko's pretty much bought off your sheriff and who knows who else down there.

I didn't like that advice much but if Syd said it's so there wadn't nuttin' I could do.

Hell, the next thing I heard, the damn Go-Go Bar had reopened like nuttin' had ever happened. People said Rocko Marchante was still runnin' it, just his name wadn't on the papers anymore. And somehow, all them charges against him got dropped— he'd slipped off the hook like a saltwater eel.

A while later I coulda used that money 'cause Momma got sick wit' a bad cancer. I don't think she was even gonna tell me. Daddy did. He come to see me and I knew the only time he came was when he'd pissed away the rent money on booze and was broke. They'd lost the cane farm we had when I was growin' up. Hell, it wadn't much, that ole house and forty leased arpents, most of it boggy gumbo soil, but the land would grow cane and it was at least *somethin'*. It all fell down the bottle and Daddy and

Momma and my sister Irene moved to a dumpy li'l shotgun rent house way up the bayou not too far from town. Most of my brothers had all hauled ass by then to work the Texas oil fields— nobody wanted to farm wit' Daddy. Paul, the smart one in our family, finished high school and got a scholarship to some college up in Nort' Loosiana and went up there and got himself a degree and become an accountant. He met a Baptist girl and married her and quit bein' a Cat'lic and joined the Baptist Church, though it nearly broke Momma's heart.

I didn't mind bein' around Momma, even though she was always on my ass to straighten up or go back to school or stop fightin', but I didn't see her much 'cause Daddy was always drunk and wantin' to fight. After I got all my money, Momma thought I was on the road to someplace and when she saw the someplace was the ditch, man, she got on me hard.

Anyway, how could I explain to Momma why I lived like I lived when half the time I don't even understand why I do the things I do?

Daddy at least had it right when he said, a long time ago, Junior, your problem is that some people are born wit' a wild hair up their ass but you, son, you got a whole pig bristle up yours.

I cain't think when I wadn't doin' somethin' crazy. When I was six years old, me and Beau would go catch frogs outta Catahoula Bayou and smear canned dog food on 'em and watch our ole hounds eat 'em alive. When I was twelve, me and some podnahs one Saturday stole a case of Jax off the beer truck when it come to unload behind Elmore's store and we run off and hid in the canefield and had ourselves a party. I sucked down six of them beers so fast that I was drunk in about ten minutes. But even though I ended up pukin' my guts out for a whole day and Daddy whupped

me good when he found out what we done, I knew I had found
the perfect fuckin' poison for me.

Me and that beer have got ourselves in some shit, lemme
tell ya.

And it's true—ever since I was little I've had the urge to beat
up on people I don't like, which includes most damn people.
Hell, some boys liked fishin'. I liked fightin'. I was big and perty
goddam good at it. Wadn't nuttin' better to me than feelin' my
knuckles upside the head of some poor sumbitch and watchin'
the bastid fall.

Back at Catahoula School, I used to get after that li'l runt
Meely LaBauve and ride him like a horse at the merry-go-round.
He ain't never done nuttin' to me but I just didn't like him—the
way he looked, the way he smelled, the way he dressed. I didn't
like nuttin' about him.

I hated his ole man worse, especially after what he done to me
and Uncle that day.

Ole man LaBauve got drowned by a gator but I thought about
killin' Meely after that rigamarole wit' the court. I was just about
crazy enough back then to do somethin' like that. I only didn't
'cause the judge in the case had the serious red-ass at me and
even Uncle figgered he'd put both of us to prison if we laid a hand
on the li'l bastid.

Anyway, I cooled down quick 'cause, like I've said before, it's
one thing to be mean, it's another to be stupid. Plus, they'd perty
much caught us—hell, I'd lied my ass off to Uncle about what
happened after me and my gang caught Meely in that corn patch.
We woulda whupped him to a pulp if that big-ass Chilly Cox
hadn't stepped in. I tole Uncle that Chilly and Meely had jumped
us and, shuh, Uncle him, he didn't need no excuse to go beat on

niggers. So we caught that big Chilly bastid walkin' down the road and roughed him up good. Meely, too. Uncle mighta done worse than that 'cept Meely's ole man come outta the field wit' his gun.

Now, if you wanna know the truth, I didn't hate that Chilly bastid any more than I hate anybody else. I hate 'em all about the same. In fack—though I'd've never admitted this to my gang—I thought that Cassie Jackson girl, who was one of them who ratted on us in court 'cause she saw us kickin' Meely's ass, was one fine thang. Fine! When it comes to nooky, I wouldn't let her bein' black stop me. To tell the truth, if I actually believed runty-ass Meely was gettin' some nooky from her, I might've axed him to join my gang!

Shuh, anyway, ain't no reason to stir all that shit again.

The thing that pissed me off about Meely is that he wadn't afraid of me. Some of 'em kids at school would wet their pants when I even looked at 'em crossways. But that li'l Meely would stare back and give me the evil eye.

He even wanted to fight *me* a few times!

One thing I come to know—you gotta watch out for them that ain't afraid of you 'cause you might have cause to be afraid of *them* one day.

Like that ole man LaBauve. Good thing that sumbitch died 'cause I'da been watchin' my back for years wit' him sneakin' around the woods the way he did. When he walked out of that canefield wit' that shotgun and got the drop on me and Uncle, I thought we were bot' dead. I ain't been scared but a few times in my life but that was one of 'em.

Uncle was scared, too, though he never would admit it.

Uncle dropped dead about five years later from a heart attack. I figger the LaBauves had the last laugh on that deal. Uncle never was the same. He got put on the desk and drunk himself out of even that job at the police station and ate himself up to about three hundred pounds. He died watchin' wrasslin' on TV. Hell, the ole judge who threatened to put us away was so pissed off that he eventually got 'em to shut down the whole damn police department.

Anyway, when Daddy came to tell me about Momma's cancer, I honestly didn't believe him, though it was the first time I'd seen Daddy sober in a long time. So I went to see Momma and she tole me it was true but that I shouldn't worry or spend my money. She said the cancer she had was real bad and anyway, she'd had a dream of the Virgin, who tole her that her time was comin' soon but she didn't need to worry 'cause she was gonna be wit' Beau in heaven. It pissed me off to hear Momma talk like that and I tole her to stop talkin' that b.s. but she said Junior, I have always believed in my dreams and I don't need you to take them away from me. That really frosted me but I at least made her tell me who her doctor was in town and I went see him myself.

Meantime, I went to the bank and I had but four thousand dollars left outta all that damn money, plus a few hundred I'd hid around the house—hell-raisin' money, I called it.

The doctor was Dr. Gautreaux, young Dr. Gautreaux, who had just come out of medical college, stedda ole Dr. Gautreaux, who used to be Momma's doctor but had died of a heart attack. He had a nice office in a nice white house under some oak trees across the bayou from Ville Canard Square.

I said to Dr. Gautreaux, how much medicine can I get for four thousand dollars?

He said Mr. Guidry, it doesn't exactly work that way. Your mother needs several massive courses of chemotherapy and there is no use doing one course if you can't do them all. Honestly, we're talking twenty-five thousand at least. And we're talking about buying your mother another year at most, not saving her life.

I said well, cain't we do four thousand dollars' wort' and see what happens?

He said no, I'm afraid not. It would just be a waste of your money and only make your mother feel worse than she does. My advice is just to make your mother as comfortable as possible and let her die in peace.

I looked at him in his starched white coat and his fancy haircut and his smooth white hands and his baby face—shuh, he didn't look old enough to drink beer, much less be a damned doctor. I was so pissed off when I left that place that I went straight to the Alibi and got drunk. Joe Prosperie saw me comin' in and said Guidry, one peep outta you and I'll have my blackjack up against your head and then I'll have the police throw you in jail. I don't care if you are a one-legged bastid.

I said don't worry, Joe. Just keep them beers comin'. I ain't here to fight nobody.

The person I wanted to fight was that damn bloodsuckin' doctor—all them damn bloodsuckin' doctors—but since this would upset Momma, I didn't. The other person who really pissed me off was ole Junior here. I'd gone from bein' rich to bein' just another broke-down coonass wit' rent to pay. The worst thing about it was that I knew nuttin' was gonna change. Not one damn thing.

We buried Momma five months later. That cancer just ate her up and the last three months she just laid there in bed sayin' her rosary, hardly able to move. But she went quiet. Irene was wit' her—I couldn't stand to be there, myself. And I took most of what was lef' of my leg money and gave her a Cat'lic funeral wit' a mass and everything.

Father Giroir said Junior, this would have made your mother very happy, and I got a belly roar of a laugh out of that. Shuh, I ain't had much truck wit' Father, anyway, but he musta thought ole Junior had gone *craque,* bustin' out laughin' in the middle of his own momma's funeral.

But you got to admit it was friggin' funny—goddam Junior Guidry ain't never made his momma happy. 'Cept when he buried her.

I still had one thing goin' for me—my job for life, at a nice salary, too.

But, shuh, that didn't last long, neither.

7

The trailer's got quiet and I'm sittin' on the sofa—sittin' up for a change. I've got my wind back and maybe I feel a li'l better, or maybe I don't.

The ghost is gone. Good riddance.

Anyway, after she tole me about killin' that man, she walked out and give me a look you'd give a pathetic, mangy dog. I don't care—I just hope I've seen the last of her. That girl give me the *frissons*.

Normally I wouldn't believe that stuff about her killin' a man, 'specially since she ain't no bigger than a sack of oysters. But I seen it in her rabbit eyes—she's damn shore runnin' from somethin'.

She could be some crazy person runnin' from the nuthouse, far as I know.

Now, in truth, ain't no way I was gonna force that girl to gimme some nooky. I was just tryin' to get her goat. It's true that I've lied my way to pussy—*Oh, yes, darlin', I love you, too!*—and

I've begged for some now and then, as most men have. But I ain't never stole it.

I do smell her gumbo now and it smells doggone good. I look around like I'm seein' my place for the first time in a while and I see she's straightened stuff up. My boots and carburetor and that stack of girly magazines are gone. Too bad about that. She prob'ly threw Miss July in the garbage.

I notice my leg is propped up at the end of the couch, so I scooch over and put it on, though it takes a while.

Then I manage to push myself up straight. I go dizzy for a second and think I might fall but I don't. I'm stiff and wobbly but I do manage to make it to my kitchen, usin' the wall along the way to hold myself up when I get too tipsy. I make the stove and take the cover off the gumbo pot.

It's chicken and okra. I stick my finger in for a taste. It's still warm, and damn if it ain't good. That girl obviously got a thang for cayenne and Tabasco sauce, which is fine wit' ole Junior.

I look over and see she's washed my dishes and put them in a drainer to dry. Mighty nice of her. I find a bowl and a spoon.

Too bad she didn't cook no rice before she went.

I fix me a bowl, not botherin' to warm it up more, and hobble to the table. My hands got the shakes and I eat it slow and dribble about half of it down my chin, but I gotta say it beats the hell out of potted meat and Three Little Pigs sausages, though I'd never tell the ghost that.

It pisses me off but the girl got that right—I do eat 'em wit' my fingers.

I get about halfway through the bowl of gumbo and I'm full— my stomach's done shrunk or somethin'. I burp and feel that gumbo settle in.

I realize I'm feelin' better and what would make me feel better yet is a drink. The ghost dumped out what was left of my bottle but I'm perty shore I got some whiskey stashed down under the sink. I go over there and bend down and open the cabinet and root around and reach way back.

Some roaches run out but I don't care. One crawls up my arm and I swat it away.

I fine the bottle—Ole Crow—and bring it out. I try to stand but I slump down dizzy. I wait a bit and try again.

Same thing.

Oh well.

I open the bottle and take a swig.

About half of it's gone 'fore I know this is where I'm spendin' the night.

I go way down deep someplace and there's ole Berta, Berta Bonvillain, my first ex. Amazin' how I still dream about Berta.

She says Junior, honey, come to bed.

I don't want to, Berta.

Why not?

I'm goin' out.

Out where, Junior?

Shuh, I dunno. Just out.

She says don't, baby, stay wit' me.

Sorry, I gotta go.

Don't do this to me, Junior.

I ain't got nuttin' to say to that.

She's yellin' and pullin' at me and slams the door behind me when I leave. She yells if you leave me now just make sure you stay gone!

Berta lays back between the corn rows. She's got her dress hitched up and her draws are but a loop around her ankle.

I say oh, yeah, Berta's got what Junior needs.

She says you got you a rubber, Junior?

I say no.

She says we need a rubber, Junior. Lucky I got one.

I say okay.

She says you want me to put it on for you?

I say no, I can do it.

She says I'll put it on wit' my mouth.

Serious?

Serious.

She tries to. She says Junior, I bit it.

What you mean, Berta?

I bit the rubber. I think I might have bit a hole in it.

You bit it? Berta, you not s'posed to bite on it!

I'm sorry, Junior. I didn't bite you, did I?

No, baby, you didn't.

I'm sorry, Junior.

Well, I gotta have it, Berta. I already got the blue balls.

Just be careful, Junior.

Oh, yeah, I will.

Me, I been drinkin' some. I just wanna go to town.

I hear Berta moanin' and when I come I feel like the moon done caved in my head. When I pull it out, I look and see. I'm like a fella who done stepped through his hip boots in the marsh.

I say you musta not bit that rubber, Berta, you musta ate it.

Ate it? What you mean, Junior? What you sayin'?

Nuttin', Berta. I ain't sayin' nuttin'.

You were careful, Junior?

Oh, yeah, baby, I was. I was real careful.

She got knocked up that night. We got married, Berta and me. Damn, I was but eighteen years ole, Berta was sixteen.

We had a baby girl. Berta named her Eulalie, like Momma. A perty li'l girl. We call her Lolly-Lee.

I just couldn't be there. I couldn't stand it. I was like a coon in a trap, slowly chewin' its leg off to get free. I knew if I stayed there I'd beat her like Daddy beat Momma.

Anyway, Berta got fat and we argued all the time but she divorced my sorry ass. Got on a diet. She got her a lawyer and got the li'l house we'd managed to buy. She met her an insurance man and married him and she left outta Ville Canard to someplace up in Arkansas wit' the girl. Sold the house for a nice chunk of money. Showed my ass.

She looked doggone good when she went. Damn good.

She used to come to town now and then and call Momma and bring Lolly-Lee over but she wouldn't call me.

Boy, Momma never lemme get over that one.

What kind of man ain't got enough sense to love his own daughter, Junior Guidry?

I love her, Momma, but Berta don't want me nowhere 'round her. And anyways, they live five hundred miles away now.

Well, she would let you see her, Junior, if you'd ever grow up and learn to be a man. You got a car. You can drive five hundred miles to see your chile. You got a phone.

I try to send her money, Momma. The damn woman sends it back!

Junior, you ain't got a lick of sense, even if you are my son.

Look, Momma, Berta divorced me, 'member? I didn't divorce her.

Junior, you hit her and ran around on her and weren't even there most of the time to help look after your chile. No wonder she threw you out.

I scream at Momma. I never hit her, Momma, not once. I lost my temper and I pushed her out of the way and she fell down! She never forgave me for that. Anyway, I couldn't stay 'cause I knew if I did, I *would* hit her. Just like Daddy done to you. Just like that, Momma. Why didn't you divorce *his* sorry ass, ehn? Ehn?

Momma looks at me and makes me sorry I said that, 'cause she turns away and says, quiet and sad, I don't know. I don't, Junior. But I'm not an excuse for you.

Shuh, I ain't never gettin' married no more. That's what I said, anyway. Never, not me. Not Junior Guidry.

But there was Alma.

Alma Barrios.

Look at that girl—damn!

I been offshore workin' a double shift. We get off the boat in Yankee City. Theriot, who's drivin' the carryall, says hell, podnahs, y'all wanna get a drink?

It ain't but ten in the mornin' but everybody says hell yes, Theriot! You a goddam genius!

He pulls into some tumbledown joint called the Rainbow Room. It's a barroom set on rickety pilings and leanin' way over the bayou. If you pushed it hard, it would fall in. Wadn't no rainbow shinin' in that place—till I saw Alma. She come on duty about an hour after we got there.

Damn, she was the finest girl I'd ever seen. Ever! Her skirt come up to about her navel. She had the leg thang going on big time.

A butt like two bulldogs in a bag.

She didn't pay me no mind for about the first two hours, but I sat there 'cause, no shit, Theriot, the only guy who was s'posed to drive the truck, had drunk about a fifth of whiskey by that time and was already *chaqued* and snorin' wit' his head down on the bar.

Anyway, I sat there and stared at Alma's perty ass and ordered about nine thousand beers and bought her some drinks and we finally talked.

Shuh, don't ax me how this works but Alma, after she thawed out, kep' lookin' at me like she knew me or knew somethin' about me. I cain't say I knew a damn thing about her, 'cept how bad I wanted to get in her draws.

I stayed there till midnight, when Alma got off, and Alma said come wit' me, Junior, and she took me home. They'd built some li'l half-assed brick apartments out on the edge of the swamp on the west side of Yankee City and she rented one of them and we got home and, honest, that girl could suck the chrome off a trailer hitch.

She said I'm gonna make you my personal lollipop, Junior.

She did, too. Damn!

Sometimes I miss Alma. Or maybe it's just that lollipop thang.

What the hell happens to women after you marry 'em, ehn?

We got married about six weeks later and I give up my li'l shotgun rent shack in Ville Canard and I was doin' so well offshore that I bought us a big-ass double-wide trailer wit' shag carpeting and the works. We rented a space in a place called Cypress Knee Estates, right near the Yankee City swamp levee. The trailer court did have some nice cypresses, though I gotta say that Yankee City might be the ugliest damn place I've ever seen. It calls itself a town but it ain't nuttin' but tin-can titty bars and rusted-out trailer parks and junkyards fallin' into the bayou and abandoned tugboats sunk and rusted and left to rot—oil-field crap thrown everywhere. But it was about twenty-five miles closer to catch the offshore boat than livin' in Ville Canard.

Plus, Cypress Knee Estates had a swimmin' pool, if you could keep the frogs, water moccasins, and nootras out of it.

Shuh, I had a net and a gun. Wadn't no problem, there.

I even took Alma on a honeymoon to New Awlins, somethin' I hadn't done wit' Berta, she bein' knocked up and all when we got married. Alma and me had ourselves a high ole time—we shacked up in some tourist court on St. Charles Street near the streetcar line and we stayed drunk and fucked through most of it and had ourselves a nice supper in some fancy-ass Creole restaurant in the French Quarter. We even drunk us some martinis, though personally I thought the damn things tasted like lighter fluid. I got the bill and like to fell over and I tole that ole boy in his penguin suit, mister, I didn't wanna buy your damn restaurant, I just wanted to have some supper!

Shuh, ole Alma already thought I was one of the funniest people alive and she laughed her ass off at that even if the waiter give me a look like I'd walked wit' muddy hip boots across his clean white tablecloth. I got even wit' him—I paid the damn bill but only left two pennies on the table for a tip and he come chasin' after us on the street and threw them pennies at me.

Alma give him the bird and cussed him lower than a dog. That's my girl!

I even talked Alma into goin' to watch one of them striptease shows on Bourbon Street and, man, I knew she was a different kinda woman 'cause even she got hot watchin' them girls swingin' them titties around. Perty soon, she leans over and whispers in my ear, Junior, darlin', take me into the bathroom and do me from behind.

Hell, it was middle of the afternoon and there were only four or five hardlegs in the place plus the bartender and some ole bouncer at the door. So I grabbed her by the hand and we made for the ladies' room and she dragged me in there and bent over the lavatory. She threw her skirt up and shucked her draws and stuck her beautiful ass up in the air and we went at it and, serious, that girl started barkin' and whinin' like a Catahoula Cur on the track of the *loup garou*!

Man, I got so hot I started barkin', too!

They called the cops but we crawled out the window and run slip-slidin' down an alley. We went got drunk on hurricanes at Pat O'Brien's. We woke up under the table at five in the mornin'. I drank Pepsi-Bismol for five days after that, my stomach was so screwed up.

What the hell happens to women after you marry 'em?

Or maybe it's what the hell happens to women after they marry *me*?

A few months went by and Alma all but stopped doin' the lollipop thang unless I begged her. She didn't want me hangin' out wit' none of my friends, sayin' all they wanted to do was keep me drunk and help me spend my money.

At first I tried to laugh and say hey, baby, that's all you wanted to do, too, and she said that's different, Junior, I'm your wife and you better get used to it.

Somethin' about the way she said that really hacked me off. I come off my offshore hitch the very next time and I went wit' Theriot and the boys back to the Rainbow Room, where Alma used to work, and I stayed all night. Blew most of my check. Started makin' out wit' some new girl there. Man, Alma's girlfriends there were givin' me the *gris-gris* eyes.

They called her, too. Alma came roarin' in the damn bar about five in the mornin', fists flyin'. I was perty far drunk but I managed to wrassle her down to the floor, though she cussed me wit' words that woulda knocked a buzzard off a shit wagon. I finally got her calmed down and we went home and I tole her I was sorry, which I kinda was, and she did give me a lollipop thang and we were okay for a while, though, 'tween us nootras, I knew by then we wadn't gonna last.

I was feelin' that trap bite into my leg again.

Momma never warmed up to Alma. She said Junior, she's a hard woman.

Alma would say livin' wit' me didn't make her any softer.

Alma pitched me out for good about six months later when she caught me bangin' Jolie Hebert, her best gal friend from the bar, on our kitchen table one afternoon.

At least we didn't have no kids.

Sometimes I still dream about Alma. That lollipop thang is kinda hard to forget.

I reach down and fine the Ole Crow and take another swallow.

I hear the door creak open and the shuffle of feet and the ghost reappears. Damn, cain't a man get no peace?

Her shadow fills the kitchen. She says are you drunk again, mister?

I say perty much.

Why do you do that to yourself?

'Cause I can.

You're killing yourself.

I tole you that before.

I'll help you to bed.

You comin' wit' me?

No.

I didn't think you were the type.

I'm not.

You're not gonna kill me in my sleep, are you?

Maybe.

I put down my bottle and look up at her. Maybe?

No, I'm not going to kill you in your sleep.

You promise?

No.

You jokin' me, right?

I wouldn't harm a hair on your head, mister. Don't worry.

Did you really kill somebody?

She don't answer. She says c'mon, I'll help you up.

She's strong for bein' so damned skinny. If she wanted to take a ballpeen hammer to my head, she could do some damage.

She guides me to my li'l bedroom stedda the couch and turns on the light and lowers me down. She takes off my leg wit'out axin' and puts it in the nearest corner.

I lie back and my head feels a pillow and I watch the ceiling twist slowly. The sheets smell washed, like they did when I lived wit' Momma.

I ax her, why'd you come back?

I see her lookin' down at me. She's a bit fuzzy.

She folds her arms and stares down at me. She says I don't know. 'Cause I like it here, I guess.

I manage to laugh hard at that. I say well, at least you got a sense of humor.

She turns and switches off the light and says good night.

I say I ate some of your gumbo.

She says did you like it?

It was okay.

Did you use a spoon instead of your fingers?

Yes, Mother Superior.

She says did anybody ever tell you that if you weren't always so crude and nasty you could be funny?

Maybe.

She says what's your name?

I say Junior. Junior Guidry.

Junior, is it?

That's right.

She says well, that's part of your problem. No man should be called Junior.

Oh, I see. I ain't just a nasty ole drunk. I gotta bum name, too.

What is your given name?

Joseph.

Well, I'll call you Joseph.

Lady, I don't give a rat's ass what you call me.

She says you're getting nasty again.

I say well, look who's talkin'. You sneak in my house and you ain't done nuttin' but insalt me since you got here.

I'm just trying to help you.

Oh, yeah? Well, I thought you already had by gettin' the hell out of here.

She's standing in the light of the narrow hall and she turns to me and she looks serious and says listen, if you really want me to go I'll go. But I need to stay here for a while longer to think things through. I'll earn my keep.

How?

I won't sleep with you but I'll look after you. Cook, clean. It looks like you could use some help in that department.

I don't like company.

So I'll leave you alone.

Like you have so far?

Cat's got her tongue again.

I look up at the ceilin'. I think about Berta. I think about Alma. I think about Lolly-Lee and Momma.

I look up at the ghost and I don't know why I say what I say but I say suit yourself.

She says thank you, Joseph.

I say you could at least make it Joe.

She says I'll think about that. But I don't know you well enough yet.

I say you got a name?

She don't speak right away. Then she says my name is Iris.

Like the flower?

Like the flower. Iris Mary, actually.

I say I ain't never seen an iris as white as you.

She says I was born like I was born.

I say you got a last name?

She don't speak.

I say you shore you don't wanna crawl into bed wit' me?

She says I'm sure.

I close my eyes and wonder if Iris Mary crawlin' in bed wit' me would save me from ugly-ass Armentau.

Shuh, prob'ly not.

I close my eyes and the dark comes down all around me.

8

I gotta get up to the top of the rig. I know he's up there.

I'm crawlin' up to the top of the rig. My leg's gone but I'm not bleedin'. I'm crawlin' up there and I'm gonna crawl in that bunkhouse and find Armentau and crack him in the head wit' my hatchet, then throw him off the rig.

I've got me a deal wit' them sharks.

That's when I hear Lolly-Lee callin' for me.

Daddy, somethin's after me.

What, baby?

The *loup garou,* Daddy.

Ain't no such thing, baby.

He's at the door, Daddy.

Lolly-Lee, where's your momma?

Momma's not here. She's gone off with Floyd. They left me, Daddy. They left me! Daddy, he's openin' the door! Help me, Daddy! Help me!

I'm comin', cher. Don't you worry. I'm comin' right now.

Where's my truck key? What did I do wit' the damn thing?

C'mon, you ole sumbitch, start.

The Plymit spits and laughs and the battery goes dead.

Ha, ha, ha! the truck says.

Laughs in my face.

Where's my tire tool? I'll show this goddam truck.

Armentau's rappin' on the window, his nose stuck up against the glass. His face looks melted and slimy, like an octopus.

He's got a hatchet of his own.

I swing at him and break the window wit' my fist but he ain't there no more. I look down and see there's glass in my lap and I've sliced off three fingers.

They look like stumpy legs. They wiggle on their own.

The blood flows and flows and flows and soon it's up to my knees in the truck and I cain't open the door. I cain't fine the door handle. The windows have turned to black iron. I try to slide over to the other side of the cab but I'm stuck. Somethin's got me 'round the belly.

The blood comes up to my waist and then up to my chest and suddenly it's in my nose and I cain't breathe.

I kick and scream and bang my fist on the ceilin' of the cab but all I can hear is Armentau laughin'.

I wake up in a cold sweat.

I see Iris Mary.

She has my head in her arms and is lookin' down at me.

She says you were having a nightmare, Joseph. It's okay. It's not real.

I blink and close my eyes again.

You want to tell me about it?

Hell, no.

Are you sure?

Hell, yes.

Is it that Armentau again?

Him and others. Hell, even my truck turned against me.

Was he trying to kill you, Joseph?

Armentau or the truck?

Armentau.

No, I was tryin' to kill him but perty much killed myself in-stead.

She says maybe your dreams are trying to tell you something.

I say my dreams don't mean nuttin'. The doc says it's whiskey and my bad liver that make me dream like I do.

What did Armentau do to you? Does it have to do with your leg?

He left me to die on the rig.

You mean abandoned you?

Somethin' like that.

Tell me how.

That was a long time ago, lady.

It must still matter to you if you have nightmares about it even now.

Maybe it does, maybe it don't.

I think it probably does.

Why should I care what you think?

The ghost looks at me. She shrugs her shoulders. She says no reason, really. You ever talk about your accident to anybody?

No.

Never?

Never.

Things get quiet for a while.

Then I open my mouth. Stuff just starts to come out. I don't know why I'm botherin' to tell her anything but I tell her the whole deal. Even the pussy boy part.

She says he called you what?

A pussy boy—a wimp, a sissy.

So instead of using your good sense, you let Armentau goad you into doing something foolish. Is that it?

Lady, you don't know nuttin'.

Well, tell me what I'm missing here?

Look, among the bunch that I work wit', the last thing in the world you can be is a pussy boy. You let 'em mark you down as that and you ain't got a chance in hell after that. They'll just keep kickin' your ass till they beat you down or you run off.

Joseph, how tall are you?

Six four.

How much do you weigh?

Now?

Hhm, no, then—before the accident.

About two thirty-five.

So what did you have to prove?

Out there? Like I tole you, what every man has to prove sooner or later.

And what is that?

What, you not listenin'? That you're not a doggone wimp.

Don't you believe in yourself, Joseph?

What the hell does that mean?

Okay, this Armentau—was he a big guy?

You kiddin'? He's a skinny li'l rat.

So you let a skinny little rat goad you into the biggest mistake of your life?

I look at her. Damn, this girl is *real* hard!

I say it wadn't just that.

What else?

See, after the boat come and chopped off my leg, it was Armentau who helped pull me up.

It was?

Yeah.

Sounds like he saved your life.

Shuh! He pulled me up off the ladder, awright, but then when he saw what happened to my leg, he run off and left me there. I was bleedin' to death, lady. If Brady Boudreaux hadn't come down in two minutes, I'd be dead.

So he ran off because he was afraid?

I guess so. Or he hated my guts and wanted me to die. Maybe both.

What does that make him?

A dirty bastid.

Not—what do you call it? What is that crude thing you say?

A pussy boy?

Yes. Isn't that what you think he is?

Damn straight! Armentau's the biggest pussy boy that ever lived!

So you let a wimp goad you off the rig and you lost your leg and, even though he pulled you up and saved your life, you hate him because he followed his nature and ran away?

I look at her again. She's got the strangest damn ideas.

I say Armentau owes me a leg.

She says can he pay it?

No.

Do you think you could let it go?

What?

Your hatred of Armentau?

Why should I?

Because what I know of hatred, it's doesn't do a bit of good.

What would you know about it?

I've hated a person or two.

You? Mother Superior? I doubt you the type.

Well, maybe there's a lot you don't know about me.

Well, there's obviously a lot you don't know about me, neither.
I like my hatred just fine the way it is. I'm perty doggone happy
wit' my hatred. Armentau ain't the onliest one I hate, either. I got
a whole list of people I hate. You wanna hear it?

She says well, look where's it got you.

Oh, you mean, stuck wit' a nosy bitch like you needlin' my ass
every five minutes?

You shouldn't use that word, Joseph. It isn't nice.

Which word? Bitch or ass?

You know what I mean.

Oooh, sorry, lady! Liked I axed you for one single minute to
butt in my business. Anyway, we got a deal, 'member? You stay
here and cook and clean but you stay off my case. Otherwise you
can go find some other place to run away from whatever it is
you're runnin' from.

She looks at me wit' them rabbit eyes and for just a blink I
think I see fear.

She stands and turns and she steps out of my bedroom into
the dim light of the hall.

She pads her way to the couch wit'out sayin' a word.

After she leaves, I lie awake, wishin' I had the energy to go get the whiskey bottle. But I don't. The ghost prob'ly pitched it out, anyway.

I close my eyes and think about freaky Iris Mary.

The nerve of that woman!

Next thing you know I'll be dreamin' of her stedda Armentau.

Well, at least she's better-lookin'.

I close my eyes but I cain't sleep. I hear a sound, soft, comin' from down the hall. It takes a while before I realize what I hear.

Iris Mary is cryin'.

9

Did I tell you how I lost my job for life?

Would you be surprised to hear that I was about half drunk when I done it? Would you believe me if I tole you it was an accident? But even I gotta say it ranks right up there in the bonehead category wit' that Vera Verret deal.

After I got out the hospital and got all my money, I went to see Nonc Deshotel, who owns Gros Bec Drilling. Nonc knew Daddy from Daddy's sober days, which is why he give me a job in the first place. I actually tried to farm cane wit' Daddy after I quit school. But I hated how he stayed drunk and picked on Momma and picked on me. He stopped pickin' on me the day I knocked him clear down the porch steps and into the yard. But, shuh, that's another story.

Anyway, big deal. It didn't stop him from drinkin' or ridin' Momma, so I finally couldn't stand to watch it anymore and moved out.

It was time. I'd just had my eighteenth birt'day. It wadn't long after that that me and Berta got hitched.

When I first signed on wit' Gros Bec, way before my accident, they had me doin' all the shitty, dirty li'l roustabout jobs but I worked my ass off and caught on quick and soon I worked my way up to roughneck on the drillin' crew. I know I raised hell now and then, and a few times I was too hungover to start my offshore shift. But Nonc and me got along okay, and the money was good for a high school dropout.

Before all the rigamarole wit' my leg, I was strong as a motorized winch and wadn't nobody could wrassle drillin' pipe in the ground quick as me. Man, we'd make some hole when I was on the job. Even Black Dugas, the hard-ass tool pusher I worked wit' most of the time, would say damn, Junior, if I had four more men like you we could take this goddam drill bit to China in six weeks. I got promoted to derrick man, which was great for a guy my age. Hell, I might've even made tool pusher myself one day and run my own damn drillin' rig. But you ain't never gonna see a one-legged tool pusher—never.

Anyway, after I got out of the hospital and all, I went to see Nonc 'cause Syd my lawyer had wrote me a letter. It said Junior, though the court has seen fit to award you a job for life, I would commend you to your superior, Mr. Deshotel, to work out the arrangements so that they might prove advantageous to you. Put bluntly, son, you don't want to be consigned to a miserable desk in the corner just staring at the wall and playing with yourself all day.

I had to get a podnah of mine who had gone to college to read Syd's letter and figger out exactly what it meant. After I figgered it out, I was tempted to say that didn't sound so bad—at least the part about playin' wit' myself—but I could see the man had a point.

So I go to see Nonc and he said Junior, what about dispatchin'?

I said workin' the radio and stuff?

He said there's a lot more to it than that. We got twenty-one hot-shot trucks on the road every day 'tween here and Lake Charles and eleven different crews on rigs from Belle Pass clear to the Sabine River. You gotta help take the work orders when they come in and you gotta make sure everybody's goin' where they need to be goin'. Sometimes you gotta wake up people in the middle of the night. Normally, it don't pay roughneck pay but we got a deal wit' your lawyer that we cain't cut your pay from what you was makin' so you'll be about the best-paid dispatcher in South Loosiana.

I said hell, Nonc, that sounds good to me.

I gotta say, I become a good dispatcher. I caught on fast and I'd get on the radio and talk shit to them drivers and order everybody to go here and go there. Most of the workers knew I'd worked the Awl Patch myself and knew what the hell I was talkin' about. Plus about half of them jacklegs had heard about my accident and felt sorry for me, and the other half had heard about that shit I stirred up at the Alibi and were afraid of me. Either way, I didn't get no guff, except from some peckerhead now and then. And when I did, usually I'd just say well, you wort'less piece of shit, if I could crawl through this radio, I'd show up in your truck right now and kick your ass into the bayou. But instead, you bein' a peckerhead and all, I'm just gonna report you to Nonc, who won't just fire you but he'll make sure you never get another job wit' another awl company as long as you live.

No lie, after about three or four months even Nonc come 'round to say Junior, goddam, son, you keep them trains runnin' on time. Had I known you was so good at this, I'd had 'em chop off that leg earlier!

Even I laughed at the joke though Betty Zeringue, one of the li'l gals who was in the Gros Bec secretary pool, tole me I shoulda tole Nonc he was out of line. But hell, I was feelin' so damn proud as a dispatcher, I went to the Maison Blanche Department Store in New Awlins and bought me some khakis, white shirts, and ties and started wearin' them to the office every day.

Man, Nonc and Stu Plauche, the fella who kep' the books in the office, give me shit about that, yeah! Oh, hell, Junior, perty soon you'll be comin' in to work in a damned tuxedo! Oh, hell, Junior, perty soon they'll be drivin' you in a damned limousine!

But I could laugh at that, too. Besides, ole Betty, who was a perty nice-lookin' gal, would sidle up to me and say oh, Junior, you lookin' sharp, oh, yes you do, cher!

'Course, that Betty girl had this weird thing for my wooden leg.

Anyway, things were goin' perty good and they might still be goin' perty good 'cept I started spendin' too much time at the dog-gone Go-Go Bar. I'd sit there some nights just about all night drinkin' beer and b.s.-in' wit' them strippers and stick my leg money in their G-strings or buy 'em overpriced Singapore slings or piss it away at the blackjack table. It was like the damn Wild West in there—between the whores and the drunks and the crooks and the dope dealers and the hardlegs and some bad-ass *cou-rouges* who were podnahs wit' Rocko Marchante, the owner, you never knew what the hell would happen.

One night one ole boy that I'd worked a coupla offshore jobs wit' was so hopped up on some kinda dope that he jumped up on the stage and went after one of them girls while she was dancin'. Man, he'd lost it bad and he whupped off her G-string and dropped his pants and had her up against the wall and was about to do the wild thang wit' her right under them revolvin' Day-Glo lights when two of Rocko's bouncers jumped up there and grabbed the idgit and threw him so far off the stage that he landed four tables out. He cracked his head on a pitcher of Pearl and was perty well knocked out and bleedin' like a heart-shot dog when them big mean bastids come off the stage and grabbed him by the ankles and drug him facedown out the bar and all away across the oyster-shell parkin' lot.

Then them sumbitches threw him in the Hollywood Bayou in front of about ten witnesses—not givin' a damn whether he was dead or alive. Bad-asses, I'm tellin' ya! Last I heard, that ole boy was still in some hospital someplace wit' a steel plate in his head.

Anyway, it's true I'd come to work hungover or even half drunk some days but I'd always stop at Po-Boy's Coffee House that was owned by my ole podnah Po-Boy Trahan, who was once in my gang, and I'd eat a big breakfast and drink about a gallon of Community Coffee before I'd show up at the office. And even though Nonc kinda knew what was goin' on 'cause, face it, I looked like shit a lot of days, I could run my mouth on the radio better half drunk and hungover than most people could sober.

The trouble started when Wiley Smurl, this snakey-assed *cou-rouge* from up around Beaumont or somesuch place in Texas, started hangin' around the office. He was what we called a sub for the drillin' crews   if somebody got sick and couldn't go out on a job, Wiley was one of the men we sent to replace them. 'Tween us, Wiley was one of them guys who talked a smooth damn game but when it came down to it didn't know his ass from a hole in the ground. Out in Texas they'd say he was all hat, no cattle. He was a tall, skinny, possum-faced guy who reminded me, unfortunately, of a cowboy version of that bastid Armentau. He did dress good, though.

Wiley took to comin' in and hangin' around the office, waitin' on jobs, even though Nonc discouraged most of the men from doin' that. But he had the hots for that sweet li'l Betty girl and he'd come in wearin' his cowboy hat and his cowboy belt and his shined up crocodile-skin cowboy boots and his damn string ties and talkin' his cowboy shit and oochy-cooin' around Betty like a horny ole hounddog draggin' his dick in the dirt. Man, even ole Junior here ain't never been that obvious! I guess I mighta been slightly jealous, though personally I thought Wiley was butt-ugly— he had so many acne scars that it looked like somebody had smashed out a pack of lit Camels on his face.

But the real deal was that I was tryin' to do my job and there he was runnin' his mouth about what a goddam amazin' fella he was and how he had a great-grandpa who had fought the Injuns and killed a bunch of Mexicans at the Alamo and how he'd gone to Vegas and won ten thousand dollars one night at the blackjack table and how he'd lost it all in one throw of the dice an hour later and how, really, he was a rodeo rider and a gambler and boxer by profession and was just down here in this here swamp among all these ignorant coonasses just tryin' to earn another stake to get him back to Vegas.

I'd heard this kind of b.s. a lot from lots of them rednecks out on the rigs and, anyway, who the hell was he talkin' to? Shuh, about the time I was dumpin' all my good money in that rigged blackjack game at the Go-Go Bar, I once bet ten thousand

dollars—serious, ten G's!—wit' this ole boy who come into the
bar one night and claimed he was connected to the racetrack in
New Awlins. He said Guidry, I got this horse, no shit, it's as fast as
a ten-dollar whore runnin' to a hundred-dollar blowjob, and, no
shit, even if he wadn't, it's rigged for him to win the third race
today at Jefferson Downs. That sumbitch is payin' thirty-to-one
odds, so if you win, podnah, you'll be eatin' steak for breakfast for
the rest of your life.

I'd been on an all-nighter and I was still drunk and I waited for
the bank to open and even the woman behind the counter tried to
stop me from takin' out that money 'cause she knew my deal by
this time. She also knew the money I was takin' out was money
Momma had me put aside for Lolly-Lee. The woman give me
a speech but I damn well took it out anyway and I give that
sumbitch the money and that's the last I saw of it.

Oh, that horse ran, awright. His name was Buzzard Bait and
they got mules in Jasper Daigle's pasture that coulda outrun that
sumbitch. He finished dead last.

Anyway, Wiley didn't have nuttin' on me so I'd finally heard
enough of his b.s. one day and stood up and said Tex—I called
him that 'cause I knew he hated it—there must not be any bullshit left in the entire state of Texas 'cause you obviously done
brought it all down here wit' you. Now, a man is entitled to bullshit all he wants to 'cause even down here in the swamps of
Looisiana we have been known to b.s. a time or two. But you
gonna have to take it somewhere else, podnah, 'cause I got work
to do and you disturbin' the hell out of me.

Oh, man!

He threw me one of them rattlesnake looks and I was hopin'
he'd come after me but he stomped out huffin' and puffin',

clickin' them cowboy boots like he was spurrin' a damn horse. Later, after I'd gone out on break, I heard he'd snuck back in and was runnin' me down to ole Betty, callin' me a ignorant coonass gimp and stuff like that.

Sweet Betty didn't tell me, 'cause she didn't wanna cause no trouble, though I think even she thought Wiley was just a blowhard. I don't think he ever got to first base wit' her, really. But they got a lot of women in the world who'll let gasbags like Wiley go on and flirt wit' 'em 'cause somehow it makes 'em feel better.

But ole Stu Plauche tole me what Wiley said. Stu was a smart man—he'd gone to college up at LSU—and was one of them refined Cajuns who talks like them smart people you meet up in New Awlins. But, man, Stu hated them Tex-asses 'bout as much as I did and used to always tell me Junior, a lot of the people down here are poor and it is true we are not as refined and educated as people in many parts of the world. But we have a nice, easygoing, fun-loving culture and it had been a pretty good place to live till those shit-talking Texans invaded us with their oil wells and money and started putting everybody—all of us—down as coonasses because our English sounds a little different and many of us can speak French. Now, of course, not everyone who comes from Texas carries on like a *cou-rouge*. But why would ignoramuses like Wiley, who talk like they have marbles in their mouth, think they have the right to make fun of other people? They make fun of *our* accent?

I loved listenin' to Stu 'cause he wadn't one of them typical stuck-up college boys. I knew he was a podnah for the home team.

Anyway, I decided I wadn't gonna stir no shit at the office. I figgered I'd just hold on to what Stu told me and I'd catch ole

Wiley out one night, 'cause I knew he sometimes even showed up at the Go-Go Bar tryin' to arrange some nooky or a card game, and I'd kick his ass good. I figgered I had to, no matter what, 'cause he was the kinda snake who'd come up behind you wit' a broken beer bottle one night if you didn't make him hurt first.

That was my plan, anyway.

Around the same time—it was tax season—Nonc started bringin' in his Aunt Annadelle to the office to help Stu out wit' the books. She was a retired schoolteacher who'd taught arithmetic at the Cat'lic school in Ville Canard for forty-four years. She was a nice lady, tall and thin wit' silver hair, and she spoke proper, like Stu. For some reason we hit it off good, me and her. Don't ax me why. Nonc had bragged on me as a worker and she was the kind of lady who would say stuff like, my nephew speaks very highly of you, Mr. Guidry, and he tells me he wouldn't want to try to run this place without you.

Mr. Guidry? Shuh, I gotta say I kinda liked that 'cause there hadn't been too many people in the world who'd broke their backs to say somethin' nice about Junior Guidry.

She come in and took over makin' the coffee 'cause she said these young Cajun women don't know anything about makin' coffee. She unplugged the percolator we had and brought in a big speckled drip pot and, man, she was right—she'd boil up some water on the li'l stove and spoon it in a bit at a time and I ain't never had coffee better than hers. Not even Momma's, and she made good coffee.

When I'd get my coffee break, me and Miz Annadelle, which is what I called her, would talk about this or that. The lady knew a helluva lot about the Awl Patch. I was surprised! You could tell her about some technical problem you'd had drillin' deep offshore and she would know exactly what you were talkin' about. She even got to where she would kid me, and now and then she would even stop me when I was talkin' and correct my grammar. She would say Mr. Guidry, *cain't* and *ain't* are lazy words and I know from my nephew you are not lazy. She didn't say it bad and I didn't take it wrong and doggone it if I didn't start watchin' how I talked when Miz Annadelle was around.

'Course I'd never talk that way around my Awl Patch buddies—that's a good way to get your ass kicked.

Well, things were goin' good when one mornin' I come in a bit early and, yeah, I was hungover and I'd been up all night. Plus I'd dropped about five hundred bucks at the blackjack table and I was feelin' about as friendly as a cottonmouth wit' his tail under a tire.

And damn it if I don't come in and see ole Wiley sittin' in my chair wit' his cowboy boots up on my desk yakkin' away on my phone!

I just snapped. I did. I shoulda just walked out but instead I walked up behind him and grabbed him by the scruff of his fancy-ass cowboy shirt and yanked him so hard that he and my chair—it was one them kinds wit' wheels—went skatin' into the wall clear across the office.

Ole Tex hit the wall goggle-eyed and it knocked his cowboy hat clean off his head and for the first time I realized he was a baldheaded sumbitch. Man, he come stumblin' toward me with his fists cocked like one of them boxers you see on TV and I squared myself up and reared back and was gonna take his goddam head off.

I never even heard Miz Annadelle come in the room.

I never even saw her try to get between us.

But when I swung, I caught her wit' about half my swing and she went down like a *dosgris* hit wit' buckshot.

When I saw what I'd done, the fight went out of me.

Ole Tex took a poke but I grabbed his wrist in midair. I'd been right about him all along—he was a boxer about like I was an accountant.

He was a damn girl.

He spit on me and said you've screwed the pooch now, you stupid coonass! You'll never get another job in this town.

I squeezed his wrist till I heard a bone crack. Then I let him go and he run wild-eyed out of the office swearin' he was gonna kill me.

By this time, Betty and Stu had come in. We picked Miz Annadelle off the floor and drove her to the hospital.

She didn't come to for three or four hours. I had broke her jaw.

I never bothered to go back to the office. I figgered Nonc Deshotel would just come find me one day and kick my ass and I wadn't gonna stop him. I was just gonna let him go at me.

People say I'm a damn whiner but I didn't even bother to call my lawyer, Syd.

Nonc never came around to kick my ass. I mighta felt better if he'da done it. I heard later that Miz Annadelle, even though she had to get her jaw wired up, didn't hold nuttin' against me. She knew I didn't mean to hit her. She knew Wiley was a jackass.

I even wrote her a letter sayin' I was sorry. I don't write wort' a damn and I don't know if she ever even got it.

But I did learn, from Betty girl, that Nonc wouldn't even let her say my name.

10

I guess you can get used to anything. Even this trailer ain't so bad in the cool weather like we got now. I drift in and out of sleep.

I dream of Lolly-Lee but it ain't a bad dream for a change. Me and her and Momma sittin' on a porch swing. Lolly-Lee is sayin' her ABC's. Momma is pleased.

When I'm awake I can hear Momma sayin' what kind of man don't know his own daughter? What's wrong wit' you, Junior Guidry?

Funny how Momma can still get on me after she's dead.

How can I miss somebody I don't even know?

I sleep. I wake. I dream of the ghost. She floats through the window like a white cloud, singing some song. It's not a song I know.

I wake up. I wonder about her, Iris Mary.

My spins have stopped. I don't know why but I decide to get up and go see her.

I wobble down the hall.

She's on the couch on her back, a quilt Momma gave me pulled up to her chin. There's a moon shinin' in the window. She looks peaceful as a child.

I wonder what Iris Mary dreams about? I wonder if she really killed somebody?

I settle in on the edge of the couch. She shifts and mumbles and then quiets down again. Her face is smooth as the moon. She breathes slow and easy. She mumbles some more. I don't know why, but I sit and watch her till the moon leaves the window.

Then I get up to go back to bed. But I stumble and fall.

I try to catch myself on the back of the sofa but I fall across Iris Mary.

She screams and then she's sittin' up and pushin' at me and punchin' at me and screamin' no, mister, no! Don't do this to me! And I'm tryin' to grab her arms but she's gone crazy and one of her punches catches me on the lip and I finally get my hands up and yell stop it! I'm not doin' nuttin' to you! Stop it!

Iris Mary stops swingin' but she scoots backwards on the couch away from me. She says what are you doing, Joseph? What were you trying to do to me?

Her voice is high and strange. I can see she's shakin' like a dog left out in the cold rain.

I put up a hand. I say whoa, lady, I wadn't doin' nuttin' to you. I come in here 'cause, uh, well, I heard somethin' and I wanted to check it out. Then I pooped out and I didn't think I could make it back to the bedroom so I sat on the edge of the sofa. But I wadn't doin' nuttin'. No reason to clobber me like that. I was gettin' up to leave and I stumbled. You know I'm not steady on my feet.

I touch my hand to my lip. I feel the warm sticky blood.

If it makes you feel any better, I say, you got me. You got me good.

I raise my bloodied hand in the bad light to show her.

Iris Mary looks at me careful and I can see, even in this light, her rabbit eyes are wild. They've got tears in 'em.

She don't say nuttin' for a while. Then she says that's what he would do, you know.

Who? I say.

The man.

What man?

The man who tried to have his way with me. The one I killed.

Did you punch him in the lip, too?

She looks at me and takes a deep breath. Then another. I realize she's cryin' but it's not any cryin' I've ever seen. She is shakin' so hard I'm afraid her head will twitch off her body.

No, she says. No. I didn't punch him in the lip. I didn't.

Then what did you do?

Iris Mary looks at me in the dim light and she half raises up on her knees. She half raises up and then she pitches forward and falls against my chest. I'm about half knocked over but I manage to steady myself and Iris Mary buries her face in my pajama shirt and she moans like some wounded animal in the deep woods.

She says God help me, Joseph. I didn't punch him in the lip. I didn't. No, I bashed in his head. I hit him over and over and over again and I saw him fall backwards onto the floor and I saw his eyes go milky as the moon and I think I saw his soul take off and fly to the devil.

Iris Mary pulls back from me and her eyes are big and red as a whippoorwill's. And then she falls against me again and she cries.

She wails like a shot dog.

I don't know what to do or say. It don't feel right to put my arms around her. It feels wrong not to. So I just sit there.

Somethin' about this makes me want to run the hell out of there. But where would I go?

Iris Mary cries and cries and then she pulls away and says look, I'm sorry I'm so hysterical. I need to pull myself together. You go on back to bed. I'll be okay. Really.

I nod.

I cain't think of what to say so I gimp on off to bed.

I lie awake for a good while listenin' for Iris Mary and I hear her pacin' up and down. She paces and paces and I half wonder if the girl might be goin' demented. I half wonder if she might come after me in my sleep.

I might feel bad for her. I might be scared of her. It's hard to know.

I wonder if I've done right lettin' her stay.

If I wake up wit' a knife stuck in my head one mornin', I guess I'll know the answer.

11

I wake up, stiff as a board. My back hurts. My neck hurts. I've been sleepin' crooked all night, or what was left of the night.

There ain't no knife stuck in me, though.

But somethin' is different and I cain't think what.

Then I know—I wadn't dreamin' of Armentau.

I look around. The sun's high up in the window. I hear the ghost rattlin' around in the kitchen again. I smell coffee and bacon and maybe eggs. I cain't quite make everything out but it smells good.

I get up and go to the bathroom then head for the couch. Iris Mary comes in after a while. She looks okay. She's washed her face and combed her hair, pinning it up high. She's still pale as a speckled trout but somethin' about her seems different to me. She don't seem as freaky-lookin'.

Maybe it's just like what happens to you in the barroom. After about a six-pack, you can drink them ugly girls perty, 'specially if there ain't no good-lookin' ones around.

She says I've made breakfast though I know you don't usually eat breakfast. But there's plenty if you want some.

I look at her, tryin' to remember the things she tole me last night. I wonder if I might've dreamed the whole thing.

I say well, I might have some breakfast if you promise not to slug me.

Iris Mary looks at me funny, like she might smile. She says I doubt if I'll need to slug you again, though I will if I have to. And anyway, last night, I didn't mean to. I—well, I panicked.

I wave my hand. It ain't nuttin', really, Iris Mary. Believe me, I been slugged harder than that.

She nods like I've said somethin' serious and then she turns and goes to the kitchen and comes back wit' two plates. She sits one on the rickety table in front of me. It's got scrambled eggs and bacon on it.

She says how do you take your coffee?

Strong and black.

She says well, lucky for you, that's how I make it.

She goes to the kitchen and brings the coffee in them cheap green plastic cups of mine. She settles in on the other end of the sofa from me. She sips her coffee and eats slowly and I do the same. We don't say nuttin' for a long while.

Then she says I need to tell you something, Joseph. I'm here and I'm in trouble and you have a right to know.

You mean about that man?

Yes, she says, about that man. See, the worst thing wasn't doing what I did to the man. It was running off and leaving Miss Laney. She's just a sweet, kindly, bony thing with nobody to care about her but me. She was his mother and he just stuck her up there in this big attic he'd converted. He just locked her up there and wouldn't even speak to her half the time, wouldn't even climb the stairs to see her but once in a while. She would say Raymond, I want to go out into the yard. Iris Mary will help me down. I want the sun on my face.

And he would look at her and say it's too hot, Momma. Or you don't need to be out there, Momma. Or he would just laugh and say Momma, this is where you're going to be from now on. Get used to it.

Iris Mary stops and shifts and fiddles wit' her dress and draws her knees up under her. When she does, she shows a bit of leg.

I gotta admit, her leg looks awful good.

She says Miss Laney would sit in the rocking chair in her room and say her rosary and she would tell me, Iris Mary, as God as my witness, I don't know the heart of my own son. Sometimes I think he can't be my own flesh and blood. He's so cold. I loved him but the love never took. He drove away his wife and his own children, my grandchildren. He terrified them. My own daughter-in-law told me. She will not even speak his name.

Iris Mary stops and takes another sip of coffee and shifts in her seat.

She says I felt so bad for Miss Laney that I tried to talk to the man about her but it was useless. He would tell me to mind my own business. He would say look, I'm paying you good money, plus a free place to stay, to take care of my mother. I don't pay you for your opinion. If you don't like it here, just leave.

I thought about it but I couldn't leave Miss Laney. I'd been there almost a year and I'd become quite attached to her. Besides, I didn't have many choices. I was saving my money, thinking I would try to make it to New Orleans one day when I had a few months' rent in my pocket. But I don't know New Orleans,

Joseph, and in a way, I was afraid. I'm bayou folk, you see, and I wasn't sure I was ready for the city.

She stops and picks up her coffee cup with two hands and takes another sip. Then she looks around like she's lookin' for somethin', then looks out the window.

She says let's go outside, why don't we? Let's go sit on the stoop. It's such a beautiful day. I think this is a story I need to tell in the light.

I look at Iris Mary. I ain't been outside in a while—I figgered I was done wit' outside, actually. But if she wants to just go and sit, fine wit' me. Anyway, I gotta hear this story. I need to figger out how freaky Iris Mary really is.

She gets up and I follow. It's a bright Injun summer day. Momma loved such days. I used to like huntin' rabbits on such days myself.

We settle in on my li'l rusted stoop. The mornin' sun's warm on my face and I look up and see a big ole chicken hawk circlin' up high in the blue sky. I wish he'd come down and eat some of them doggone nootras, or at least some of the mice that keep movin' in wit' me.

Iris Mary says you know, this is actually a pretty handsome swamp. If you lived in a proper house, and if you didn't throw all your whiskey bottles in your yard, it wouldn't be too bad out here.

I say well, you can go pick up my whiskey bottles if you want to. Help yourself. And you ain't been here in summer. When the rains come, there's water halfway up these steps. Mosquitoes like you wouldn't believe. Doggone cottonmouths crawlin' every-where.

She says a lot of people mistake common water snakes for cottonmouths.

Oh, so you think I don't know the difference?

I didn't say that. I was just pointing out a fact.

Well, I can tell you I know the difference. One of them things come swimmin' up from my toilet when I first moved in—no kiddin'. And if you think this is such a great place, I'll sell it to you, no money down. I'll move to town.

Iris Mary looks at me hard at first, then smiles. She says now there's an offer I can refuse.

Even I gotta laugh at that.

Then she looks way over by the swamps, then looks up at the sky and says well, I want to tell you the rest. But I need to back up a bit.

My parents died when I was fourteen. They were, well—they were murdered. I told you I'd seen some hard things but nothing was harder than that. For years, in fact, I believed it was my fault. Maybe I still do. I'm convinced they were murdered by voodoo, by—

I put up my hand. Wait, wait, Iris Mary. Voodoo? Some kind of bad *gris-gris*? You ain't tellin' me you believe in that stuff. You don't look like the type.

Iris Mary shifts on the stoop and looks at me. She shrugs. It's a strange story, I admit. Just hear me out.

We lived way down in the salt marsh at a place called Bayou Go-to-Hell. I was close to my parents. They were kindly and they understood me. I was born this way, you see—I am an albino. Maybe it's not easy being an albino anywhere. But down where we lived, people are not very sophisticated. Some are terribly superstitious. Some could be cruel.

Papa, especially, would try to toughen me up. He loved me but he refused to treat me like some delicate flower. He was a shrimper and in the summer I would go with him on his boat. I wasn't really strong enough to help him set the trawl, but when we pulled it in, full of glistening white shrimp, I could *trier* the catch with the best of them. We would pick through the trawl, sorting out the trash fish and throwing them over the side, and have these nice long talks. Usually, these were little homilies about how you can't live down to bad people. People like the Carencros.

See, we lived near a big Creole family called the Carencros. They claimed to have the voodoo and they told everyone that I was a child of the devil, a freak of nature. People were afraid of them. Their eldest son, Elgin—they called him Pick—would follow me around at school, saying vile things. He was big and a bully. He picked on all the kids but he seemed to especially have it out for me. He would taunt and torment me. For no other reason, as far as I could tell, except that I looked different.

Some days I would have traded everything I had to look normal. To have blue eyes or brown eyes or green eyes like everybody else. To have color in my skin like you do, Joseph. To have black hair or brown hair. Anything but *this* hair. Sometimes I would look in the mirror at my eyes and think maybe the devil *had* made me.

One day at our little school on the bayouside—I was in the seventh grade—Pick caught me alone as I waited to be picked up by Papa. He yanked my hair. He called me a red-eyed bitch and cursed me with some other words I can't repeat. I don't know what happened but I snapped. I turned on him like a bobcat and clawed him good. I raked deep slashes in his cheek. I never knew I could be so angry. If I had had a gun or knife, I think I could have killed him—seriously.

He was stunned, but he slapped me and I fell to the ground and he fell atop of me.

Next thing I know he had a knife and was holding it to my throat.

That's when we heard the boat. We lived three miles down the bayou from school and Papa would come most days to pick me up in his putt-putt, his little swamp runabout. Sometimes he would even let me take the boat by myself.

Pick knew the sound of my father's boat—putt-putts have a signature throb—and he also knew my father. Papa was a big man and not one to abide foolishness. He knew of my trouble with Pick. Once, he overheard Pick taunting me and Papa had a word with him. I don't know what he said, but people said Pick went pale and slunk away like a dog that's been kicked but hasn't learned a lesson. I was mortified. I didn't want Papa messing with the Carencros.

When Pick heard my father's boat, he ran off, but not before vowing to get me good next time. Papa saw the state I was in and asked me what happened but I couldn't tell him. I was afraid—afraid mostly of what Papa might do.

The next day at school, Mr. Broulet, the principal, called me into his office. Pick was there, as was a teacher named Odelle Samanie. Miz Odelle, as everyone called her, was a Carencro by birth. Pick's aunt. She was a widow, prim and severe, and cross as a hawk. All the children feared her.

Pick said to Mr. Broulet that I had attacked him and tried to scratch his eyes out.

His aunt said she'd seen the whole thing.

I was suspended from school.

I was driven home by Mr. Broulet—Papa and Momma didn't have a phone. He wouldn't look at me. He dropped me off without coming in.

I started crying as soon as I got in the door. I had no choice then. I told my parents the whole thing. My father just looked at me and said now don't you worry about this, Iris Mary. I'm gonna straighten this out.

I said don't, Papa. It won't do any good. Miz Odelle will lie and so will all the other Carencros. And it will just make things worse. Just let it be, Papa.

He said Iris Mary, cher, you worry too much. He kissed me on the cheek.

I only found out the full story of what happened next much later.

When Papa couldn't get satisfaction from Porter Broulet, he drove his pickup over to Caillou Carencro's house—that was Pick's father. He knocked on the door. I know Papa tried to reason with him but one thing led to another.

Caillou had been drinking and became angry. He told Papa I was evil—*une putain diable*—and that I was the cause of all the trouble. That's all it took. Papa lost his temper and grabbed Caillou by the shirt and dragged him off the porch and marched him to the bayou. He threw him in and said if Pick bothered me one more time he would come back, and all the Carencros would be sorry.

He turned to leave and saw the rest of the Carencros had come out on the porch—Pick and an older brother, a big oaf named Buster, and Caillou's wife, the one they called Tante Lo-Lo. Buster had an oyster knife. Pick held two giant dogs by their chains—some kind of bulldogs that the Carencros entered in dogfights they held at night way over on some lonesome *chenier* in Daigle's Swamp.

They sicced the dogs on Papa, who ran for his truck. He snatched a tire iron out the truck bed just in time and took the first dog down with a blow to the head. But the other dog lit into him and knocked him to the ground and bit into his calf. Papa managed to kick free and swing the iron again and hit the dog as it came at him again. He hit it hard and it went down in convulsions. Next he knew, he was scrambling backwards on the ground as Buster swiped at him with the oyster knife. It caught him on the right hand and sliced it open.

Papa went into a rage. He scrambled to his feet and wrenched the knife from Buster and knocked him to the ground—knocked the fight right out of him. Pick attacked from behind. Papa peeled him off like a sweaty shirt. Tante Lo-Lo began hitting him with a stick. Papa put up his hands and snatched the stick from her.

Buster was still down on the ground, so Papa grabbed Tante Lo-Lo and Pick by the scruffs of their necks and marched them to the bayou and threw them in. He went back and pulled Buster off the ground and marched him to the bayou, too. There they were, the whole lot of Carencros, sputtering and cursing and trying to claw their way up the muddy bayou bank.

As Papa started to leave, one of the dogs came to and went for him. Papa was halfway in the truck when the dog grabbed him by the arm. Papa slammed the dog's head in the door. It released him but Papa wouldn't release the dog. He held its head in the vise of the door and started the truck and drove away. He dragged the dog along the shell road for miles, hoping to kill it. When it wouldn't die—when it kept trying to bite him—he sped up as fast as he dared and opened the door.

The dog flopped out and bounced hard.

Papa braked the truck and looked back. He said he was going to turn around and run over the dog—finish him off if he wasn't dead.

But when he looked back, the dog wasn't even there. It had vanished.

Papa came home in a bloody mess. He was dazed. Momma wanted to drive him to the hospital way in town but he said no, just bandage me up. He sent Momma and me to the back of the house. He got down his shotgun and loaded it and sat out on the front porch saying his rosary and waiting for the Carencros.

The night passed and nothing happened.

I spent the week at home, glad to be suspended. When I went back to school, Papa made a point of coming with me. It was a strange experience.

Miz Odelle had suddenly quit teaching. And no Carencros had been in school all week. I had a bad feeling about all of it, and I told Papa we should go away.

He said Iris Mary, go where? This is our home, cher. Our family goes back on this bayou to my great-grandpa. We sure not gonna be run off now by those ignorant Carencros.

A month later, I went to school feeling uneasy and depressed. It was a rainy winter day, gloomy. The day dragged on. Something was wrong but I couldn't put my finger on it. The Carencros still hadn't been at school.

In the late afternoon, Mr. Broulet came into my class at school. When I saw him look at me, I knew.

He called me out in the hall. He said Iris Mary, there was a fire at your house. Your parents were trapped inside. They are dead.

The men came from town to investigate. They said it must've been the wiring that caused it. They said they had been overcome by smoke before they could get out.

I knew better. I knew in my heart of hearts that the Carencros had done it.

At the funeral, I could barely stand. And suddenly I saw her standing in front of me, a woman in black with a black scarf pulled tightly around her head. It was Miz Odelle. She pressed something into my hand. It was a doll of some kind. She said Child of the Devil, you are next.

I fainted.

Papa's family had mostly moved away, except for the old great-uncle who owned our house and who was too frail to look after me. I'd heard about a distant cousin or two on my momma's side who lived someplace around Ville Canard but I'd never met them and had no idea if they were even still around. Momma had an older sister, Prosperine, who was a nun teaching in the Catholic school way up the bayou and living in the rectory. My aunt made arrangements to take me in. She got me into the school, though for weeks I was in a daze and couldn't go.

I slowly came out of it and I finally had the courage to show my aunt the doll. I told her the whole story.

I saw it in her eyes—anger and fear. She said come with me now, child. We have to see Father.

Father DeLaBreton was his name. He was an old priest of the old school, a Jesuit, very well educated. He listened to my story and examined the doll that Miz Odelle had given me.

He said Iris Mary, don't worry about this thing. I will take care of it.

Now, I consider myself a good Catholic. I love being in the quiet of the church. I love the smell of incense and the statues and the light pouring through the stained-glass windows. But like a lot of children I didn't necessarily believe in all that hocus-pocus. My parents were devout but not superstitious. But word about what happened next spread slowly up and down the bayou far, far into the salt marshes, way down where the people live poor and isolated and ignorant on those lonesome *cheniers* near the Gulf. Father had gotten out the old books and he found the ritual and he took the doll and the gold crucifix from the altar and some holy water and he drove to the Carencros. And he walked onto the lawn and he threw the doll on the ground and he held up the cross and said the prayers.

And Caillou and Tante Lo-Lo came out onto the porch and screeched at him. They cursed him and called him unspeakable names and vilified him and threatened to shoot him if he didn't leave. But he held up the cross and he said the rituals and commended the doll back to Satan.

People who had happened along, who had been walking or driving down the road, people who had stopped to watch this spectacle, said the Carencros piled off the porch with knives and guns, threatening Father.

People said the knives became hot and couldn't be held and the guns would not shoot.

I'm not sure I believe that, Joseph. I honestly think the Carencros just realized they would never get away with killing a priest—not with witnesses around. I think they never really tried to kill Father, only to scare him away.

But to this day, many people believe the saints were protecting Father. In the old days, you know, this is what the people believed—that the saints are alive with God in heaven and can intercede on our behalf.

Anyway, Father fell to his knees and threw himself facedown into Carencro dirt and then, after a while, he rose up again and dug a shallow pit with his hands. And he threw the doll into the pit and raked dirt on top of it and stomped on the mound with his foot while he said his prayers in a big, booming voice.

And those who watched say the doll rose from the ground and then burst into flames. And up on the porch, Tante Lo-Lo swooned and toppled from the top step and fell dead to the ground.

Iris Mary stops and looks at me.

She says I honestly don't know what to believe, Joseph. I can't explain the doll, and it is possible Tante Lo-Lo died of a heart attack or something. Anyway, the Carencros, the whole lot of them, picked up and moved to the deep swamp, plotting revenge. At least, that's what people say.

Father DeLaBreton got sick soon thereafter and never really recovered. He died a year later of pneumonia.

I lived in a little room at the back of the rectory for six years. Then my Aunt Prosperine passed away of cancer. And once again I was utterly alone in the world.

12

Iris Mary sits there on the stoop lookin' at me as if she expects me to say somethin'. I don't know what to say. Of the stories I've heard in my life, I can only think of one stranger—my brother Beau gettin' married after he was dead. Most people think that was a freaky thing, and maybe it was. It made Momma happy, though.

Iris Mary says Junior, I know I could be boring you with all this. There's more to tell and I—

I put up my hand. I say no problem, Iris Mary. You got my attention, I mean it.

She says do you think this is too crazy?

I say you talkin' to Junior Guidry, girl. I been in some crazy things myself.

Iris Mary looks away, up into the clear blue sky. The sun on her face makes it shine like a gold moon. I have to say, Iris Mary has a pretty face.

She says after my aunt died, I became very angry, particularly angry at God—I hated Him. I'm sure I hated Him worse than you've ever hated Armentau. What right did He have to take everybody I loved away from me? What did He want from me? Couldn't He see inside my heart? Didn't He see how I bled? Still, I blamed myself. If I had just stayed quiet about Pick Carencro and kept things to myself, none of this would have happened.

The Mother Superior came to me and said I could stay attached to the convent as long as I wanted to. She wondered—and I know you will laugh at this—whether I might want to follow in my aunt's footsteps, become a nun. I would have to go off to New Orleans to study, but this could easily be arranged. I thought about it briefly but decided it wasn't for me. I'd lived so little in the world as it was. And, of course, I was still mad at God.

This was the path that led me to Miss Laney. For in the meantime, I needed to support myself. Mother Superior came to me to tell me about a school in Ville Canard that had a program to train nurse's helpers, people to care for the elderly, things like that. I decided to enroll and I did well and the woman who ran it told me about what seemed like a perfect job. A man—a rich man—had advertised for someone to live in and look after his aging mother. The salary was generous and it offered a free place to live.

At first it seemed too good to be true. The man lived in a beautiful new house a few miles north of town in the middle of a big sugarcane field. There were no other houses for a mile or two but that suited me fine. There were azaleas and wisteria and gorgeous old moss-draped oak trees and a man who came in once a week to look after it all. I had my own little suite, with a bathroom of my own and a kitchenette.

Raymond, as his mother called him, was a mystery to me. When I went for my interview, he barely spoke to me. He said he would agree to anyone his mother picked. There was something cold about him. He had this look in his eyes—he never looked at you, but through you. His eyes were always darting around.

I went upstairs to meet Miss Laney for the first time and we hit it off right away. Within a half hour she told me I had the job. She seemed thankful that there would be someone else in the house—someone to talk to. I moved in the next day. I had very little in the way of possessions, except for my clothes and a picture of my parents that my aunt had copied for me, and a keepsake statue of the Blessed Mother that she had given me as well. It wasn't some fine artifact. It was one of those two-foot-high ceramic kinds that you see on lawns everywhere, fairly heavy. People buy them and then paint them, usually white and blue—

I put up my hand. I say hey, wait, hold on. I know about those things. Momma had one. In fack, most of the ladies down this bayou have 'em in their yards.

Iris Mary stops and smiles. She says oh, of course you'd know what they are. Anyway, this particular statue was a cheap thing but it had special significance to me, since my mother had given it to my aunt as a gift to decorate the little patio outside her room at the convent. So my aunt left it to me—that and her rosary. Honestly, I felt a little sheepish about carting it to my room and putting it on my bedside table. But I had so few keepsakes of my family, I wanted it near me.

Good thing, too.

Things were fine at first. The man kept strange hours but he was generally civil. He seemed to sleep through a lot of the day, then get up in the late afternoon and spend his whole time talking on the phone. Whenever I was anywhere near him, he would lower his voice so I couldn't hear what he was saying. But sometimes, when I came down to the kitchen to fetch something and he didn't know I was there, I'd hear him shouting or saying ugly things into the phone. He seemed always in a state of agitation.

Then he would go off to attend his business, though he never told me what that business was. When I once asked Miss Laney, she simply lowered her head. She refused to speak of it.

I'm a light sleeper. Sometimes I would hear him come in and I would look at my clock and it would be very late—sometimes near dawn. Now and then I would hear other voices, usually women. Often they were boisterous. Sometimes angry.

The man had a wing of the house that was off-limits to me. I didn't make much of it—I like my privacy, too. But now and then, when he was gone, the door would be ajar and I would peek in. The first room was a den of some kind. As far as I could tell, it was nothing unusual—a black leather couch and chair and one of those mock fireplaces. I also noticed a cabinet full of guns. I didn't make that much of it. Lots of men down here have guns— Papa had three of them himself. I noticed at the rear of the den was another door, which I assumed led to his bedroom. But I dared not go in there. I already knew enough about the man that he gave me the creeps.

Months went by. The only time I ever really spoke to him was when he paid me, every two weeks. Sometimes he'd just leave the money in an envelope on the kitchen table. Sometimes he would call me into the kitchen and take the money from a clip in his pocket and pay me. It was always in cash. He would say things like, Is my mother all right? Does she need anything?

Once I made the mistake of saying well, perhaps you could ask her yourself. She might like your company. He glared at me and said I was to mind my own business.

Iris Mary stops talkin'. She looks up, hands shaded over her eyes, into the bright blue sky, like there's somethin' she expects to see. She stares out for a while and then looks at me. She says this is not easy to tell, Joseph, but you need to know.

I look at her careful. I say well, you wanna take a break?

She says no, if I take a break, I might lose my courage.

I say well, just keep goin'. Go slow. Take your time. I ain't got nowhere to be.

One night, she says, I awoke to hear voices. I looked at my clock and it was just after two—earlier than Raymond usually came home. I started to roll over and go back to sleep when I heard someone scream and then what sounded like scuffling.

I got out of bed and went to my door and listened. I heard a door slam and then another and then what could have been another scream but it was too muffled to make out. I opened my door and tiptoed down the hall in the dark and made my way to his door. I put my ear against it and listened. I thought I could hear a woman sobbing, then silence. I tiptoed back to my room and closed my door quietly and crawled back into bed. I worried that something horrible was going on but I was too afraid to do anything about it. If I could have locked my door, I would've. But there were no locks, so I pulled my sheet up over my head and eventually went back to sleep.

I was startled awake again by voices—they sounded angry. This time they were outside. It was still dark. Then I heard doors slam and a car start. I got up and crept to the kitchen window, where I peered out. I could see the taillights of the man's car as it drove away. When the car reached the main road, I heard the engine gun and it sped off, tires squealing.

I started back for my room but I noticed the man's door was

ajar and a light was on. I should have just gone back to bed and minded my own business. But something powerful pulled me toward the door.

I walked down the hall to the light.

What I saw stopped me in my tracks. There was blood on the floor—splatters of it—in a trail leading to the second door.

I almost turned and ran but then I heard a sound, muffled, like a voice. I listened carefully and, against my better judgment, began edging toward the second door. As I got closer, the sound became clearer—it was definitely a voice of someone moaning, of someone in pain. I got to the door and opened it.

I could've fallen down.

It was the man's bedroom, all right, and in the center of it was a huge four-poster bed made of heavy wood. It was like something you'd see in one of those old plantation houses up on the river. There was a woman—no more than a girl, really—kneeling at the foot of one of the posts. She was naked and her hands were lashed to a bedpost.

She had been badly beaten. I can't tell you the look of surprise and fear on her face as I untied her. She began to scream and I put my hand to her mouth to shush her for I couldn't be totally certain that the man hadn't returned.

I couldn't think of what to do. I found myself saying who did this to you? Who would do such a thing?

She looked at me, as if in a daze. She didn't answer. She turned away and began looking for her things. She finally found a dress, a short shiny blue thing, and her shoes. She put them on. She didn't bother with anything else. Then she turned to me and said, her voice faint and trembling, who are you?

I said I work here. I take care of the lady upstairs.

Do you have a car?

I said no.

She said is there a way to town without taking the highway?

I said there is but it's a bit complicated.

She looked around, as if lost.

I said tell me what happened to you.

She said you don't want to know.

I said I need to know. I live here.

She said he's a bastard.

The man who lives here?

He lives in hell. He's a monster.

Did he beat you?

She looked at me, her eyes wild. She said beat me? Oh, he beat me all right. Beat me and more. God, for what he did to me I wish he'd killed me! They trapped me, both of them. They put something in my drink . . . They . . . she—oh, God!

I tried to go to her to comfort her but she just backed away, fear in her eyes. She said I'm not like that. I know what it may look like but I don't do those things. I work for him but it's just a job. It's—I never thought, I, uh—

She stopped and then began screaming. I have to get out of here! I've got to! He's coming back—coming back with those animals he calls his friends! If they catch me, they'll—

She began to choke on her sobs.

I was so shocked by this, Joseph, I didn't know what to say. I'd never imagined such things. She just pushed past me and I could see she was unsteady on her feet. I followed her out of the room and down the hall and said why don't you call the sheriff?

And she turned and a look of terror came over her and she

said the sheriff? The sheriff? You must be joking. He *owns* the sheriff and if I called them they, well, they would . . .

She stopped and looked at me hard and said miss, I don't know you but I'm begging you not to call the cops. Just pretend you never saw me. Just pretend like this never happened. If he catches me I'll just say I managed to untie the ropes. I won't tell on you. 'Cause if he finds out you cut me loose, he will do unspeakable things to you, too. He'll make you sorry. Very sorry.

I followed her to the door. She looked around like a scared animal and then disappeared into the night and I stood for a long while in the hallway, trembling with fear and rage. I was determined to call the law. It was the only way. But as I began to dial the number, I heard a car pulling in the driveway.

I panicked and ran to my room and shut the door and crawled under the sheets and tried to calm my breathing.

I heard them enter the house. I heard a loud pounding, like someone beating their fist on a wall. I heard shouts and curses and the awful sound of footsteps as they came down the hall.

And then my door burst open and my light came on and the covers were snatched off of me.

There he stood—the man, and a woman and two other men— his face twisted in rage. He pulled me out of bed and said, uh—

Iris Mary looks at me. I see her eyes are big as the moon.

He said, Joseph, a thing I would not normally repeat but I want you to know the kind of man he was. He said where the fuck is she!

Suddenly, I felt myself slip from my own body and I looked down on myself and I heard myself speaking in a voice that was strangely calm. I found myself rubbing my eyes and saying I'm sorry, but where is who? What is it you want? Why are you in my room like this? Please be quiet or you will wake up your mother.

He looked at me and a small flicker of doubt crossed his face. He shoved me back down roughly on the bed and leaned close and whispered in my ear, if you're lying to me, you bitch, you'll pay.

Then he turned away and they all left and I trembled in shock for hours.

I should have run away, or I should have been brave and gone to the sheriff. But I didn't. I was afraid. I remembered what the girl had told me. And I also worried about Miss Laney.

I couldn't go back to sleep, so at an appropriate time, I went upstairs to be with Miss Laney. I asked her if she'd slept well, thinking maybe she had heard the ruckus. She looked at me with complete innocence and said she'd never slept better. I wasn't going to burden her with what I knew. Maybe I hoped that being in her company would protect me.

Nothing else happened for a while. I steered clear of Raymond and began to convince myself that it was all a bad dream. I kept thinking maybe I *had* imagined it.

But, staying—well, it turned out to be an awful mistake.

About a month later I'd gone to bed and fallen into a deep sleep. I was dreaming about my mother when I was startled awake by a presence or a feeling.

The man was leaning over me in the dimness, a knife in his hand. He pressed it to my throat and said what did I tell you would happen to you if you lied to me?

I was too rattled to answer. I tried to shrink away from him but he grabbed me by the hair and yanked me toward him. I was too shocked to even scream.

He said we caught her, finally, in Texas. It took a while but we tracked her down. And we got it out of her—how you invaded my room, how you cut her loose.

He said I gave her to my boys. They played with her for a few days and then they took care of her.

He said if you don't do what I tell you to do, I'll bring them here one night and give *you* to them.

Iris Mary stops and shifts on the stoop. She looks at me again. There's tears in her eyes. But some fire, too.

She says he yanked off my covers and pulled up my nightgown. I scrunched up like a mad cat at the end of my bed.

He looked at me with utter contempt. He said I just wanted to see. Next time I come I'll want more. I'll take it, too.

He said don't try to run. She ran and we tracked her down. We'll hunt you down, too.

He turned and left. I lay there, paralyzed with fear.

I should've run, of course. I could have run back to the convent. But I knew he *would* track me down. I'd told my parents about Pick Carencro and look what happened. What if I brought such a fate to the sisters? This man would stop at nothing.

I was trapped. I couldn't believe something so monstrous was happening to me again. I prayed and prayed and prayed. I said if there is a God, He must spare me this. I remembered how the people on the bayou said the saints had protected Father De-LaBreton. I prayed to the Blessed Mother that she would protect me. It's not that I prayed with much hope, but I prayed constantly.

The man didn't return right away. In fact, that's when I knew how evil he really was. He was mocking me—giving me every chance to run, knowing that he had me in terror, knowing that I wouldn't run. I thought about trying to move into Miss Laney's room under some pretext but then thought better of it.

What if his mother wouldn't matter? What if he took his liberties with me in front of her? What mother could—should—endure that?

Eventually, I began to hallucinate. I couldn't sleep. I couldn't rest. I had this fantasy about stealing one of his guns and hiding it under my pillow and when he next came to me shooting him dead. One minute I would be resolved and brave and defiant. The next I would be a trembling mass of tears. I'm sure this is what he intended for me.

So one night, in utter exhaustion, I went to my bed and collapsed.

And next thing I knew, there he was, hovering above me. At first I thought it was a nightmare. But I smelled his foul breath— liquor and cigarettes.

He said it's time, Iris Mary. Don't make trouble for yourself or me.

He said I will make you my slave like I made her my slave.

He said sit up.

I found myself obeying.

He pulled my nightgown off over my head.

He said lie back.

I did.

He said don't say a word. Don't even breathe.

He kneeled down before the bed. I felt his tongue on the inside of my knee.

And then I heard my papa talking to me. He said you don't have to, Iris Mary. You don't have to do as he says.

I suddenly sat up.

The man tried to push me down but I found myself reaching out to him. I found myself saying it's okay, it's okay, and tousling his head. I found myself saying you don't have to force me.

And he said oh, oh yes. Oh, I know your kind. You really want it, don't you? Don't you?

And I heard myself saying oh, yes, I want it. I truly want it.

And his tongue moved higher and I spied the statue of the Virgin on my nightstand. *That's* what I wanted and that's what I prayed God I could reach. I reached oh so slowly with my left hand for I knew I couldn't give away my motions. I found myself gripping the statue and raising it and then getting both hands around it.

And when his tongue moved higher still, I slammed it down with a force I didn't know I had. His head jerked up and there was fire in his eyes.

I knew I had to put out the fire or die.

So I hit him again, and again and again until he rolled away from me and slumped faceup on the floor, his eyes still wide open, his mouth in a snarl. I stood above him and raised the Virgin again and I saw the flicker of fear in his eyes but I didn't care.

I raised the statue again and would have hit him again but he suddenly twitched and his eyes went milky and his head slumped to one side. It was as if the air was sucked from the room and I knew something had changed.

That he was gone and couldn't hurt me.

I dropped the statue and walked from the room, not even bothering to dress. The air felt thick as butter. I was soon in his den and then in his room. I turned on the lights and looked around carefully. I was in no hurry. I had a strange sense of calm—as if nothing could hurt me.

I rummaged through drawers and closets and found things I hadn't dreamed existed. He had stacks and stacks of magazines—filth, Joseph. Men, boys, women, animals. I noticed another door that I thought was a closet. I opened it and found it was another den, but different. It had a cot against one wall and all kinds of devices—chains, whips, things that looked like dog collars with spikes. At first I couldn't conceive of what he did with these things, and then it hit me—this was some sort of torture chamber.

This is where he brought women like the woman I had freed.

This is where he intended to take me.

I noticed a filing cabinet against one wall. I found a shoe box stuffed way toward the back of the top drawer. I took it out and opened it. It took me a while to realize what I was seeing. They were Polaroid pictures. There were dozens of them. The man was in every one of them. I can't tell you what he was doing, Joseph, I can't. But I can show you. I stole them, you see, or some of them. I knew if I didn't have them no one would ever believe me. No one.

Then I rummaged around some more. In a drawer by his bed, I found a pistol, a shiny thing, not too big. I took that, too. Maybe I thought in desperation I could figure out how to fire it.

I went back to my room and stepped around his body. I got down my little suitcase and put the pictures and the gun in them. I put on my simplest dress and gathered the rest of my clothes and my things from the bathroom. I was about to leave when I decided I should take the statue, too. It had saved my life and I knew I wanted it, heavy as it was.

I reached down and picked it up. It was splattered in blood but I didn't care. I put it in my bag.

I thought about Miss Laney but I couldn't face her. How could I tell her something so awful? She has a phone in her room. I figured that when I didn't show up for a few hours, she would call someone. I couldn't think any more clearly than that.

I walked out into the dark, not sure where I was going. I just walked and walked and walked, sticking mostly to back roads, until the sun came up and I found myself on a bigger road. A cane farmer in a pickup truck came along and slowed down and offered me a ride. He asked where I was going. I said as far as he could take me.

He dropped me off at the junction of your little road. I just started walking. I napped in the canefields and then I stumbled on your place and, well, here I am.

Iris Mary stops and she looks at me. She seems calm.

She says wait here, Joseph, I want to show you the pictures. You have to see them.

Iris Mary gets up and goes inside again and brings out her bag. She kneels besides me and upzips it and gets out a small shoe box.

She hands it to me and I open it up. The pictures are turned upside down. I grab a handful of them and flip them over.

I have to say I've seen some nasty pictures before but none quite like these. In one of 'em, the man is leadin' the woman around on all fours with a big chain attached to a dog collar.

The next one causes even ole Junior here to flinch.

The man is gettin' it on wit' a dog. It ain't really a big dog, neither. In fack, it looks perty much like a beagle.

Now, there ain't much that's ever disgusted me but I find myself turnin' the pictures back over and puttin' them in the box.

Iris Mary says was that the dog, Joseph?

I look at her and nod. Yeah.

She says you should keep going.

Why? Is there more stuff like that?

Worse.

Worse?

I turn the pictures over and flip through them again. Iris Mary ain't kiddin'. There's one of an old woman tied up in ropes.

She says have you ever seen such a horrible thing?

I realize the cat has got *my* tongue this time. Then somethin' slams me like a ballpeen hammer.

I say oh, my God—it's not? He's not—he's not a—

Iris Mary holds up her hand. She says please don't say that word. And, honestly, no, I looked at it carefully. It's not his mother.

I say well, it's somebody's momma. Or, actually, somebody's grandma.

Iris Mary looks at me, dazed.

I don't know what to say. I force myself to flip through all the pictures, every one of them.

I feel sick to my stomach.

There's somethin' else about this that bugs me. I turn the picture of the old lady over so I don't have to see it and I go through the pile again slowly. I feel like I'm lookin' for somethin' and then I know what it is.

These are Polaroids and the light ain't always good and most are fuzzy and the man is in the background but when I look close enough, a light flickers on.

I think I know this sumbitch from someplace.

But where? Where?

13

It's been more than two weeks since Iris Mary tole me all this. I've got that sumbitch—that man she knocked dead—in my head but I still ain't placed him. Maybe it's all the whiskey I've drunk.

Iris Mary, meantime, is a mess. The girl's fallin' apart. She can be fine, act normal, for hours, then she just loses it. She starts cryin'. Talkin' to herself. Blamin' herself for just about every bad thing that's ever happened in the world.

My first thought was that we oughta somehow check wit' the sheriff's office to see what they know—hell, maybe just go in there and explain the whole friggin' mess. Maybe talk on the sly to my podnah, Roddy, the deputy. Wit' them pictures, ain't nobody gonna blame her for what she done.

But Iris Mary went nuts on me. She hardly ever raises her voice but she screamed at me. She said she knew the man and the law were in cahoots and if she went in they'd just turn her over to the man's friends and they would take turns doin' what the man was gonna do himself. She screamed at me and then broke down cryin' and begged me not to call.

So I didn't. Anyway, hell, I ain't gotta phone. They disconnected that a long time ago 'cause I wadn't up to payin' the bill. For all I know, she's prob'ly right about the law.

Three nights ago I woke up and Iris Mary was curled up at the foot of my bed. She was cryin', though I could barely hear her.

I sat up and said look, if you cain't sleep on the couch, just sleep here. I'll take the sofa. It ain't no big deal.

She said no, Joseph, that's not it. I'm afraid. Sometimes I'm just afraid to be alone.

I said afraid of what? The man? He's dead, girl, he cain't hurt you. Plus, think about it. If the ole lady liked you, she probly ain't told nobody about you. You could be free and clear of the whole thing.

She sat up and crossed her legs and said no, they're after me. I just know it. I've done an awful thing and I have to pay.

Awful thing? Iris Mary, you gone *craque* on me? Far as I'm concerned, you done the right thing, shuh, the only thing you could do. After I looked at them pictures, I wanted to kill the sumbitch myself. You done the world a favor.

Iris Mary said all this violence is wrong. Look where it's got me.

I said talk sense, girl. You think you could have reasoned wit' that man? Was your own daddy able to reason with the damned Carencros? He went there to talk to them but when they tried to kick his ass he did what he had to do. He defended himself, and you. I woulda done the same thing.

Iris Mary said I'm so tired of it all. I'm so weary of my past. Sometimes I wish I could just start my life over.

I looked at Iris Mary and said hey, tell me about it. When I was fifteen and bustin' everybody's ass, I thought I could rule the world. Now look at me—a damn gimpy drunk livin' in a pigsty out in the middle of nowhere.

Iris Mary said well, as I keep telling you, you don't have to be a drunk. Nobody's making you. And I know you think I'm a nag. What is it you said—I'm harder to get rid of than fleas on a dog? But you have to admit I've kept up my end of the bargain. This place isn't a pigsty anymore.

I couldn't argue wit' that, though I figgered the girl was gonna start lecturin' me again. But she surprised me for a change.

She smiled and said hhm, we're some pair, aren't we, Joseph? Imagine you and me in the same boat.

Even I had to laugh at that.

I gotta say I hadn't thought about me and the ghost bein' a pair. Or exactly in the same boat, either. But I gotta say—though I ain't about to tell Mother Superior—that the girl might be growin' on me.

That must show how fucked up my life really is. Maybe I been lonesome and didn't know it. Maybe I don't really wanna die. Or maybe I'm just gettin' desperate.

When Iris Mary is feelin' normal, she goes for walks or she cooks. I like the cookin' part. Be a cold day in hell before you see ole Junior warmin' up a pot. Just about everything that comes in a can, I've eaten. But I don't mind eatin' real cookin'. It's not just the gumbo thang she's got goin' on. The girl cooks a jambalaya spicy enough to burn a hole in a gator hide. And that's just how I like it.

She said I don't have to be a drunk, and maybe I don't. I haven't had a drink in six days. Don't ax me why. Maybe it's easier not to drink than to have the flea bitin' into my ass. Or at least givin' me them looks. I get them shakes now and then but eatin' helps.

I even threw out my whiskey. Imagine that.

As soon as I threw it out I wanted a drink so bad that I cussed myself. But it was too late then.

One afternoon, when she wadn't feelin' bad, Iris Mary gave me a haircut and a shave. That girl seems to know how to do just about everything there is. She said you clean up well, Joseph. If you took care of yourself you'd be presentable.

I didn't have nuttin' to say to that but I did look in the mirror later, somethin' I hadn't wanted to do in a while. I awmost didn't recognize myself. Them girls used to think ole Junior here was a good-lookin' devil. Maybe I was. Maybe I could be again.

It's October now and cool. The mosquitoes got chased off by an early frost. At least the day don't start like a damp rag and end like a damp mop like it does in summer out here. The sky's blue and there's a bit of color in the hackberries, and the sugarcane up my road is head high.

I know about the cane 'cause Iris Mary has gotten me to go on a couple of her walks—shuh, it's sometimes easier than arguin' wit' her. She says you need the exercise, Joseph. She said you need to get out.

I said I need a damn sight more'n that.

She said well, it's a start.

Iris Mary takes it slow and we don't go too far. She likes to walk along the li'l canal that skirts the swamp. There's a low levee that we take and the goin' is easy. The girl seems to know a hell of a lot about the swamp, too. She says her daddy taught her. She stops every now and then to point out some tree or plant. She can name every doggone bird she sees, even them little dickey birds. I can barely see them bastids, much less tell what the hell they are.

I hunted some when I was a boy but I cain't say I know much about the swamp, 'cept it's full of cottonmouths and mosquitoes and gators and you can bog your ass down real quick if you're stupid enough to try to walk it. As for birds, about the only ones I ever cared about were the ones I could shoot.

One night Iris Mary said tell me about everything, Joseph.

I said what you mean?

About your life. Tell me about your life.

I shook my head and said you already know too much about me. Don't get me started.

She said well, tell me about the parts you liked.

I said I would if I could think of any. Maybe it's when I had all that money after my accident.

But that money didn't get you anywhere, did it?

I said it got me somewhere. Least for a while. Hell, I had myself a good ole time—what I remember of it.

She said it got you here, too.

I said well, I cain't argue wit' that.

She said do you think that could be the point?

Of what?

Of your money—maybe it was only given to you to teach you something.

Oh, yeah? What did it teach me?

That it can't buy you love or happiness.

I said it bought me love now and then.

She said well, I doubt that's the kind of love you could depend on.

I said it was there long as I had money.

She threw me one of them looks. She said you are *so* exasperating sometimes, Joseph.

I said what the hell does that mean?

It means you're ornery. Stubborn. Like this plow horse my papa once ran for a man who had a big potato patch way up our bayou. Every time Papa hitched that nag to the plow, she wouldn't move. The man that owned the horse told Papa, hit her on top of the head with this—just not too hard. He handed Papa a sawed-off two-by-four. Papa did and that horse would go to work. But she never learned. Every day Papa would have to apply the two-by-four.

I said what, you wanna do that to me?

Iris Mary smiled for a change. She said maybe I do. Go find me a two-by-four and we'll start today.

I laughed, too, but then I just said Iris Mary, you got some crazy ideas in that head of yours. There will be some things you'll never understand.

She said tell me about your mother.

I said why would you want to know?

She looked around and said well, you don't have a television. And I doubt if you can sing. So you can at least tell me a story or two.

I said you're bein' a smart-ass, right?

She smiled and said I guess I am.

I said I already tole you about my accident.

She said I know. We can talk about that some more, too, if you want.

I waved my hand at her like I was battin' away a gnat. I didn't say nuttin' right away. In fack, I didn't say nuttin' for a coupla more days. But I thought about it.

And then I started talkin' to Iris Mary one night and, shuh, I ended up tellin' her about awmost every damn thing there is. About my fucked-up drunk of a daddy and my poor momma and my dead brother and Irene my sweet but scatterbrain baby sister and the rest of the six Guidry kids who couldn't wait to get the hell off Catahoula Bayou. About all them boys I beat up at school. I tole her about Berta and Lolly-Lee and crazy-assed Alma, though I left out the trailer-hitch part, knowin' what I know about Mother Superior.

I tole her about my fight at the Alibi. I tole her about gamblin' away all my money, even the part about how I pissed away the ten thousand dollars I'd put aside for Lolly-Lee. I tole her about wreckin' all them cars. I tole her about losin' my job for life 'cause of that stupid deal wit' Wiley Smurl. I tole her about gettin' evicted from my castle and livin' for a while in a flophouse, just like that damned Armentau, till some drugged-up guy tried to stick me wit' an ice pick one night. I tole her about how I was about to go live in a ditch someplace till I went through some clothes I'd stashed in Roddy's garage and found fourteen hundred dollars. I tole her how I used that money to buy this wreck of a trailer and this patch of swamp it's sittin' on and moved out here figgerin' I'd had enough of just about everybody and everything.

There was one deal I wadn't gonna tell her. One deal I wadn't gonna tell nobody. But I tole her anyway.

I said you know, Wiley and his *cou-rouge* buddies got me not too long after I got fired. They caught me wobble-leg drunk one night wanderin' around the back parkin' lot of the Go-Go Bar lookin' for my car.

Them boys come up from behind and they held me while

Wiley kicked and punched me. All I can really remember is Wiley sayin' I'm gonna make you bleed, coonass. Wiley, if you ax me, still punched like a girl but he did a good job makin' me bleed. I got a concussion, a busted lip, a black eye, and three broke ribs outta the deal.

Another thing I remember. Wiley got it out and pissed all over me while I was down on the ground. Laughed while he did it.

I said so, Iris Mary, I got turned into a pussy boy after all. I'm shore they woulda killed me 'cept some guy come to make out wit' his girlfriend and saw what they was doin' and yelled at 'em. They run off like cowards.

Iris Mary said oh, Joseph, I'm sorry. That's awful. Beyond awful.

I said was it my fault?

She said no, of course not. How could it be?

I said well, then what happened wit' you and that man, or wit' Pick Carencro—that cain't be your fault, neither.

She just looked at me, sad like Momma sometimes did.

I said that wadn't the end of it. An ambulance come to pick me up and when they found out I was broke and out of work, they carted me off to the Charity Hospital in New Awlins. They dumped me in the emergency room and drove off. I laid there all fucked up for hours on a stretcher. They finally sewed up my head and put me in a room wit' some ole boy they pulled from the ditch after a motorcycle wreck. He screamed for three days wit'out stoppin' before he finally died. I think the doctor come to see him once. I think I heard that he was biker trash from up by Mississippi someplace. They looked at me about the same way.

After nine or ten days, I'd seen my doctor twice. I couldn't even get them sour-ass orderlies to change my sheets. I was still dizzy and sore but I threw what little I had in a paper sack and walked out of that hellhole the minute I could stand on my feet wit'out fallin'. I took the Greyhound back to Ville Canard and realized nobody I knew even knew I was gone. Maybe nobody gave a damn. Maybe that was best. I didn't want to have to tell nobody what Wiley had done to me.

Iris Mary reached over and put a hand on my head and touched the scar that Wiley left me. She said does it hurt still?

Iris Mary has the soft hands of a child.

I said nah.

She said did you think you were going to die?

I said no, but I mighta wanted to die.

But you decided not to?

I said I'm not shore if it's a thing you get to decide.

She said sometimes I think it is. When you came off the rig after the accident, you were certain you weren't going to die, as I recall it.

I said yeah, but that was different. It was that rathole of a hospital that got to me more than Wiley's beatin' on me.

She said well, now you see how it is for a lot of people.

I said what you mean?

She said how a lot of people live in despair in terrible places or situations without hope.

I said well, I got my ass out of there.

She said well, what about the people who couldn't—people who were too poor or tired or sick or confused to get out?

What about them, Iris Mary? Was I s'posed to get them all out, too?

She said no. But maybe now you know how it feels to be trapped and helpless. Maybe now you know how it must've felt for those boys you beat up when you were younger.

I said I don't see how one of them things has to do wit' the other.

She said there is a connection, in a way. You just have to try harder to see it. Stop and ask yourself how they felt.

I looked at Iris Mary and I could feel the red-ass comin' on. There's somethin' about the way Mother Superior always puts things. It's worse than the doggone third degree. She don't put you under the lights and make you sweat—shuh, I could take that. No, she needles you and puts them damn questions in your head and then there they are, rattlin' around stirrin' up shit.

I said okay, you got me. Yeah, I felt like a helpless gimp. And, yeah, it felt rotten.

She said when you got back to town, Irene would have looked after you.

I said I guess so. But Irene gets on me, bad as Momma. Bad as you.

She said it's probably that Irene loves you. She probably hates it that you've lived the way you've lived. Maybe she just wants you to clean up your act.

Maybe.

You shouldn't run from the people who love you, Joseph.

Yeah, well, I can tell you for a fack there ain't that many.

'Cause you've chased them all away?

Maybe.

I'm sure Lolly-Lee would love you if you gave her the chance. I can tell you for a fact that little girls want to love their daddies.

I said well, I don't even know her. She's not so small anymore.

Who's fault is that, Joseph? She's a child. You're her father. She needs her father's love. Maybe you need to grow up.

That gave me the red-ass, too. I said you sound like Momma. Anyway, Lolly-Lee's gone. They live far away.

She said Joseph, do you know what you sound like now?

I said no, what?

What do you think? The one thing you hate to be.

What? A pussy boy? Bullshit, lady!

She said think about it. You're afraid. Afraid! You'd have a lot of explaining to do—about why you haven't been around, about why you never went to see her, about why you never called. Maybe you're afraid she won't forgive you.

I said are you tryin' to make me feel better or worse?

She said I'm just trying to make you feel.

That's the thing about Iris Mary. The girl always wants ole Junior to feel this or that.

Maybe I ain't wort' a damn at figgerin' out how I feel about anything and why I feel that way. Or maybe the last thing in the world I wanna do is feel them things—shuh, you go there and you might not come back.

Iris Mary has perty much moved into my room now. She comes in after she thinks I'm asleep and she lies with her back to me, though not touchin' me. And soon I hear her breathin' soft as a baby and I know she's asleep.

Sometimes I roll over and watch her sleep in the dim light. Sometimes she whimpers and cries in her sleep. Sometimes she looks peaceful as them statues on the wall at church.

I don't know what to make of this—a damn woman in my bed and I lie there and pretend she ain't there.

Sometimes I wake up in the middle of this and I'm all man. I got me a boner bigger'n a Lake Palourde alligator and there's Iris Mary sleepin' right next to me. And it's not that I cain't touch her—what would stop me if I wanted to?

I been eatin' regular and I gettin' my strengt' back.

At the very least, I could cop me a good feel and ole Junior here could use one, lemme tell ya. Hell, she wouldn't even know it.

No, I don't touch her 'cause I know I shouldn't.

And you know why I know that?

'Cause Iris Mary put them questions in my head.

How would you feel, Joseph? How would I feel?

Sometimes, when I feel hornier than a two-dicked goat, I go to the bat'room and jack off.

Mostly I try to think 'bout Alma and all them women I've had. Mostly I try to think about Alma and the trailer-hitch thang.

But sometimes I think about Iris Mary—oh, yeah. Like I said, the girl's a bit skinny for the way I usually like my women but I gotta admit I've noticed a few things lately. For one, she's got a cute butt though I cain't imagine ever sayin' such a thing to Mother Superior. She'd prob'ly fall over dead. Or slug me. Or say oh, you're *so* crude, Joseph.

But when I'm done gettin' hot over Iris Mary, I say damn, Junior, what the hell is wrong wit' you, son? Man, you are *losin'* it. Losin' it big time.

Even I can see what a joke I've become.

Joseph sleepin' in bed wit' the Virgin Mary, just like that fool in the Bible.

14

I hear a car bangin' up the narrow road.

Wit' all that stuff 'bout the dead man, I guess I'm spooked. I jump up quick as my leg lets me and hobble to the window.

It's my podnah Roddy. I've lost track of the days, otherwise I might have remembered it was about time for him to show up.

Iris Mary ain't here, which is lucky. It's mornin' and she wanted to go for a long walk, so I said go wit'out me. I don't go on long walks.

She said we'll take a short walk together this afternoon.

I said I knew you wadn't gonna let me get out of it.

She laughed and said you know, you *are* trainable, Joseph.

I said what the hell does that mean?

'Course, I knew what it meant.

I watched her go along the swamp path. She had on blue jeans and a green sweatshirt. That girl looks okay in them jeans. She looks better than okay, actually.

I wonder what Iris Mary would do if she saw ole Roddy pullin'

up. He's in his truck, not his police car. She'd still prob'ly haul
ass, and I'd never see her again. Somethin' about that gives me
the *frissons*. I hope that girl's gone on as long a walk as she said
she needed.

Roddy comes bouncin' up the steps of the trailer carryin' a big
paper bag. I've already made the door when he raps loud.

I say hey, podnah, I'm right here. Keep your damn shirt on.

I open the door and let Roddy in. He steps inside and looks up
at me with his usual grin. Roddy grins a lot but it don't mean he's
bein' friendly.

Roddy ain't but about five foot seven, though he is a strong
sumbitch. He's got a crewcut and a wide, blocky head. He's built
squat like one of them pug-nose mutts—ugly as one, too. He's all
neck.

Roddy steps through the door and says Junior, how the hell are
you, son?

I say okay.

He says sorry I ain't been out in a while. The goddam sheriff's
office keeps me busier than a one-legged man at an ass-kickin'
contest. We been up to our necks in crooks every doggone day.

Then he looks at me careful and then he looks around. He
says goddam, Junior, what the hell is goin' on here? Somethin's
different. Uh, what the hell?

I say Roddy, there ain't nuttin' ever different in this damn place.

He looks at me again. Then he says, I got it—you're sober,
podnah! Man, what happened? Didn't I bring you a big supply
last time?

I say you did bring me a good bit of whiskey but I busted
a couple of bottles by accident—dropped 'em, you know me.
Drunk up the rest of it.

He says well, damn boy, you must be desperate.

I say I could use a drink, if that's what you mean.

He says damn straight that's what I mean. Well, you're in luck. I brought you six fifths. Some Ole Crow, some Canadian Club. I don't want you to get bored with the same ole shit.

He takes a bottle out and walks over to my coffee table and puts it down. He turns and carries the bag to a closet where I used to keep my whiskey. He opens the door and puts the bag in there, then closes it. He comes over to the table and picks up the bottle. He unscrews the cap and takes a big drink, then holds the bottle out to me.

Damn that's good, Junior. You ready?

I gimp over and take the bottle. Actually, I ain't ready. But I ain't ready to explain nuttin' to Roddy, neither. I act like I'm takin' a big sip but I don't. But even a tiny sip tastes good. Too good, really.

I hand the bottle back.

Roddy looks around good and takes another swig. He looks around again. He says goddam, son, what the hell happened to this place?

What you mean?

Junior, look at it, boy. Your dump of a trailer is clean. Clean!

Aw, shuh, ain't no big deal.

He sniffs the air.

Damn, podnah, I think you even took a bath! Got a haircut! Shaved! What the hell's got into you?

Aw, nuttin', I say. One day I was lookin' for somethin' I'd lost and I started pickin' all my shit up and, well, one thing led—

I see Roddy's not listenin'. He's lookin' over in the corner.

I know what he sees.

Iris Mary's bag is over there.

His eyes go wide and he says Junior, stop bullshittin' me, man. You got you a woman out here now? You shackin' up, podnah? You holdin' out on me? Damn, Junior, you dirty ole dog!

I ain't never been that good at thinkin' on my feet but I hear myself sayin' aw, man, I wish. It's my sister, Irene. She come yesterday and got on my ass about livin' like a *cochon* and she went to town. You know how she is. She all but threw my ass in the tub and then she threw half my shit in the garbage. I myself sat right there on the couch and tole her well, Irene, whatever it is you wanna do, do it. Just don't ax me to do it.

Roddy looks at me wit' his head cocked sideways. He says what's her stuff still doin' here?

I shrug. She left this mornin' before I got up. When I come in, there it was. I figger she'll be back when she finds out it's missin'. You know Irene—the girl's sweet but a scatterbrain.

Roddy looks at me hard for a second and then that grin comes back. He says oh, yeah, I know Irene is a sweet thang, but the girl's got *étouffée* for brains, no foolin'. Did I ever tell you, podnah, that me and Irene got it on one night at a party up the bayou at Deek Cancienne's? We did it in the barn, doggy-style. That girl got wild!

I stare at Roddy, not knowin' what to say. He could be bullshittin' me—far as I know, Irene ain't never had a serious boyfriend or much interest in men. But, true, what the hell do I know? When's the last time I axed Irene about her life? About anything, really?

One thing I do know—before I busted my ass offshore, Roddy woulda never said somethin' like that to me, b.s. or not. He knows I'da kicked his ass good.

I decide I'm gonna ignore what Roddy said about Irene and

file it away. Who knows—if I keep eatin' Iris Mary's gumbo, I might get all my strength back. Then one day Roddy will come over with his b.s. and I'll clobber the bastid.

The only thing I wanna do right now is get rid of him before Iris Mary comes back. He don't usually stay long anyways—just long enough to drop off my whiskey and my disability money. He cashes my check for me, buys my liquor out of it at Shack's in Ville Canard, and brings me the rest.

Sometimes I count it and it's twenty, thirty bucks short, even after subtracting the whiskey money.

I ain't complained about it yet because who else would do it? Irene would cash my check and bring me my money, but she shore as hell wouldn't bring me my poison.

I stare at Roddy, tryin' not to give one damn thing away, and say so, hey, well, I appreciate you comin' out but I know you got a lotta shit to do so—

Roddy puts up his hands. He says Junior, podnah, I ain't in no rush, bro. I thought I'd catch you up on the gossip. I mean, you way the hell out here in the middle of nowhere livin' like a damn caveman.

Roddy is still holdin' the whiskey bottle. He sits down on the beat-up couch and takes another sip and hands the bottle back to me. I do what I did before. I pretend to take a big swallow but I don't take much at all. I screw the cap back on and put the bottle down on the table.

He says well, it's mostly the usual shit. Drunk rednecks at the Alibi and bustups between the Pas-dahs and the Billiots way down the Salt Marsh Road. I'm glad I ain't assigned to patrol down there, Junior. Them people are a bunch of savages. A coupla days ago, one of them ole boys run through his best friend wit' a oyster knife. They was drunk and arguin' 'bout whether a *gasper-gou* is a fresh or saltwater fish. Can you believe that shit? Man, that damn liquor ruins some people, don't it, Junior?

Roddy stops and looks at me. He says yeah, buddy, I guess that's somethin' I don't have to tell you, ehn?

Roddy cackles like a *poule d'eau* when he says this.

He reaches for the whiskey again but I get my hand on it before he does. I say hey, podnah, I ain't tryin' to be stingy but I wanna go slow on this. I got some catchin' up to do.

I don't want Roddy sittin' here gettin' drunk on me. He'll never leave.

Roddy throws up his hands, like I've just arrested him. He says hey, no problem, bro. It's a li'l early for me to get *chaqued* anyway. You keep that bottle all for yourself. In fack, Junior, I'm gonna get out of your hair 'cause I can tell this is one of your red-ass days. But there's somethin' I gotta tell you. 'Tween us nootras, the real news in town is what ain't made the news yet.

I say what's that?

He says it involves an ole podnah of yours.

Of mine? One of the gang?

Junior, no, man. Get serious. You don't have a gang no more, remember? And I guess this guy ain't really a podnah since he helped steal about half your leg money.

What the hell you talkin' about, Roddy?

I'm talkin' about that bad-ass Rocko Marchante—you know, the asshole who runs the Hollywood Bayou Go-Go Bar. The guy who rooked you out of all that money by runnin' that crooked blackjack game.

What about him?

Well, let's just say the mean sumbitch ended up in Canard

General wit' his head up his ass. Some of his podnahs drove him there, said he'd fallen down the stairs at his house. He laid there for six days in a coma—people thought he was a goner. Then he come out of it. But one of them doctors who came in later to look at him didn't believe the b.s. about him fallin' down the stairs. To the doc, it looked like somebody had kicked the shit out him. So the doc, bein' a do-gooder, calls the sheriff's office. Anyway, we sent a man over there to talk to Rocko but his goons were in the hospital room and basically they tole our man to get lost. Well, when the detective starts insistin' on axin' Rocko some questions, the goons pick him up and are about to do the Roto-Rooter up his ass wit' a blackjack. Then ole Rocko speaks up and his mouth is all twisted from havin' his brains beat half out and he says, like some record player at thirty-three-and-a-third, mister, get the fuck outta my face. Go back to your office and tell the sheriff himself to come see me. Tell him to come today or he'll be sorry and you'll be scrubbin' out the toilets in the courthouse for the rest of your career.

Roddy stops so I can let this sink in.

Now, Junior, had it been me, I wouldn'a put up wit' that shit. I don't give a fuck if the guy is s'posed to be Mafia—Mafia guys die, too. I'da pulled my gun and shot the bastid. And his damn goons.

I look at Roddy and wonder if he was always such a bullshitter.

Roddy says anyway, our man goes back and tells the sheriff and damn if Go-Boy ain't at the hospital quicker than a rough-neck runnin' for a beer joint. I don't know the whole deal but basically Rocko tells Go-Boy that some woman who was workin' at his house takin' care of Rocko's ole momma had knocked him on the head and left him for dead. He tole the sheriff he didn't

wanna file no charges, no sir. No, he wanted the bitch himself
and he'd give anybody one hundred thousand dollars who found
her and brought her to him, alive, no monkey business. He told
Go-Boy that he should spread the word to a few of his men he
trusted and if it was a deputy who found her, Go-Boy himself
would get a twenty-five-thousand-dollar bonus. Anyway, we both
know Go-Boy's gotta do just about anything Rocko says. That
sumbitch has a ledger a mile long of the bribes he done paid the
sheriff.

Roddy stops again. He says c'mon, Junior, how 'bout another
pop of that whiskey? Be a podnah.

I look at Roddy, hopin' he don't see what I'm thinkin'. I say
help yourself, and slide the bottle over to him. He unscrews the
cap and takes another big swig.

He says now, the sheriff didn't tell me this hisself—I guess
I ain't one of the ones he trusts. But he tole my podnah, Soileau. We got drunk together a coupla nights ago and Soileau
tole me. Man, oh man, Junior, can you imagine? One hundred
grand? Damn, bro, that's awmost as much as you got for your
leg!

He says anyway, ain't nobody actually got a clue where she
is. It's been long enough now she could be clear to Kansas.
And 'tween us chickens, I figger Rocko Marchante musta done
somethin' perty fuckin' bad to her to make her wanna kill him—
everybody knows that sumbitch is into some real nasty stuff. The
damn Go-Go Bar is always overrun with jailbait—most of 'em
runaways from Texas and places like that, some of 'em not more
than fourteen, I've heard. Anyway, that sumbitch and the woman
who helps him run the bar—what's her name, Junior? You oughta
know.

I say Roddy, hell, I don't 'member my own damn name most days.

He says well, whatever her name is, so said she and Rocko have this racket goin' where they promise to hire them girls to dance for big money and then a few nights into the job they put shit in their drinks and then take 'em home and tie 'em up and both of them would take turns doin' 'em. The woman has a big ole dog and sometimes they bring the damn dog, too. Serious! When them girls come to and complain, Rocko beats the hell out of 'em, then threatens to kill 'em if they say a word to anybody.

Roddy looks at me and says damn, Junior, we shoulda sucked up to Rocko a long time ago. Imagine the parties we missed! If you'da been gettin' all that young pussy, maybe you might not care that that sumbitch stole all your money!

I look at Roddy, wonderin' how the hell I can get rid of him. I stand up from the couch like I'm stiff and gimp over to the screen door. I look out. If I see Iris Mary comin' down the road, I'm fried.

Roddy says that ain't all, podnah.

No?

He says no. First of all, we know who the woman on the run is.

Yeah?

She's a Parfait or some name like that. She comes from down in the lower end of the parish way down near Bayou Go-to-Hell.

So?

Hold on, Junior. Follow me. Now, there are some damn strange things about her.

Like what?

She's a freak—an albino. People say her eyes shine like a rabbit's in a bulleye.

I swallow hard.

She ain't got no more kin. Her parents burnt up in a fire. Some people think they were murdered but they ain't nobody ever proved nuttin'. Somethin' to do with one them voodoo clans down there. Like I said, it's the Wild West down there, Junior.

Roddy looks at me and that grin comes back. He gets up from the couch and walks over to me and looks out my screen door.

I don't like this one bit. I step in front of Roddy to block his view.

He says you lookin' for somebody, Junior? You seem fidgety.

Me? Nah. I get them shakes when I ain't had a drink in a while. Sometimes it helps to stand and stretch.

Roddy gets up close in my face, like he's got some secret he's gonna tell me. He says well, gettin' back to this woman, guess what else?

What, Roddy?

Her daddy was a damn half-breed—Injun, Cajun, God knows what else—a *sabine*. Oh, hell, he could pass for white. But the ole grandpa—everybody knew him down there. He was darker than a blacktop road after the rain. Imagine that. Some people thought the ole grandpa was one of them *sabines* descended from the slaves. If that's true, that makes that girl a vanilla nigger!

Roddy leans even closer. He says Junior, you shore you ain't seen nobody like that, have you?

I look at Roddy and I swallow again and I say, straight as I can, podnah, I ain't, but if I do I'm damn shore gonna try to chase her down.

Roddy slaps me on the back and laughs so hard I think he's gonna fall down. He says Junior, you gimpy bastid, you couldn't chase down a three-legged turtle.

Then he pulls back and says but imagine, if you the one who caught that girl, you'd be rich again stedda some bum livin' in this piece-of-shit trailer. You'd be back in tall cane again.

I say well, like you said, the girl could be anywhere by now.

He says well, she ain't down the bayou no more, that's for sure. Rocko sent his goons down there 'cause she'd been livin' wit' an aunt at that convent over on the northern end of Bayou Go-to-Hell. Them bastids broke into the damn convent and searched the whole place and started messin' wit' them nuns. One of the sisters who was off clackin' her rosary in a back room heard the ruckus and called her brother who's the constable down there. Before long about ten men showed up wit' shotguns. They went in and there was a Mexican standoff for about an hour and them damn rednecks had to grab one of them nuns and threaten to slap her around so they could get out of there alive. Can you imagine that? That damn Rocko thinks he's one mean sumbitch but he's gonna bite off more than he can chew one day. If he ain't careful, about half the Cajuns on that bayou are gonna show up at his bar one night and shoot the place up, and him wit' it, you watch.

Roddy stops and walks back to the coffee table. He picks up the whiskey again. He says I hate some of them damn *cou-rouges* myself. How 'bout one more pop for the ditch, Junior? I'm workin' the night shift tonight. I gotta go home and take a nap.

I say help yourself, Roddy.

He drinks deep. He says you want more?

I say no.

He says well, if any albinos come wanderin' down your road, you catch 'em and call your podnah Roddy here. I'll come get her and we'll take her to Rocko together and split the money, what you say?

I say fifty thousand bucks still wouldn't be bad. You're right. I could get the hell out of here.

Roddy stands to leave. He says Junior, you want me to take Irene's bag to her? Hell, I pass by that li'l shack she rents on my way toward town.

I say aw, don't bother, podnah. When she comes back out here to get it, maybe she'll cook me some dinner.

Roddy laughs. He says I wish my ole lady would cook me some dinner. You seen Donna lately, Junior? Well, no, I guess you haven't. That girl's got a bad case of the fat ass. She don't do nuttin' but lay around watchin' the damn soap operas every day. If I wadn't gettin' so much pussy on the side, I might be upset.

Roddy squalls like a duck when he says this.

Roddy walks out the door and clops down the steps in his cowboy boots. It seems like it takes him a damn hour to make the truck. I hear it crank up. Roddy puts it in gear and turns wide. I hear the truck thumpin' away over the potholes and ruts.

I look out to make sure he's gone and I go to Iris Mary's bag. I open it and get out those pictures again and take 'em to the coffee table. I sit down on the couch and sift through 'em to find one where the man is clearest.

And, damn, it's true.

Iris Mary has fucked wit' Rocko Marchante, the baddest man in all of Catahoula Parish.

That sumbitch is still alive and he wants her ass.

And Iris Mary is even freakier than I thought she was.

I put them pictures back and go back to my whiskey.

15

I got just enough whiskey in me so that I want some more. Any drunk can tell you how that works. That's just how the poison is.

I pick up the bottle. I put it down. I pick it up again. I put it down again.

I pick it up and take a long, long drink. I wipe my mouth wit' my sleeve.

I wish flaky Roddy hadn't showed his sorry ass. I wish I didn't know any of this stuff. But I know it—oh, I know.

But Roddy's right—imagine what I could do wit' a hundred thousand dollars. Damn!

I think of how much I hate that crooked Rocko Marchante and how I'd like to pay that bastid back for a coupla reasons. My money, plus Wiley ambushin' me in the Go-Go Bar parkin' lot. The bastid owes me.

I think about Iris Mary.

Hell, what do I owe that girl? I shore in the hell didn't ax her to come here. She ain't really nuttin' to me.

Anyway, if that sumbitch Rocko is dedicated to findin' her, he's gonna find her. I might as well be the one who collects the money.

He prob'ly won't kill her. Just rough her up a bit. Maybe I could make a deal wit' him. I deliver the girl, they could teach her a lesson and let her go. He already knows she ain't gonna go to the police—she'da already gone if she was goin'. Hell, maybe I could even give her some of the money!

I think about Iris Mary and how sometimes she ain't more'n a child. She said she tole me everything but she didn't. She didn't tell me about her *sabine* daddy or her grandpa who could be any damn thing.

I think about Iris Mary and how she sleeps in my bed 'cause she's scared. She's scared of a man she thinks is dead but she ain't scared to sleep in my bed 'cause she's got big ole Joseph to protect her. She knows Junior ain't gonna lay a hand on her.

Ha!

I don't think I can turn Iris Mary in myself. But I could do what Roddy said. I could just call Roddy and he could come and make like he's arrestin' her. Hell, what would she know?

She's the one who went to Elmore's store to get groceries that day. Maybe Elmore saw her. Maybe Roddy went over there to ax questions and Elmore tole him what he saw. *Why, Roddy, podnah, a girl who looked just like that was drivin' Junior Guidry's truck.*

It makes sense he'd come out here to look.

Like Roddy said, fifty grand is a lot of money, too. It shore in the hell is. *Damn, it is!*

He prob'ly wouldn't kill her, Rocko. He'd prob'ly just mess her up some—bat her around.

But what if he did kill her? Or somethin' just about as bad? How would you feel, Junior? *How would you feel, Joseph?*

I'd kill any man who turned over Lolly-Lee to that asshole. I'd kill him and laugh while I done it.

How would you feel, Joseph?

Anyway, the ghost ain't my daughter. She ain't really nuttin' to me.

I pick up the whiskey again and, though I know I shouldn't, I take another big swallow.

Roddy's such a dickhead. That bastid would sell his momma to Rocko Marchante for the right price.

I owe him a pop in the nose for what he said about Irene.

I ain't gonna split no money wit' Roddy. No way. Never.

I gotta think about this.

I cap the whiskey. I gotta hide it before Iris Mary gets back. I gotta act like nuttin' has happened, nuttin' at all. I gotta think about what I'm gonna do.

I realize I've thought this too late when I hear a rustle up the steps. The screen door opens and there's the ghost.

She's got color in them cheeks from the sun and sweat on her brow and she smiles at me big.

Till she sees what I got in my hand.

Iris Mary has a perty smile, I got to give the girl that much.

That smile goes fast as it come. She says Joseph, what are you doing? Where did you get that?

Somethin' about the way she says it just pisses me off.

I say it ain't none of your business where I got this.

She says I thought you were trying to quit.

I say maybe I was, maybe I wadn't.

She says well, if you're planning to stay drunk, I can't be here.

I say suit yourself. You're s'posed to stay out of my business, 'member?

She says I thought maybe we were past that.

She looks at me, then looks down and shakes her head. She looks up and shrugs her shoulders.

There ain't no fire in them big rabbit eyes. It's a look like Momma used to give me.

She says I guess I'll go. I can't see a reason for me to be here. I can't help you if you won't help yourself. You don't need to stop drinking for me. You need to do it for yourself.

I look at Iris Mary and wonder if she knows how she *really* ain't got no place to go. If Roddy knows about that reward, by now every other jackleg in Go-Boy's office has prob'ly heard of it, too. She'd be lucky to make it off the Catahoula Bayou Road, much less to the parish line.

I hear my voice risin'. I say where the hell would you go, Iris Mary? You ain't got no place to go, 'member? Far as you've tole me, you ain't got a family and no friends in the world 'cept some nuns down the bayou and maybe some cousin someplace that you don't even know.

She says well, I'm not strong enough to stay here and watch you kill yourself. I'll find someplace.

I say so, that's it? Mother Superior sees a man slip down and she takes off, just like that? Maybe I *am* tryin' to quit drinkin'.

She says a person trying to quit drinking doesn't stand around in the middle of the morning with a bottle of whiskey in his hand.

I say maybe it's hard to quit.

I'm sure it is, Joseph. How much have you had?

Not much. I ain't drunk, if that's what you mean.

She looks down at the floor, then up at me. She sniffs the air, gentle as a cat.

She says has somebody been here? Did somebody bring you that whiskey?

I look down. I hope I ain't looked down too long when I look up to answer. I look her square in the eye and say no, why would you think that?

She don't answer.

I say nobody ever comes out here.

She says when I was walking I thought maybe I heard a car on the road.

I keep my eyes on her. *C'mon, Junior. Don't fuck up.*

I say them cane farmers sometime come down here to turn around. But I ain't heard nuttin' myself.

She says well, then where did you get the whiskey?

I had it hid outside in the bushes.

She looks at me like she don't believe me.

I say it's been hid out there in the bushes long before you come here. I'd forgot about it and then I remembered. When you left I went out and got the bottle and brought it back in. I just looked at it for the longest time, wonderin' if I could avoid temptation. And then I took a li'l sip to see how it would feel. It felt too damn good and I didn't wanna drink more but I did drink more. But not much more.

I straighten myself up and realize I've got to tell this story good. Iris Mary is my ticket out of here.

She says that bottle is half empty, Joseph.

Well, it wadn't full when I fetched it.

I think you're lying to me.

I feel the heat rise up in me and for a second I think I'm gonna throw the bottle at her. But I don't.

I say I know what it looks like but it ain't that way. Look, I'll show you.

I walk toward the ghost. I brush past her to the door, then walk out onto the stoop. I open the bottle and I pour the rest of the whiskey out into the yard. I put the top back on and throw the bottle as hard as I can.

It thumps on the spongy ground and bounces once and then rolls slowly toward the swamp. It kerplops into the water.

I just hope Iris Mary don't look in that closet where Roddy stashed the rest of that whiskey. She'll be out of the door before I can catch her.

I look at Iris Mary. There, I say, that make you happy?

She says you shouldn't throw garbage in your yard.

I say well, excuse me.

She says we can pick it up later.

Then Iris Mary looks at me curious. She says anyway, it's not me you need to make happy, Joseph, it's yourself.

Nobody says nuttin' for a while. Then she turns from me and says I need a drink of water. She goes inside and walks softly down the hall to the kitchen. I hear her rummaging in the cabinet for a glass. I hear the tap running. Somehow I know it's not a good idea to follow Iris Mary in there right now.

I stand at the door, thinkin' about what she said.

Make yourself happy, Joseph. Make yourself happy!

A hundred grand would make me a happy man. Oh, yes, it would.

16

The whiskey and the warm fall sun have made me drowsy. I sit on the stoop for a while, listenin' to Iris Mary rootin' around in the kitchen.

I'm wishin' I hadn't drunk none of that whiskey so I could think clearer about what to do. Junior needs a plan. Actually, Junior needs a nap to clear his head. It ain't the best time to be needin' a nap but I gotta be able to think straight.

After a while I get up and hobble in there and tell Iris Mary I'm not feelin' so great. I'm gonna go lay down.

I find her standin' still at the stove. I think maybe she's makin' coffee but I don't smell it.

She says sleep well.

I say you wanna come wit' me? I try to make it sound like a joke.

She keeps her back to me. She says no.

I say I didn't think so.

She don't say nuttin'. Makes me wonder if she's about to have one of her nervous spells—fall apart again.

I say we can go for that walk later.

She says sure, if you feel like it.

I say I'm shore I will.

She says all right.

I say Iris Mary, you're not still mad at me, are you?

She don't turn around to face me. She says no, I'm not mad at you.

I say what are you, then?

She don't say nuttin'.

I say you're not plannin' to run off, are you?

She turns slowly to face me.

I can see tears in her eyes.

Damn!

She says it all just reminds me of the truth, Joseph—that I really have no one and no place to go.

Well, I ain't chasin' you out, in case you've noticed. I might get the red-ass now and then, but you know me—

She says I know that. But it was wrong of me to sneak in here like I did. It was wrong of me to intrude on your life.

Well, you got my sorry ass off the sofa.

Maybe you were happier on the sofa.

Trust me, I wadn't. You the one who's got me to try to stop drinkin'. I'm tryin', honest. Maybe I could even go see that outfit it town—whatcha call it? Alcoholics Unanimous?

I can see Iris Mary almost smile. She says I think you mean Alcoholics Anonymous.

Whatever. That bunch.

Well, like I keep saying, that's a decision you have to make for yourself.

Then Iris Mary looks at me with them big rabbit eyes. She says I've thought about my own decision and I really have to go. I—

I listen to my voice risin' again. We been over this, Iris Mary. Go where? If all that stuff you tole me about that man is true, you prob'ly *are* wanted by the cops—or worse, his podnahs. And it ain't like you can hide. If that's all true, everybody in Catahoula Parish knows what you look like. And there ain't nobody else who looks like you, who looks like—

Looks like what, Joseph? A freak? A ghost?

I didn't mean it that way. You look fine to me, Iris Mary. In fack, you look awful doggone good. But you know what I mean— it ain't every day people meet people like you.

Iris Mary stares down at the floor. She says I know exactly what I look like. And I know what you say is true. But sooner or later I have to face up to what I did.

What you did? Iris Mary, we've been over that, too. What you did was defend yourself.

Still, I killed a man, Joseph. I killed a man in rage and then I ran. It's all so wrong.

Iris Mary has tears rollin' down her cheeks now.

I cain't tell her that that's not true—that she actually didn't kill the fool.

I find myself walkin' to Iris Mary and puttin' my arms around her. The girl don't resist. She collapses against my chest and starts to sob.

I know I ain't wort' a damn in these situations. But this is what I know.

I cain't let her go on her own. A man needs to keep his eye on his prize.

So I just hold on to her. She cries for what seems like minutes, then looks up at me, them rabbit eyes both bright and sad.

She says you can really be nice if you put your mind to it. I appreciate everything you say but I know I have to go sometime. I can't hide out here for the rest of my life.

I say well, okay, I can understand that. But you cain't go runnin' off wit'out thinkin' where it is you wanna go. Tell you what—Junior here has a plan. Let's both sleep on it overnight. If you still wanna leave in the mornin', I'll crank up the ole Plymit and take you as far as I can take you. If you're plannin' to leave Catahoula Parish, that's the best way. I'll hide you in the pickup bed under a tarp. Hell, if the truck will make it that far, I could drive you all the way to Texas or someplace like that.

Iris Mary looks up at me. She steps gently out my arms and dries her eyes on the sleeve of her sweatshirt.

She says I must look like a mess.

I say you look okay to me.

Nice of you to say, Joseph, but I know better.

I say well, you ain't goin' to the dance, anyway.

Iris Mary smiles that perty smile of hers. She says no, but maybe I wish I was. Did you ever dance, Joseph?

Ever? Iris Mary, I may be a washed-up gimp but, damn, girl, I can still zydeco better than most two-legged men.

She gives me that Iris Mary look. She says hhm, well, I'd like to see that one day.

I say okay, one day we'll go dancin', me and you.

She says that's a nice thing to think about. No doubt we'd be the oddest couple on the dance floor.

Damn straight we would. Shuh, let 'em look, that's what I say, girl. We'd get that zydeco thang goin' and they'd all be jealous just to see us. C'mon, check this out.

I step toward Iris Mary and put out my hands and give her that two-steppin' pose. She smiles and slips into my arms and I take her around once.

I gotta say, well, maybe I ain't the zydeco dancer I used to be. But the girl giggles, and leans against me again, her cheek on my shoulder.

Then she steps away and says okay, Joseph, I'll take your advice. I'll sleep on it and we'll talk about things in the mornin'. But I know I have to do *something*.

Iris Mary then does a surprisin' thing. She steps back into my arms and puts her arms around my neck and kisses me lightly on the cheek. She says thank you. Now you go get your nap and I'll cook us up a gumbo.

I feel the *frissons* rise on my neck and somethin' stirrin' down below. Iris Mary pulls away and I hear myself sayin' you know, girl, if you came and took a nap wit' me, you might be the perfect woman.

Iris Mary turns to me and her eyes are sad again. She says well, Joseph, I'm not ready for that. But I can tell you a small secret. I'm flattered you would ask. I really am.

Then she gets this li'l twinkle in her eye and says oh, and something else. That night I got you in the tub, I have to confess, I *did* notice.

I look at Iris Mary and realize my mouth's hangin' open. The cat don't just have my tongue. He's swallowed it.

She says you go on now and take your nap. I'll be fine. We'll sleep on everything and decide in the morning.

I nod and hobble off to my room and shut my door. I flop on the bed, not even botherin' to take off my clothes, or my leg. I close my eyes and drift off toward sleep, thinkin' about Iris Mary and what I'm gonna do.

Wishin' that bastid Roddy had never showed his sorry face.

Anyway, the main thing is that Iris Mary ain't leavin'. She's gonna sleep on it.

I drift off to sleep and somewhere down there all jumbled up is Momma and Lolly-Lee and Iris Mary. They all know each other but nobody knows me. They're carryin' on, havin' a good ole time. I'm feelin' left out and it don't feel so hot. I wake up callin' Momma's name.

I look up at the ceilin' and I suddenly know what I'm gonna do.

I'm gonna get up in the mornin' and I'm gonna put Iris Mary in the truck and we gonna drive away from this friggin' place and we ain't never gonna come back. Not ever. To hell wit' Roddy, to hell wit' Rocko, to hell wit' the law, to hell wit' the money. I'm gonna sneak us outta Catahoula Parish, maybe all the way up to Texas. And maybe after we get there, I'll stir some shit—maybe sic the State Police on Rocko's sorry ass, send 'em some of them Polaroid pitchers in a plain brown envelope wit' a li'l note about what that sumbitch does in his spare time. They busted his ass for gamblin' so you know they'd love to get their hands on them things. Man, the shit would hit the fan!

And when they put that sumbitch away, Iris Mary will think I'm a hero. And Rocko, Roddy, and the rest of them bastids will know what it costs to mess wit' goddam Junior Guidry.

I look around my li'l room and I listen and I'm still sleepy as a church after mass. I hear the ghost in the kitchen and my nose picks up the smell of gumbo.

Man, that girl can cook.

I close my eyes again and I fall into a deep, deep sleep. I'm way down there in some warm place where nuttin' bad's gonna get me.

When I wake up, the trailer's quiet and I can tell by the light comin' in the li'l window that the afternoon's grown late. I can smell the gumbo and it smells great. I get up and stretch the stiffness out of my bones and go to the kitchen.

Iris Mary ain't there. But a note is.

It says, *Sorry, Joseph, but I had to go and thought it would be easier this way. I've left you food enough for a few days. I left you the gun I took from the house. I can't bear to have it. I can't tell you where I'm going but it's all for the best. Don't worry about me. And be good to yourself.*

—*Iris Mary.*

I feel somethin' awful rise in me, somethin' I'd awmost forgot I could feel. I feel the mad dog rise in me and there is a poundin' in my head and a fire in my chest and I pick up the note and rip it to pieces and throw it in the air. I slam my hand down on the table and sweep the pot of rice that Iris Mary has put there onto the floor. The pan hits and spins and rice flies everywhere. I turn and go down the hall toward the closet where Roddy stashed the rest of that whiskey. I trip once and bang hard against the wall. But I pick myself up and make the closet and rip open a bottle and take a big gulp, then another.

I find my truck keys.

I see the pistol lyin' on the rickety coffee table. I pick it up and

I break open the chamber and count the bullets—four. I close it up and stick it in my waistband. I head for the door, totin' the whiskey in my right hand, and a curse rises to my lips.

Damn her! Damn her for lyin' to me! Damn her for runnin' out on me! Damn her for turnin' me into a pussy boy!

I'm gonna find Mother Superior and it ain't a ride to Texas I'm gonna give her.

17

I pull myself up into the truck and throw the whiskey and the gun on the seat. I put in the key and turn it. The Plymit coughs and sputters and coughs and sputters, then fires up. I manage the clutch and put it in first and start to pull out. It jerks and groans and dies.

I crank it up again. It dies again.

I know what's wrong. There's a choke that sticks. It sticks all the time.

Why the hell does it have to stick *now*?

I throw open the door and climb out, realizin' I'm already wheezin' like a beat-up diesel. I go around and crack the hood. I gotta take off the air filter to get to the choke.

The wing nut on the filter is rusted—it won't give. I need a tool. Pliers, or a hammer to beat the shit out of it.

I step back and take a deep breath.

I know I ain't never in the hell gonna find Iris Mary. I know ole Junior's screwed the pooch one more time.

Who knows when she left? I slept for three or four hours, best as I can tell. The girl could be anywhere by now. She coulda got lucky and made the parish line. Or she could already be dead in a ditch.

I walk back to the truck bed where I remember there might be a pair of rusted pliers. I find 'em under a greasy rag and I pick 'em up and go after the wing nut. It's stubborn but I get the bastid loose. I unscrew it and toss the filter into the yard. I fiddle with the choke, then close the hood.

I pull myself back up into the cab and turn the key. The truck starts.

I sit there for a minute, wheezin' like a broke accordion. I put the truck into gear and see the bottle of whiskey on the seat.

I take a few deep breaths and I feel myself calmin' down.

I realize I don't really want the whiskey. I realize I don't even like the goddam taste of whiskey. I pick up the bottle and throw it out the window.

I don't throw good, though.

The bottle hits the rim of the open window and shatters. Whiskey and glass fly all over me.

How come you're such a fuck-up, Junior, ehn?

I smell like a barroom at closin' time.

I put the truck in gear and take off.

I rattle slow down my narrow road. It ain't a good idea to go fast. There's a slough on my left where the swamp presses close up, and a fair-sized ditch on the right. You get a wheel off in that slough and roll over and they'll need a dredge to find your sorry ass.

I figger Iris Mary would be walkin' on the road, at least for a ways. Ain't no choice for the first mile or two. Then the canefields start up on the right but it's a bit hard goin' 'tween them cane rows. The cane's tall and thick this time of the year and them leaves will rake you like razors if you're not careful. One time, some crook busted outta parish jail and they got the dogs on him and chased him through the canefields and that sumbitch come out on the other side lookin' like somebody had took a dagger to his face and arms.

I bump along like this for three or four miles and there ain't no sign of Iris Mary. I slow down even more when I reach a li'l rise where another narrow road comes into this one. It's a twisty oil-field board road, just one lane wide and made of planked cypress. I know the road—it dead-ends back at a played-out well at the edge of the woods. Ain't nobody ever goes down there but coon-hunters now and then.

It's late afternoon. I bump past the road and happen to look down there when somethin' catches my eye.

I brake and back up slow and look again.

It's the tail end of a car, about a hundred yards away. I look closer and it looks like some kind of fancy black car—maybe an Olds or a Caddy.

What the hell would a car like that be doin' back here?

I feel the *frissons* rise on the back of my neck.

I back up some more and nose the truck in. I gotta run in low, the first stretch of the road is so bumpy and rutted. I wonder how a fancy car like that, sittin' so low, could even make it back here.

I get closer and see I'm right. It's a Caddy pulled up into a sharp curve. There are people sittin' in the backseat, one or two—I cain't exactly tell. I get about twenty yards away when a man emerges from around the bend, followed by another. Past the bend, on the other side of the Caddy, is a cop car.

The first man is Roddy. I see he's got a revolver in his hand.

The second one is wearin' a cowboy hat and carryin' a shotgun. It's Wiley Smurl.

A herd of wild horses have got loose in my chest.

I brake the truck and put it in neutral. My hands are already shakin'. I slowly reach over wit' my right hand and pull Iris Mary's pistol toward me and shove it under my good leg.

Roddy comes to the driver's window and Wiley makes the other side.

Roddy says goddam, Junior, I didn't know you ever drove this ole truck anymore.

I look at him and wonder if Roddy would actually put a bullet in my head.

I say I do now and then.

He says you out lookin' for somethin'?

I shrug. Goin' to the store, actually.

Roddy says shuh, you ain't outta whiskey yet, are you?

I don't answer.

He says well, if it's your girlfriend you're lookin' for, you're late, podnah.

Roddy laughs his *poule d'eau* laugh when he says this. He points to the car.

He says she's over in the backseat wit' ole Rocko. I think the man's tryin' to talk her into a blowjob. Hell, if it's good enough, he might not really kill her—just fuck her up some.

He says Junior, podnah, you were holdin' out on me, bro! Your best podnah, and you were tryin' to keep her all to yourself!

I say I don't know what you talkin' about, Roddy.

He says don't bullshit me, Junior. We only had to slap her around a bit 'fore your girlfriend tole us how you put her up.

I say Roddy, you drunk too much of that whiskey at my house this mornin'.

He says ha, Junior, you lyin' bastid! That story about Irene leavin' her bag—what a crock. I went by Irene's house, podnah. She said what, I went to see Junior? I didn't go to see Junior. My fucked-up brother must be drinkin' again. Man, your sister knows you well, don't she?

Roddy nudges me on the shoulder wit' his pistol. He says so, when I heard that, I come back to pay you a li'l unexpected visit, 'cause I figgered if that bag didn't belong to Irene I had a good idea who it might belong to. But damn, the girl made it easy on me. I caught her on the straightaway about a mile from the highway. They'd already cut that cane and she had no place to run, really. It was the open field or the swamp. Oh, she run like a deer and fought like a bobcat, but I got my cuffs on her. We had us a bit of a scuffle, if you know what I mean.

She give me this. He points to an ugly scratch on his cheek.

He says anyway, your girlfriend was awful disappointed to hear that I'd paid you a visit and you didn't even tell her you knew the whole friggin' world was lookin' for her.

Roddy puckers up his lips and says in a woman's voice, *Oh, Joseph would never do a thing like that to me! Oh, Joseph!*

He leans in close and says why, hell, Junior, you even changed your name wit'out tellin' me, bro! What kinda podnah are you, anyway, ehn?

Roddy sniffs the air like the pug-nose dog he is. He says damn, this truck smells like the Go-Go Bar at closin' time.

I know I'm fucked now. I got no choice but to play along wit' Roddy.

I say I've had a pop or two.

You got any left?

No. But we can go back to the trailer and get some more.

Aw, forget it, Junior. Anyway, we got business to attend to. So you best get your sorry ass outta here.

I say well, look, the bitch wadn't nuttin' to me. She come sneakin' in my house wit'out permission. You know the shape I been in—when she first come I didn't even have the strengt' to throw her out. Then she started cookin' gumbo and, what the hell, I tole her she could stay so long as she stayed out my business.

I say anyway, Roddy, you the one who put it in my head that if I turned her in I'd be rich as when I got my leg money. Shuh, I had already decided to come look for you so you could make like you were arrestin' her. I was gonna split the money wit' you, like you said. Then next thing I know the freak run off on me.

Roddy shakes his pug-dog head. He says what a bullshitter you are, Junior. I always knew you were a greedy bastid. But you know what they say—sooner or later, *cochons* get slaughtered.

I hear a rustle to my right. Wiley has stuck his shotgun in the window, pointed at me. He looks like a damn snake wit' acne.

Roddy says oh, I think you know Smurl here. He works for Rocko.

Wiley says Roddy, I already kicked this bastard's sorry ass once and now I gotta kill him. Makes me sorry I didn't do it the first time around. He knows we're here and he knows we've got the woman. He squeals on us and we're dead.

Roddy looks at me and then he looks at Wiley. He says hey, podnah, c'mon. Junior here's a pathetic damn drunk. Smell this truck. This sumbitch can hardly remember his name, much less us.

I turn toward Wiley and then look down. Them coupla pops of whiskey have got my head bobbin' like a fishin' cork bein' yanked down by a *sac-à-lait*.

I say shuh, y'all can shoot me if you want. But I'd take a part of that girl, if you passin' her around. She's good.

Roddy cackles. He says Junior, you tellin' me you were humpin' that overgrown rabbit?

I say hell, Roddy, you throw a sheet over her head and what the hell—pussy's pussy. Right?

Roddy slaps me on the shoulder. He says well, there you go. That's the Junior I know. Okay, you can join the gang bang, but you don't get any of my hundred thousand dollars. But maybe I'll buy you a beer after it's all over.

I see Wiley has shoved the gun further through the window. I'm just waitin' for the blast. He'll shoot me and they'll dump me and Iris Mary in this swamp and we'll never be found.

But Roddy says put the gun away, Wiley. I'm vouchin' for Junior. He won't remember nuttin' in the mornin'. Besides, the sheriff don't want more dead bodies than necessary. Them's his orders.

Roddy says c'mon out here, Junior. I cain't really promise you no nooky 'cause Rocko might want her all to hisself. But maybe you can talk some sense into her. She don't seem to want to listen to Mr. Marchante. If she cooperates maybe he'll go easy on her.

I wait till Roddy and Wiley have stepped away from the truck and I ease that gun from under my leg and lower it to the floor, then push it under the seat wit' my boot. I climb out the truck, not botherin' to turn off the engine. My peg leg hits

the ground, then my good one and I feel myself tiltin' and I have
to grab on to the door to keep from fallin' over.

Roddy puts a hand rough on my shirt collar and hauls me up-
right. He says damn, drivin' drunk again, huh, bro? I just might
have to take you in!

Oh, Roddy is really gettin' a kick outta this. He pulls me away
from the door and says let's go talk to your girlfriend. *Joseph!*

I wobble over to the Caddy, wit' Roddy steerin' me by the collar. Wiley walks on the other side, his shotgun tucked in the crook
of his left arm, like a squirrel hunter. In the ole days I'd already be
goin' for the bastid but he'd cut me down like a waddle-ass possum if I made a move now.

The window of the Caddy slides down and I look in. Rocko
Marchante is lookin' up at me. I ain't never really met the guy,
though I'd seen him plenty of times at the bar. I can see he's a
beat-up ugly bastid. He's got a bandage clear around his head and
one eyelid is droopin' about half closed and there's a sag on the
left side of his face. He prob'ly never was Rock Hudson, but he
looks like friggin' Frankenstein now.

Ole Iris Mary really put a whuppin' on him. Somethin' about
that makes me proud of that girl.

I look past Rocko and see her. She's hunched up against the
opposite door, her hands pinned behind her. I figgered she's still
handcuffed.

One eye is black and partly closed. There's blood at the corner
of her mouth.

At first she don't even look up at me.

Rocko says to Wiley, ooo da fuck ees diss ah-ah-ass-hole?

I cain't make it out at first and it's clear that ole Rocko done
took some bad licks to the brain since he talks like a retard. Then

Roddy says Mr. Marchante, this is the fella I was tellin' you about, Junior Guidry. The woman was hidin' out at his trailer down at the end of the road back there.

Rocko says whu-uhtt ees doo-in eeere?

Roddy says he come lookin' for her hisself 'cause he knew about the reward, too. By the way, ole Junior here was one of your best customers at the Go-Go Bar. That sumbitch lost about a million dollars at the blackjack game you was runnin'.

Roddy laughs hard again.

Rocko raises his ugly face and trains his good eye on me. His other eye droops like the moon about to fall from the sky. I know I ain't got but one chance.

I say yeah, Mr. Marchante, Roddy's right. I was a damn good customer of yours. Shuh, your bar was practically my second home. Anyway, I heard about that reward you were offerin' and I was gonna turn the woman in myself till she run off on me. Her li'l stunt done cost me a hundred fuckin' thousand dollars 'cause my podnah, Roddy, found her first. Anyway, she ain't nuttin' to me and I don't care what you do wit' her. Just give her a pop for me while you workin' her over.

I look over at Iris Mary and the one big rabbit eye that she can still open is lookin' at me in a way that damn near knocks me over.

I say lemme tell you somethin' else, Mr. Marchante. She might act like she's the Virgin Mary but she's a damn whore and a damn thief. She'd talk all that holy stuff then she'd come into my room every night and give me a two-handed blowjob. You ever had a two-handed blowjob? Ole Junior here ain't never had better and Ole Junior's had a few blowjobs in his day—some real expensive ones. That's the only damn reason I let her stay. One other thing. She stole my damn pistol. I hope you frisked her good 'cause she could be armed. I had it on my coffee table and it was loaded for bear and when I woke up from a nap this afternoon I was gonna stick it to her head and march her to your office. But she was gone, and so was my gun. It was a damn nice pistol and if I had it now I'd be happy to do the job for you. If I had that gun now, there would be hell to pay. I mean hell.

I see Rocko lookin' at me cross-eyed. But then he says yea-aah, shee tole muh-muh-my gun, tooo, duh too-pid bih-itch!

It takes me a second to understand what Rocko said and when I do it's all I can do to keep from laughin' in his face.

I say Mr. Marchante, couldn't you give me at least some of that reward money? I'm broke—real broke—and I barely get enough to eat wit' what the Relief pays me. Shuh, wadn't for me keepin' her in my trailer, she wouldn't be here now. I, uh—

I feel a hard hand on my collar and Roddy yanks me back like a chained dog.

He says I'm sorry, Mr. Marchante, but as you can see, Junior here's got shit for brains.

Roddy looks at me ugly and says Junior, don't even try to lay a finger on a penny of my money.

Roddy lets go my collar and I stagger back. I throw my hands up in the air and say hey, podnah, awright, awright. Just take it easy on me, okay?

Roddy says get your ass over there to your truck, Junior, and let us men do what we gotta do.

I say well, I can still be fourth, right?

Roddy sneers. He says Junior, drunk as you are, I doubt you can get it up.

I glance in the car and I can see Iris Mary has got her good eye on me. And it's wide open and wild and I take a chance and I wink at her.

I don't know what a wink can say. I want it to say I hope you got that b.s., girl. I was talkin' about that gun you left on the table. I got it, baby, and it's loaded and Junior here is gonna raise some hell.

I say Mr. Marchante, don't forget what I said. If you uncuff ole Iris Mary there and free up that girl's hands, she'll do you right. If you promise not to kill her, that girl might take you to a place you ain't never been.

Roddy pushes me hard and says Junior, where'd you get all this bullshit?

I push Roddy back, but not hard as I could, and say Mr. Marchante, I'm only tryin' to make you happy—that girl's got the thang goin' on. I could use some of that money and—

Roddy grabs me rough by the shoulder again but I push my head around him and look at Iris Mary and I say when that girl goes to town, you gonna feel like you been run over by a truck. Get ready. By a truck!

Roddy grabs me by the collar again and shoves me back hard.

I stumble and fall on my ass.

Roddy says get back to your truck, Junior. Don't make me tell you again.

I pick myself up, which ain't easy in my shape.

Then I hear Rocko say tuh-ake 'eeem off, Wi-lee. Tuh-ake uh, off thu-uh cu-uffs!

Wiley don't understand at first, then Rocko screams at him.

Roddy says Mr. Marchante, Wiley ain't got the key. It's me. I'll do it.

I turn and head back to the truck.

I hope Wiley don't shoot me in the back.

It seems to take forever but I get there and open the door and pull myself up into the cab. I put my head down on the steerin' wheel like any drunk would and I reach down wit' my right hand and find the pistol.

I pull it out and put it on the front seat.

I look ahead. Roddy's done what I suggested. I see him raise and fold the cuffs, then put 'em back on his belt. Iris Mary's hands are free.

That's all I can hope for.

Wiley's standin' between me and the Caddy. Roddy's still got his head stuck in the Caddy window, sayin' something to Rocko.

It will be a bit like pickin' up a 7-10 split to get 'em both and ram Rocko, too, but that's all the chance I got.

I push in the clutch and ease the truck in reverse. I start to back out and Wiley looks away. That's all I need.

Then I, Junior Guidry, goddam Junior Guidry, pray.

I pray to Mary and Joseph and all the saints and God and Jesus. I pray to the nootras and the hootowls and the alligators.

I pray that goddam Junior Guidry, please Lord, will not screw the pooch one more time.

I brake soft and shift into first. I gun the accelerator and pop the clutch and grab the pistol wit' my right hand.

The truck lurches forward and I'm about ten yards from Wiley. He's on my left and he looks up and I'm about halfway to the bastid when he realizes what I got in mind. As I hit second gear, he raises the shotgun.

Out the corner of my cye, I see Roddy divin' away from the Caddy like a shot-at *dosgris*.

I fall down to the right on the seat, grippin' my pistol like a nun holdin' her rosary in a hurricane, and I push as hard as I can on the accelerator.

My windshield explodes and I'm covered wit' glass and then I hear a thump and some sumbitch screamin' and then I ram Rocko Marchante's Caddy.

My truck slams into the Caddy and I feel it start to tilt over left and I'm thrown against the dash and bang my head hard. I bang hard and I know I've drawn blood. But I still have the pistol and all I can hope is that I've at least killed Rocko clean and not taken Iris Mary wit' him.

And then the truck rights itself and sputters and dies and all sound seems to have been sucked out of the world 'cept for those horses poundin' in my chest again.

The next thing I know I see Roddy's face in the window lookin' down at me and it's all twisted and he says goddam you, Junior, I'm gonna blow your brains out!

He points his gun at me and I reach to grab it wit' my left hand. I raise my pistol and I say Roddy, this one's for Irene.

Roddy's eyes go wild wit' surprise and he shoots and I shoot and bombs go off and the world slows down to syrup and I reach out to fend off Roddy's bullet and I feel my left hand explode and there's blood everywhere.

But I got my eye on Roddy and I see his pistol fly out of his hand and I see his other hand grab for his face and then I see him fall away like a crazy man dancin' backwards and suddenly I'm lookin' out the window at a clear sky.

From somewhere far away, them hoot owls start up but there ain't another sound on earth, except the sound of my heart and the tick of the Plymit's radiator.

I look down at my left hand and I count my fingers. The tips of two or three of 'em are gone down to the knuckles.

Then I hear the slow clomp and shuffle of boots on the board road and my door opens and there's Wiley the snake.

I gotta say, the boy don't look too good hisself.

I musta smacked him clear into the slough 'cause he's holdin' on to the door frame and his right leg looks like a gator chewed it and spit it out. He's got mud and blood plasterin' his face and that fancy cowboy shirt he's wearin'. He won't be dancin' in them crocodile cowboy boots—there's a tire track across his left toe.

I fucked him up good but I didn't kill him.

He's got his shotgun, and though it's got water grass danglin' from the barrel, I figger that unless it's stopped up wit' mud, that's my ass. Even though I still got my pistol I don't have the strengt' to raise it.

I feel awful damn bad that the last thing I'm gonna see on earth is his ugly face.

He bends down toward me wit' the barrel of that gun in my belly and says you're dead, coonass.

I say bite me, Wiley.

I see him raise the shotgun and I stare the bastid in the eye and he sticks the barrel to my forehead and then there's a shadow that falls on both of us and there's a sound I cain't make out, like *thwuck*.

Wiley's eyes go crossed and his shotgun falls into my lap and he staggers back from the truck. He staggers back and flops loud to the ground like a horse that's been throwed from a tree.

Iris Mary is lookin' down on me and she crosses herself and I see she's holdin' somethin'.

I finally make it out—it's that statue of the Virgin she has. She drops the statue and comes to me and kneels down.

I point to the shotgun, which is cocked and pressin' up against my leg. I manage to say careful, it's cocked and loaded. Iris Mary reaches down and picks it up gentle and carries it out in front of her like it was a snake.

She tosses it into the slough. When it hits the water, it goes off. *Pow!*

Iris Mary jumps like a frog in hot grease.

There's a fire in my arm and a fire in my head and I feel like a ship full of water pitchin' down to the bottom of the Gulf of Mexico and I say that sumbitch is close, Iris Mary, it's real close.

She comes over and reaches down and takes the stump of my fingers into the hem of her dress and then starts to tear at her dress to try to make me a bandage. She manages a strip or two and ties them around my stumps, then she gets down in my face and there's fire and tears in her eyes. She says soft, real soft, don't you dare die. Don't you dare, I mean it.

I say well, it's not like I want to.

She says well, then don't. Don't! I'm going for help!

I close my eyes and feel my head roll to the side and I hear Iris Mary all but screamin' at me.

She says don't you dare go being a pussy boy on me, Junior Guidry!

I don't feel like openin' my eyes but I gotta smile at that.

I say hey, don't you remember?

The name's Joseph.

18

There's a buzzard doin' cartwheels way up in the sky and I figger that sumbitch is comin' down soon to peck out my eyes. The way I feel, I wouldn't care if he did.

Armentau's over by the edge of the canefield, but for a change he ain't got nuttin' to say to me. He's like that ole buzzard. He's watchin' and waitin'. He'll wait till I die, then come steal my wallet.

Shuh, he'll be doggone disappointed by what he finds.

I see Momma and Irene. I see Lolly-Lee and Berta. I see Alma.

I see a deer—a doe—standin' at the edge of the field. It goes as quick as it come.

I see the ghost floatin' above it all.

Ain't none of it matters to me. I see myself lyin' there on the board road. I notice the bandage on my hand has done bled through.

From where I am, I can see I put a hell of a whuppin' on

Rocko's perty black car. The back door is caved in. But I don't see that sumbitch nowhere. I hope he's dead down there on the seat. I hope I knocked his crooked brains out. I hope I finished what Iris Mary started.

I hear a clunkin' on the board road and next I know a man is standin' over me. At first I think it might be that bastid Rocko or even Wiley—maybe they like them four-headed snakes that cain't be killed. But it's some ole man wit' a baseball cap pulled down hard against his eyes. He standin' against the sun so I cain't make him out too clear.

He says how you doin', podnah?

I say I've been better.

He says I'm shore you have. Your friend ran to fetch help. I hope she'll be back soon.

Me too.

Who are these guys?

Bad-asses.

It seems that they are. Here, let me check your tourniquet.

I say I'm cold.

I see him shuck a coat. He kneels down and lays it over me.

I feel him fiddlin' with my shot hand. He unwraps the bloody bandage and tosses it away. He says hold still, this might sting a little. I see him reachin' behind him in a vest of some kind. He comes out with a wad of gray stuff.

Spiderwebs, he says. I pulled 'em off some palmettos across the slough. An ole Cajun remedy. They'll slow down the bleedin'.

I feel him packin' my hand wit' the webs. He takes out a white handkerchief and reties the bandage. He says I shore was fond of that handkerchief.

He says you left-handed or right-handed?

Right-handed.

Well, at least you can still bowl.

You think that's funny?

The man pushes back his cap some. He says normally I wouldn't but, face it, son, everybody knows you're too doggone mean to kill.

You know me?

Yes. I know you. And it's obvious you still cain't stay out of trouble.

How you know me?

Well, you *are* Junior Guidry, ain't you? Now, I have some water in my canteen here. Try to have a little.

I see him slip a green canvas canteen from the pouch of a khaki vest. He unscrews the top and holds it up for me to drink. I take a sip.

Best water I ever had.

He says I cain't stick around too long. I'm gonna watch from the woods there. At least I'll keep the buzzards off you till help comes.

I say you a hunter?

I used to be. But I don't travel with a gun anymore. Otherwise I mighta tried to help you out. I could see you were badly outnumbered by them outlaws.

I say you live around here?

Used to. I've come a fer piece, walkin' all the way.

I nod. I'm feelin' woozy again. I want to go to sleep.

I say if I go, tell Iris Mary I'm sorry.

He says is that your friend?

I say yeah.

So, tell me, what are you sorry for, Junior?

She'll know.

You shore?

Oh, yeah. She'll know.

He says I'll see what I can do.

I look at him close, though there's big spots in my vision.

Do I know this sumbitch?

The man stands and I close my eyes and I hear him walk away. Then the day grows quiet, except for some chirpy redwing blackbird scrabblin' in the *roseaus* over by the slough.

I close my eyes and drift off. I drift way down deep inside of ole Junior, to places I ain't never been.

19

Maybe I *am* too mean to kill.

There's a woman standin' over me in a room of bright lights. Somebody in white. If I'm dead, maybe she's an angel. But then I see her nurse's cap. I groan.

I hate friggin' hospitals. I been in enough of 'em.

I see her mouth movin' like she's talkin' but I don't hear her right away. Her voice fades in and out, then comes clear. She says he's coming around.

A man steps into the light. He's got on what looks at first like a cowboy hat. I think it must be ole Wiley risen from the grave. But then I see him better.

It's a cop.

He leans over me. He says can you hear me, podnah?

I nod.

He says can you talk?

I shrug. I'm not shore I can. I open my mouth but no words come out.

He says okay, don't try too hard. But you can understand me, yes?

I nod.

He says your name is Joseph Guidry? Also known as Junior Guidry?

I nod again.

He says I'm Captain Mouton, St. Madeline Parish Sheriff's Office. You're bein' held under guard in the charity wing of the parish hospital under suspicion of three counts of attempted murder, including the attempted murder of a Catahoula Parish sheriff's officer, Roddy Bergeron. I believe Mr. Bergeron was once a friend of yours. You are also under arrest for the attempted murder of Wiley S. Smurl. Both of these charges are based on an arrest warrant issued by Canard Parish, based on an affidavit by Raymond J. Marchante, who says he witnessed both crimes. You are also under arrest for the attempted murder and armed robbery of Mr. Marchante. Do you understand what I'm tellin' you?

I nod. Then I find my voice and say yeah, I understand you. But it's all bullshit.

He says I'm required to read you your rights. You have the right to remain silent. You have a right to an attorney. You need to realize that anything you say may be held against you in a court of law. Do you understand these things, Mr. Guidry?

I nod again.

Captain Mouton turns to the nurse. He says Nurse Hotard, please note that the accused nodded in the affirmative.

Nurse Hotard says yes, Captain, that's what I witnessed.

He says well, Junior, do you have anything you want to tell me?

I look at Mouton careful. He's a short sumbitch, built like an oil drum. He's got a mustache and dark eyes and a jaw like Popeye the Sailor Man. He's one of them guys you just know it ain't good to fuck wit'. It's not that he looks mean. He reminds me some of the last tool pusher I worked for offshore. He wadn't the kind of man who starts a fight. But if you wanted a fight, he'd give you two or three.

I clear my throat and search for my voice again. I say how long I been here?

He says four days.

Where's Iris Mary?

Your accomplice, Miss Parfait? She was here briefly but she's now being held in parish jail. We understand you two were a regular Bonnie and Clyde.

Me and Iris Mary? You gotta be jokin'.

This is no joke, Junior, I can assure you. Your girlfriend somehow managed to drop you off at the hospital and skeedaddle before we got here. But those duty nurses call us when people come in shot up like you were. They reported the girl as well. She'd obviously been injured but refused treatment, which is suspicious in itself. We caught her as she was tryin' to leave town on her thumb. She wasn't hard to spot.

Captain Mouton stops and folds his arms. He says that was some mess you two left out there on Catahoula Bayou. If people hadn't survived, the investigators would still be tryin' to puzzle it out. As it is, Mr. Marchante may not make it, in which case we'll add a charge of capital murder to the gumbo.

I say yeah, well, I thought I'd finally got rid of that nasty sumbitch.

So you admit to tryin' to kill Mr. Marchante?

Hell, yeah. Considerin' that he was plannin' to do about ten really bad things to Iris Mary and then skin her alive, it was the least I could do for the girl.

So she *was* your girlfriend?

I bat my good hand in the air. I say Iris Mary was hardly my girlfriend. And you got it all wrong.

I tell him about Iris Mary workin' for Rocko and what she saw. I tell him about the bounty. I say go look in my trailer and check out some Polaroids we got. That'll show you what kind of guy Rocko Marchante is. The man's a granny-fucker, for God's sake!

Captain Mouton looks at me. Well, we would go look in your trailer—we asked the sheriff over in Catahoula Parish to investigate it for us—but it seems you burned it down to destroy evidence.

I did what?

Burned your trailer down. It's gone, podnah. Doused with gasoline, set fire to—whoosh!

I look up at Mouton. The man cain't be serious. You could fill up the entire Gulf of Mexico wit' the bullshit I've heard in the last two minutes.

I shake my head. I say well, it's them goons that work for Marchante then. They musta known we had them pictures.

Good try, Junior. We found a half-empty gas can in the back of your truck.

Oh, like that proves somethin'. Like a man cain't drive around wit' spare gas in his truck. Anyway, Captain, you a hound on the wrong trail. I mean, go ax Iris Mary. She was there. I'm shore she's told you the same thing.

Captain Mouton grins. He says aw, Junior, that's absolutely true. You lovebirds obviously got a chance to compare notes and decided to sing the same song. But it won't hold up.

Compare notes? Officer, I don't hardly remember nuttin' after Iris Mary kept ole Wiley from blowin' my head off. You might know a few things but you ain't got a clue about Iris Mary. That girl couldn't lie if her life depended on it.

You don't say, Junior?

I do say.

He says well, if Mr. Marchante or any of the victims die, her life *may* depend on it.

Then Captain Mouton looks at me hard. He says anyway, we know what kind of witness you are, Junior. We've been sniffin' around down in Catahoula Parish and dredged up some business some years back involving one Emile LaBauve. As we understand it, you lied your ass off to the police, tryin' to get Mr. LaBauve and his father arrested.

I shake my head. This cain't be happenin' to me. Man, how many times is that LaBauve deal gonna come back to bite me on the ass?

I say that might've been true then, but then ain't got nuttin' to do wit' now.

He says of course it does, Junior. You're a perjurer, son! That gets right to your credibility as a witness. Besides, there's a drunk-drivin' arrest a few years back and several unpaid speedin' tickets since then for which you were finally arrested and thrown in jail. You're gonna have a hard time convincin' a judge and jury that you're some poor beat-up Boy Scout with a bum rap.

I shake my head. I say I ain't sayin' I'm a Boy Scout. I'm just sayin' I did what I did to protect Iris Mary and she did what she did to protect me.

So you two lovebirds were coverin' for each other? Is that right?

I close my eyes. I been awake about ten minutes and this has already wore me out.

I keep my eyes closed and say Captain, one more time— we ain't lovebirds and, no, I ain't a Boy Scout. But now here's a fack—Rocko Marchante is about the best-known crook in all of Catahoula Parish. Why don't you take your bloodhounds and go sniffin' around that saloon he runs there? That sumbitch stole my money and screwed about two hundred other guys, too. Hell, the State Police know this. Don't you law doggies talk to one another?

I open my eyes and Captain Mouton is perty well in my face. He says you're pretty cocky for a man who could be starin' at the death penalty.

I shrug my shoulders. I say I'm Junior Guidry and I'm too dog-gone mean to kill, don't you know that?

He says we'll see about that, podnah. We'll see. Then he backs up and looks at me sharp.

He says maybe for grins we'll run a report on your podnah Marchante. Just to see how good of a liar you are.

20

Three more days pass. I got a fever. I hurt like hell. Half the time I wake up not knowin' where I am. I expect ole Wiley to be standin' over me.

A woman come in my room, dressed in a suit. I don't know when, exactly. She said she was my lawyer sent by the court—Maureen somebody. She started axin' me a bunch of questions but I wadn't in the mood to talk—my hand was on fire. She went away and ain't been back.

Otherwise, I guess it ain't too bad in here. They feed me when I feel like eatin', which ain't often, though the food ain't nuttin' like Iris Mary's gumbo. I had mashed potatoes and Jell-O one night and I couldn't tell which was which. They gimme dope to make me feel better but it don't always work.

Captain Mouton basically lives outside my door, him and coupla other cops. I don't know what they think ole Junior's gonna do. They took my leg and stashed it way up in a closet, and they keep me drugged up enough so that I'm always drowsy. What they think—I'm gonna crawl outta here stoned one day on my one good hand and my one good knee?

I don't remember nuttin' about comin' here. I wonder how Iris Mary managed it? She musta thought we'd be better off across the parish line, otherwise I'd be in Canard General, wit' Go-Boy Geaux's deputies tryin' to stick knives in my back every night or Rocko sendin' his henchmen to skin me like a gator.

In the daytime, Nurse Hotard comes in the room about every two hours to check my bandages and dope levels. She ain't been bad to me, considerin' everybody thinks I'm a cold-blooded gunslinger. I guess I popped ole Roddy good, though Mouton won't gimme no details.

I hear the door swing open and there's Nurse Hotard again. Two doctors are following her.

She says Junior, this is Dr. LeMoine, the physician assigned to your case, and Dr. Authement, a surgeon. They need to talk to you.

I say fire away. I got nuttin' else to do.

Dr. LeMoine says I'm sorry to say, Mr. Guidry, but your injured fingers below the knuckles are turning gangrenous.

What's that mean?

It's a very serious infection. We'll give your antibiotics another twenty-four hours, but if you don't get better, we may have to amputate.

Cut my fingers completely off?

Actually, our concern is your hand. It depends on how far the gangrene has spread. You could refuse surgery but I wouldn't advise it. If you do, the gangrene will continue to spread. You could lose an arm. You could die.

I got two things I'm thinkin'. The first is I don't wanna lose no more body parts. The second is I gotta see Iris Mary. I worry about her. It's possible I might even miss her.

I tell this to Dr. LeMoine.

He says a request like that is not up to me. It's up to the police.

Is she all right?

I wouldn't know.

Well somebody must know.

The doc shrugs.

I say you know, Iris Mary was hurt, too. I don't know why she ain't in the hospital wit' me.

Dr. LeMoine says that wasn't our decision to make. The parish jail has an infirmary and a duty doctor. I'm sure she's well cared for.

Well, I gotta see for myself, doc. The girl's not made for jail. I gotta know if she's okay.

The doc shrugs again.

I say well, why don't you tell Captain Mouton I'll confess to everything if I can see Iris Mary.

Dr. LeMoine says Mr. Guidry, again, we're your doctors, not your lawyers.

Okay, how 'bout this. Tell Mouton that unless I get to see Iris Mary, I ain't gonna have no operation, gangrene or not. I'll die and they'll never get the whole story. But if I get to see her, I'll tell 'em everything. Everything.

The docs look at each other like they're not shore what to do. Then Dr. LeMoine says we'll see what we can do.

21

Iris Mary is hovering over me.

I say is it really you?

She says yes, I'm here, Joseph.

I say touch me.

She puts her hand on my forehead. I gotta say I ain't felt nicer hands than hers.

I say okay, then it's you. You awright?

She says I'm fine. How are you?

I been better.

They told me about the gangrene.

They wanna take what's left of my fingers. Maybe my whole hand. If they keep cuttin' on me, there won't be much left.

I'm sorry, Joseph. I did my best, I ran to that store across the bayou and got the first person I could find to come. I—

Shuh, you sorry? You got nuttin' to be sorry about, Iris Mary. I'm the one. I—

Iris Mary puts her hand on my mouth. She says hush. I know

you're sorry. The man in the woods told me what you said. And I know what you did. You saved my life.

I say well, you returned the favor. And I wadn't shore that's what I was gonna do. I was so pissed off that you left. I didn't want you to leave me, see, though I did think about that money and, uh—

She shushes me again. She says you mustn't die. I couldn't stand it. We'll get out of this somehow.

I smile best as I can. I say they think we're Bonnie and Clyde. What's funnier than that?

Iris Mary manages a smile, too. Nothing, she says. Nothing is funnier than that.

I look around and for the first time I see Captain Mouton standin' in the corner. I say hey, Captain, soon as they finishin' slicin' me up, you and me can have a long talk.

The captain nods.

I look at Iris Mary. I say the captain don't believe nuttin' I say. But I'd forgot about the man in the woods, Iris Mary. He come and looked me over and redid my bandages. He tole me he saw it all. I don't guess you got his name?

Iris Mary shakes her head. No, I didn't. Everything was such a blur. I saw you coming to ram us. I pulled away from Marchante and scooted back against the far door and braced myself. Then there was a bang—the next thing I know, I'm on the ground and then scrambling for my bag. I honestly don't remember grabbing the statue. I don't even remember hitting that man, Joseph. I just wanted to get him out of the way so I could get to you. After I tended to you, I ran to Elmore's. A farmer was pulling up in his truck and I begged him to drive me back to you. I'm sure I frightened him—God, I was a wild-eyed mess—but he told me to get in. I begged him to drive as fast as he could and we got back and got you in the truck and then I ran back to the car hoping to get my bag. I was running half crazy and I literally ran into the man. He was standing by the car holding the bag and he just handed it to me like he knew what I was looking for. Then he told me what you said, then turned and disappeared into the woods.

I say do you remember what he looked like, Iris Mary?

Not really. He had a cap on but I never really saw his face. I'd say he was grandfatherly—he had gray hair sticking out from under the cap. He had on faded khakis. A hunting vest maybe? Other than that, I don't know—if only I'd been thinking, I could have maybe asked him to come with us. Maybe I—

I hold up my good hand. I say Iris Mary, you done all you could do.

Then I look at the captain. I say so there you go, Captain. Go sic some of your detectives on findin' the man in the woods. He'll tell you everything we say is true.

Captain Mouton walks toward my bed. He says that's real rich, Junior. I have to say you and Miss Parfait can tell a good tale. A phantom old man emerges from the woods, doctors you, tells you he witnessed your heroic acts of self-defense, then delivers Miss Parfait your love message. Well, he's a mighty, mighty fine fella. Too bad he's not real.

Iris Mary looks at the captain and she has fire in them rabbit eyes. She says as God is my witness, I'm telling you the absolute truth.

I can see the captain starin' hard at Iris Mary, tryin' to size her up. I can tell this throws him a bit.

He says well, for grins, we'll take a description from Miss Parfait. We'll—

Iris Mary interrupts. She says Captain, as I said earlier, I never really saw his face. I can only tell you generally what he looked like. But I swear he was there. I swear.

The captain nods. Okay, well, I'll put out a bulletin. Let's see—an old man wearin' a baseball cap and khakis and maybe a huntin' vest. That's not much to go on but miracles happen. Maybe he'll march right into our office and give us a statement. But just in case he doesn't, either of you two have any idea what color the cap was?

I see Iris Mary shakin' her head. I speak up. Green, I say, the cap was faded green.

The captain takes a small pad out of his hip pocket and gets out a pen and stares at the pad like he's puzzlin' over somethin'.

I say green. I spell it slow, G-R-E-E-N.

Mouton looks at me and a tiny crack of a smile forms on his face. He writes it down.

He says Junior, if it ends up that you don't spend the rest of your miserable life in prison, maybe you could become a comedian, son.

The doors to my room open and men in white coats come in. It's time to go to surgery, one of 'em says.

As they wheel me out, Captain Mouton says remember, podnah, you and I have a date when you're done.

22

I'm comin' out of the fog and I hear somebody sayin' it's Friday. That's three days later than when I went in to get my fingers chopped off. There are a few things I remember from the fog.

The doctor sayin' Nurse Hotard, it was bad but not quite as bad as we thought. We've saved the hand.

I remember wakin' up from a dream. I'd dreamed they'd taken my other arm and my other leg and I was just a stump sittin' in the middle of a highway, cars racin' around me. Next I know, there's a big-ass eighteen-wheeler haulin' drillin' pipe and it's thunderin' down at me, a front wheel on each side of the yellow line, and the road is shakin' and I know I'm about to be splattered like a slow-footed possum crossin' the New Awlins highway.

I screamed my head off till the duty nurse come and calmed me down. She squeezed my right arm and my right leg under the blanket to show me they were still there. She said you'll be all right, Mr. Guidry.

I axed for Iris Mary but she looked at me like she didn't know what I was talkin' about.

I'm comin' out of the fog and the first thing I do is pat my hand to make sure it really is still there. I expect to see Captain Mouton. But I got a surprise waitin' for me.

Syd Shainburg, my leg lawyer, is sittin' by my bed.

Now I *know* I must be outta my mind.

But it's gotta be Syd. Nobody I know looks like Syd. He's got a black beard and a mustache. His hair comes down long on the sides. He's wearin' one of them funny beret-type hats. A hat like that would get you beat up in some barrooms I been in. Syd's eyebrows arch up like the Huey P. Long Bridge.

He says I trust you've had a restorative nap, Junior?

Now I'm positive it's Syd. Them big-ass bullfrogs in the Catahoula Swamp don't bark deeper than Syd talks. Plus, he likes them two-dollar words. A man like me talks in quarters.

I say podnah, I've had better naps. Lost three fingers. If they keep sawin' on me like that there won't be nuttin' left.

I heard. How's the pain?

There's plenty of pain, Syd. You want some?

He smiles. I'm glad somebody can smile.

What the hell you doin' here, Syd?

Let's just say I'm on a reconnaissance mission, my friend. I heard you were involved in an altercation with a certain high-ranking member of the Ville Canard civic community, namely Raymond "Rocko" Marchante.

Syd, if an altercation means trouble, I'm up to my ass in altercation.

He says Junior, as far as I can tell you're always in trouble.

But this time you're famous. You and your Miss Parfait even made page 14-A of that paragon of journalism, the *New Orleans Review.*

Syd reaches down and shuffles through a stack of papers on his lap and comes up wit' a newspaper clipping. He starts to hand it to me but I brush him off.

I'm cross-eyed wit' them pain pills, Syd. Read it to me.

He starts to read:

VILLE CANARD—A Ville Canard man and a south Catahoula Parish woman said to be his accomplice are under arrest in neighboring St. Madeline Parish on three counts of attempted murder and one count of attempted robbery in what Catahoula Parish sheriff's officials are calling a bizarre and bloody act of revenge.

The man, Joseph "Junior" Guidry, whose last known address was lower Catahoula Bayou, and the woman, Iris Mary Parfait of the Bayou Go-to-Hell settlement about 30 miles south of Ville Canard, are being held without bail by St. Madeline Parish authorities.

Catahoula Parish Sheriff Ervil "Go-Boy" Geaux, in a press conference yesterday, identified the victims as Raymond "Rocko" Marchante and Wiley Smurl, both of Ville Canard, and Sgt. Roddy Bergeron, a Catahoula Parish sheriff's officer who makes his home on Catahoula Bayou. Mr. Marchante, according to the sheriff, is a well-known Ville Canard civic leader and nightclub owner. Mr. Smurl is a Texas native in Mr. Marchante's employ. All are in fair to guarded condition in Canard General Hospital with various head injuries.

Syd clears his throat and looks at me. He says I'm not going too fast am I, Junior?

I say I don't like the sound of this but you goin' just right.

Syd starts to read again.

Sheriff Geaux provided only sketchy details of the alleged crime, saying the matter would soon be brought before a parish grand jury. He said Guidry, who had a previous arrest record, had apparently blamed Marchante for a series of gambling losses he had incurred in private poker games with some of Marchante's friends. He had also been in a previous altercation with Smurl at an office where they were both employed, the sheriff added. He would provide no details.

Sheriff Geaux said the alleged attack happened about a week ago in a remote part of Catahoula Bayou and details were only now being pieced together because the victims had been too weak or disoriented to speak to authorities. He said investigators believe Guidry used the Parfait woman as a lure to coax Marchante and Smurl to the area; Sgt. Bergeron, the sheriff said, stumbled upon the robbery in progress and tried to intervene.

Sheriff Geaux said the incident involved weapons, including a religious object, and a motor vehicle. He said Guidry was also wounded in the fracas and is being held under guard in St. Madeline Parish Hospital. Miss Parfait, who also suffered undisclosed injuries, was treated and released from the hospital and is being held in the women's lockup of St. Madeline Parish Jail. Sheriff Geaux said he hoped both suspects would soon be returned to Catahoula Parish to face trial.

The sheriff added that should any of the victims die, he would ask prosecutors to seek the death penalty for both of the accused. "It's a sad day in our parish when law-abiding citizens, including one of my most talented deputies, are subject to such wanton violent acts," Sheriff Geaux said. "I ask you all to pray for these men and their recovery."

Syd lowers the paper and says damn, son, I didn't realize what a vicious bastard you were. And a religious object as a weapon?

Now, of course, I am an observant Jew, but don't you people down here in the swamps have any respect and reverence for your Lord and Savior? Why, this is appalling! Appalling!

I see Syd smilin'. I never quite know when Syd is yankin' my chain.

I say it's all lies, Syd—total bullshit. Plus, Rocko Marchante a civic leader? Hah! That sumbitch is a thief and a pervert. We'd have proof of that last thing if his goons hadn't burnt my trailer down and all them pictures wit' it. You know the bastid cheated me and a bunch of others at cards. But that was nuttin'. You shoulda seen the stuff Iris Mary took outta his house.

I see Syd is still smilin' at me. I don't see nuttin' funny about it.

He says oh, I've heard most of your side of the story, Junior. I paid a jailhouse visit to Miss Parfait, who filled me in on everything she knows. By the way, they love her over there in the jail. Even those hard-assed deputies act like altar boys when they're around her.

No shit?

Indeed. I happened to be there yesterday when they brought a young girl into juvenile lockup, which is a small wing just off the main jail. I didn't get the full story but it was one of those unfortunate domestic imbroglios. You know—the girl was pregnant. Her lousy boyfriend had skipped town. The parents were religious types who wanted to send her off to a nunnery or the equivalent. The girl had run away instead and was caught shoplifting a loaf of bread at one of those country grocery stores over near the next town. She was arrested. She came in hysterical and threatening suicide. They had to put two deputies in her cell to keep her from banging her head against the wall.

Finally, one of the jailers comes over to see Iris Mary. He says we don't know what to do. Could you please go talk to her?

Iris Mary says why me?

The jailer says because everyone thinks she'll listen to you.

Of course, Iris Mary went to see her. In twenty minutes she was calm.

Syd looks at me and shakes his head. He says I'll let you in on a little secret. Even your pal Captain Mouton is shook up by the steadfastness and calm with which Iris Mary repeats her story. She'll make a very credible witness, if it comes to that.

I look at Syd. I still think I might be dreamin'.

I say well, hold on before we get too far. See, I ain't got no money to pay you if you're thinkin' about bein' my lawyer. That leg money? Gone. I blew it. Every damn penny. I'm poor as a crawfish in a concrete parkin' lot.

Syd leans over close. He says Junior, to be perfectly honest, I knew you were a poor candidate to take care of your money and that's too bad because I won you some respectable cash. Invested wisely, you could be rich by now. And when you first called me way back when to sue the Go-Go Bar over your gambling losses, I knew you were burning through your money like a marsh fire in a hurricane. But anyway, I don't want any money, at least not from you.

Syd leans even closer so that he's practically whisperin' in my ear. He says Junior, not only is Rocko Marchante probably all those things you just called him but he's—ah, how would you put it?—up shit creek, too. You know how I once told you he was connected to the New Orleans mob, thus it would be best not to try to litigate your gambling losses?

Yeah, what about it?

Well, *was* is the right word. It turns out that our Mr. Marchante wasn't just screwing the good working men of Catahoula Parish at blackjack and fixed horse races and crooked slot machines. He was also cooking his books so that he was cheating the Mafia, too. They provided him with the slots and the feed to the horse track—my sources tell me they staked the guy so that he could buy the bar in the first place. Now, being crack businessmen concerned with their investments, they felt like their returns were falling somewhat south of expectations, if you follow me. So they decided to conduct a little audit.

I stop Syd. What the hell is an audit?

Well, to put it in layman's terms, they planted a snitch in the bar and the snitch found out he was skimming from the till—big, big bucks. Basically, the esteemed Raymond Marchante, the sheriff's favorite civic leader, owes the mob about five hundred thousand dollars. And that's just for the last six months. No wonder he could afford to throw ten thousand a year at the Ville Canard Little League! I did a little checking on his level of civic generosity and that's exactly how much he gave.

I look at Syd. I say that's all very interesting. But what's it got to do wit' me?

Okay, yes, well, I'm coming to that. As you may recall, my knowledge of the Go-Go Bar's mob connection goes back to a divorce matter. The man I represented was actually one of Caro Marcelli's top enforcers—have you ever heard that name before?

I say yeah, Caro Marcelli's like the *loup garou* around here. Everyone's heard his name. He's the guy in charge of the New Awlins Mafia, right? He's always bein' investigated for one thing or another but the cops cain't ever catch him. Now and then you'll hear about him on the TV.

That's the guy, Junior. This fellow I represented in the divorce was Caro's nephew and just like a son to him. Mafiosi are like Cajuns in a way—big, close families, devoutly Catholic, many of them. Even though he is personally rumored to have murdered ten or twelve people on his way to the top, Caro prays the rosary every day. Anyway, the nephew had married outside his faith and the woman happened to come from a nice New Orleans Jewish family. Now, why she married this man is a mystery. He was physically ugly and prone to violence. He was not a man of great intellect, I can tell you that. Maybe he was great in bed. Maybe he had an enormous putz—who can say?

I stop Syd. I say is a putz what I think it is?

Syd smiles. He says yes, Junior, it is. Anyway, perhaps this particular lady liked the rough, ugly types. Alas, the honeymoon was short and she was making his life miserable and threatening to expose him, since by this time she had a pretty clear knowledge of his particular business. Now, I know what people say about the mob but these guys aren't stupid. They didn't *want* to kill her if they could help it. So the goon comes to see me and let's just say I used my connections and influence in the Jewish community to work out a quiet and tidy settlement. The woman got a fancy house up by her sister in Scarsdale, New York, and a ton of money and a clear understanding of the consequences should she talk about family business. After it was all over, I got a visit from Caro Marcelli himself. He showed up at my office unannounced. An interesting man. Dapper, well-spoken, clearly intelligent. Polite, generous. One story circulating about him in New Orleans is that he'd stopped one day on the freeway to change the tire of a woman in distress. A black woman, yet! Anyway, he came to express his appreciation. Among other things, he wanted to know if there was anyone who was bothering me, causing me grief. You know—as in we'll take care of them if they are.

Syd draws his finger across his throat like a knife. He smiles at me again. He says I'm serious, Junior. I could have named anybody and they probably would have murdered the poor unfortunate. Can you believe it?

I look at Syd and I nod. I say this is still an interestin' story, but what the hell does it have to do wit' me?

Syd says well, Mr. Marcelli read with great interest what had happened to our friend Rocko, not to mention the local sheriff's description of him as such a fine, upstanding citizen. He knew—don't ask me how—that I'd had some business dealings down in Ville Canard, and the next thing I know, I'm being paid another visit.

Syd stops for a second and folds his arms. He says now, the mob has many ways of collecting its debts and getting even with deadbeats. As demonstrated by the case of the goon's ex-wife, they don't *automatically* kill people. In the case of our Mr. Marchante, well, they obviously know certain things about him that would be extremely embarrassing to him and would undermine his position as a luminary of civic charity, the statements of your fine sheriff notwithstanding. Normally, they would not tell such things because it would place their own interests in jeopardy as well. But as luck would have it, Mr. Marcelli and his boys just beat a big racketeering case that was tried in federal district court over in Mississippi. This had to do with allegations that the Marcelli gang was trying to muscle in on casinos there—

your basic protection racket. One of the casino owners went to the feds, and as a result, the feds planted one very broad wiretap on the Marcelli operation and, well, they were busted. But Caro can afford the very best legal defense and he beat the feds at trial—my opinion, he had a brilliant lawyer, a gullible jury, and a judge who was probably on the take. Some of those rulings from the bench with regard to evidence were—

I throw up my hand one more time. I say Syd, podnah, I'm lyin' here in this friggin' hospital where they keep whittlin' away at my body parts while the sheriff in Catahoula Parish wants to fry my ass in the 'lectric chair and you're in here tellin' me bedtime stories about the New Awlins Mafia. What the hell you *doin'* here, Syd? Ehn?

Syd shuffles in his chair. He says okay, Junior, calm down, son. I'm actually here to make you feel better. Just let me paint this picture a little more fully for you. Caro, upon his last visit, enlightened me about some peripheral matters that never made his trial. It turns out that in the feds' investigation of the casino matter, they cast their net fairly wide to look at other protection scams the Marcellis might be running. They heard about the Go-Go Bar down here in this neck of the swamps. To cut to the chase, they got a wiretap on the Go-Go Bar's phone and one on Marchante's home phone. One of the things they picked up was a conversation between Marchante and the ever-eloquent Sheriff Geaux. In it, the sheriff waxes grateful for all the donations that Marchante has bestowed upon him so far to keep the bar operating smoothly but, well, Christmas *is* coming and the sheriff has his eye on a duck-hunting camp out in some swamp someplace and Rocko is going to have to find fifty thousand dollars to finance the sheriff's purchase of it. Now, on this tape we hear our friend Rocko growing, shall we say, indignant and saying he doesn't have a spare fifty grand and casting various aspersions on the sheriff's character and making miscellaneous threats to his person. But your sheriff, to his credit, remains remarkably composed throughout this tirade. I know this because I have a transcript of this conversation in my very possession. Let me read it to you, Junior. It's the sheriff speaking first.

Syd shuffles through his papers again and takes a page out of the stack and starts to read.

Rocko, Rocko, podnah, calm down. Them threats ain't gettin' us nowhere. My boys are in your place all the time. The fuckin' joint's a gold mine, everybody knows that. You pop fifty thousand, hell, a hundred thousand dollars in profit on a good Saturday night.

Go-Boy, how come you're bein' such an asshole about this? Don't be such a greedy cocksucker. I pay you good goddam money already. You get the pick of my dancers. Hell, I know you like the young ones and I send you the youngest ones I got. I got expenses, too, man. I gotta pay my help. I gotta pay my girls. I gotta pay them boys in New Awlins. I gotta—

Rocko, listen to me, podnah, and listen good. I know for a fack you'll have an easier time payin' me than explainin' to them fuckin' dagos in New Awlins why you cain't keep your bar open. I hear they got a lot of money invested in you. You don't pay me and we shut you down, bro. It's that simple. And then you cain't pay them and they'll come down here and we'll find you at the bottom of some bayou wit' a garfish swimmin' up your ass. (Chuckle.)

Syd don't do a bad imitation of a Cajun accent, I got to give him that much.

He lowers the paper and says Junior, I was reading from a

deposition—the actual testimony from the federal agents who made the wiretap. Now, for a long time, these depositions were sealed, which means nobody could read them but officers of the court. But now that the trial's over, guess what? They're unsealed—they're public information. If certain parties knew of their existence, they could cause great trouble for Rocko Marchante and the sheriff.

I can see Syd is pleased wit' himself, and even though sometimes I'm thick as a gator, I can kinda see what he's gettin' at.

I say okay, that proves that Marchante's a crook. And the sheriff, too. But it still don't prove that I didn't lure Rocko out to Catahoula Bayou to rob his ass and run him down wit' my truck.

Syd smiles again. He says ah, Junior, my boy, you are absolutely right. But let me give you a little lesson in lawyering. First of all, as to the facts of your case as the sheriff has spun them out, I've already found a few weaknesses. The big one, and I'm sure your buddy Captain Mouton didn't tell you about this, is that the sole witness who is able to testify to these events at the moment is our Mr. Marchante.

I say why's that? Roddy and that snake Wiley can lie as good as Rocko.

Aha, Junior, that's probably true. But it turns out that Roddy and Wiley are, well, incapacitated.

Speak English, Syd.

You shot Roddy's ear off, Junior. His left ear, by the way. Normally that's not a debilitating injury, but for some reason Roddy's developed an inexplicable roar in his head. He keeps hearing the gunshot over and over again. They've got him locked up in a padded cell over in some secret wing of Canard General. He keeps running around and yelling out Irene! Irene! You have any idea who that could be, Junior?

I look at Syd. Maybe my mouth's hangin' open. I say well, that's prob'ly my sister.

Your sister?

It's a long story, Syd. I'll tell you about it later. What about Wiley?

Oh, yes, your charming friend Smurl. Well, you'll probably be happy to know that you broke his leg in about seven places when you struck him with your truck. Amazing that he could even crawl out of that ditch to come after you. But that's not his real problem. He seems to have bitten off most of his tongue, this after Miss Parfait hit him on the head with the religious object in question. He can't talk, unless you call babbling incoherently talking. And he can't write, either. He's developed tremors in his hands, probably from a bruise on the brain, so that he can't even hold a pencil. A mysterious thing, the brain. So he can't write his testimony, either. Of course, his condition could change. As could Roddy's. But for now, neither one of them is able to perform as a witness, which is convenient for us. Highly convenient, I'd say.

I see Syd is smilin' again.

If I didn't feel so friggin' bad, I might smile, too.

I say well, but there's still Rocko.

He says that's right, and for a couple of days they thought he might die. But in a way, it's better that he's alive. Short of being able to disprove his story, our immediate strategy is to cast doubt upon the integrity of your accusers, namely Mr. Marchante and Sheriff Geaux. Which means that these depositions have to become public.

What? You mean we gonna tell people about 'em?

Not just people, Junior. The press! The papers, and not just any paper. Your local paper, Junior. See, being your lawyer—and by the way, Caro Marcelli has said he will pick up any legal bills that have anything to do with matters antagonistic to Rocko Marchante, including yours—I've taken it upon myself to do some snooping around. You have a feisty little paper here, the *Ville Canard Call.* For years, they've been chasing after Go-Boy Geaux. They haven't gotten on to anything big. It's mostly low-grade matters like the sheriff fixing speeding tickets for his cronies or using parish jail prisoners to plant sugarcane on his farm. In more genteel places, this might get you thrown out of office, but in South Louisiana politicians are *expected* to dip their snouts in the public trough from time to time. But this is different. This is dynamite, Junior. Dynamite!

I say okay, wait, back up a bit, Syd. Are you sayin' the Mafia is payin' you to be my lawyer?

Syd's got that smile on his face again. He says well, Junior, let's just say that you and Caro Marcelli have converging interests and leave it at that.

And Iris Mary is part of the deal?

Absolutely. In fact, Mr. Marcelli, who was terribly irritated by the sheriff's use of the word *dago,* was quite taken with Miss Parfait's choice of a defensive weapon.

The statue, you mean?

Yes, the statue.

I look at my lawyer and shake my head. I say okay, well, so what we gotta do now?

We're going to spoon-feed these depositions to the local press. Of course, before we do, we'll have to get a guarantee that they won't rat us out as the source. That way we can be as shocked as everyone else when these awful things hit the streets. I've got my statement ready. *Oh, how dreadful for this poor community, but these sordid revelations do cast a ruinous shadow on the testimony of Mr. Marchante and Sheriff Geaux regarding my clients.*

Syd slaps his knee and laughs loud. It sounds like a thunderclap.

He says now, I could simply Xerox a couple of pages of the depositions and send them anonymously, with a little note attached about where the full documents can be found. But I've got a better plan. See, the *Call* is already on to the story, Junior. The New Orleans paper has published just the one piece I just read to you, but the *Call* has now had two longish articles. Happily, it appears that they are a bit more skeptical than is your sheriff about Mr. Marchante's character—they did bother, for example, to dredge up Rocko's previous run-in with the State Police over his gambling operations and the subsequent controversy when the charges were dropped. The same reporter wrote both stories, and I think he's a digger, which is exactly what we need. My plan, unless you object, is to slip into Ville Canard unannounced and have a little cloak-and-dagger meeting with the guy. Just like in the movies.

Syd is smilin' again and what can I say to his plan? Beats the hell out of anything I can think of to do.

Syd says at any rate, I've brought the *Call* articles with me. You don't have to read them now if you don't feel like it, but you should read them at some point. For better or worse, you're now infamous in your hometown.

I look at Syd and I gotta say, I don't like the sound of that word. I say okay, give 'em to me.

Syd shuffles through his papers again and hands the stories over. I'm seein' a bit blurry but the first headline catches my attention right away. It says MYSTERY ON A LONELY CATAHOULA BAYOU ROAD.

Somethin' else catches my attention, too, and I hear myself sayin' holy shit.

Syd says holy shit what, Junior?

I hand the papers back to Syd and say read me the name off that story.

He says you mean the byline?

I say yeah, the byline—the name of the person who wrote it.

He says by Meely LaBauve.

I say Syd, we gotta talk, podnah. You done put your money on the wrong horse.

23

I ain't seen him in a coon's age and here he is standin' by my bed wit' Syd at his side. He ain't givin' away nuttin'. He's just lookin' at me.

Syd brought him here. Syd said they went over everything yesterday for hours and hours and he agreed to come, finally.

He ain't a runt no more, for one thing. He could be six foot, which is perty damn amazin' considerin' how small he was. He's still a bit scrawny—but definitely no signs of a beer belly like some people I know. I wonder if he even drinks beer. He prob'ly does. All Cajun men do.

He's got a mustache, which I'd say is kinda wimpy, same as his hair, which is long in a way I'd never wear mine. People wit' hair like that are tryin' to tell you somethin' about themselves though don't ax me what the hell it is. It's perty close to bein' hippy hair, though not quite.

He ain't dressed so great, if you ax me. He's got on blue jeans wit' a white shirt and one of them tweedy-lookin' sports jackets.

He's got on them boots the roughnecks call fruit boots. At least he ain't wearin' a tie. It's true I bought me some khaki pants one time but I ain't never got low enough to wear a tie.

I gotta admit he don't look too bad. I figger I'm two, three years older than him at most, and some days I think I look like a fifty-year-old man. He looks like a friggin' college kid, which I guess is what he used to be.

Way back when, I thought he was some kind of retard 'cause he never went to school much. His momma was dead and his ole man was always gone or drunk or in jail, so there wadn't nobody makin' him come. But he always had smart-ass answers for the shit I give him, so I shoulda figgered he had a brain. The sumbitch could play shortstop, too, though I never wanted to admit that.

He went to college, even though it was just the local college up the bayou. I had a podnah who went there for one semester before he flunked out and become a welder. He said believe me, Junior, it ain't igzackly LSU.

Still, the runt went on to college and got one of them sheep-skins and now he makes a livin' wit' his head, not his back. I know all this 'cause Irene tole me about him a coupla years ago. I don't know why she did but she did. I don't know why I remember it but I do. Somethin' 'bout that sumbitch has stayed wit' me all these years.

I notice his hands ain't got a nick or callus on 'em. He's got all his fingers, too. And both legs. He looks perty doggone good next to me, and somethin' about that *really* pisses me off.

After I told Syd the whole story of Meely LaBauve, he said well, son, he may be totally furious with you after all these years, or maybe he's forgotten. But no matter what, you've got to be calm and reasonable—no temper, no wisecracks. We have to appeal to his journalistic instincts.

I said that's fine, Syd, just tell me what that means.

He said look, our depositions are explosive. When Iris Mary tells her story, people have a hard time doubting it. I'll get LaBauve into jail to interview her and he'll feel the same way. Then there's that mystery man in the field. Maybe he'll resurface, maybe he won't. But looking at it from LaBauve's standpoint, it has to be the best story he's stumbled into in a while—likely the best story of his career so far. It's a whole morality tale—greed, corruption, honor, valor—unfolding right here in Ville Canard. Plus, I know for a fact he's been chronicling the shenanigans of Go-Boy Geaux for a few years. Nothing so far has stuck but, this, well—this could bring the sheriff down. And we're serving it up to him like a free platter of salty oysters.

I didn't get all them words but I more or less got the point.

Syd said I'm gonna go talk to him, Junior, and if I'm any kind of lawyer at all he'll be here tomorrow night.

Here he is.

Syd's some damn lawyer, I got to give him that.

Syd tole me one other thing after he'd talked to Meely. He said Junior, I gotta be honest—I really liked the guy. I think he's smart and a square shooter.

I said whose side you on, Syd?

He said Junior, with any luck, it'll all be the same side.

That sounds like somethin' Iris Mary would say. I wonder about that girl in jail. Maybe they do love her over there but she has to be freaked out. Iris Mary ain't made for jail, I know that much. Plus, she's probably in there sayin' prayers for ole Wiley, even though the bastid deserved to be knocked on the head or worse. Maybe Roddy, too. Maybe even bad-ass Rocko. That's just how she is. Myself, after what Wiley did to me and after what he and ole Rocko tried to do to Iris Mary, I'd zydeco dance on their graves if they died. I would—serious.

And if I tole that to Iris Mary she would say Joseph, you'll do no such thing!

But I might do it anyway. I just wouldn't tell her I did it.

I have grown sweet on Iris Mary Parfait. I realize how I've never really worried much about anybody or anything in my life, 'cept maybe Lolly-Lee now, and Momma after she got sick. All that worryin' was a bit late, I guess. But I'm plenty worried about Iris Mary. Not that worryin' does anybody any damn good. Maybe that's why I never cared to worry about nuttin' before. Where the hell does it get you?

Iris Mary would have an answer to that, too. I'm perty shore I know what she would say. People who love each other look after each other, Joseph. Worryin' about them is just another way of lookin' after them.

Lawd. The things she expects a person to do.

I look up from my bed and, hell, I got no idea what to say to Meely LaBauve.

Syd sees that and he says uh, I believe you two know each other. Junior, I've filled Meely in on our version of the events but, of course, he'd like to hear them directly from you. Our deal is that he is free to use anything we tell him, he simply can't quote you or me or Iris Mary directly.

I nod. I say well, shoot, Meely. Talkin's about all I can do these days.

It's clear he ain't gonna shoot right away.

He says well, well, Junior Guidry, the world is full of surprises.

I think last time I saw you up this close you had me tied up in knots back out on Catahoula Bayou—literally, I was tied to the post of our old garage and I could hardly move. And now, here you are, crippled and wrapped up in bandages, and I doubt you could get very far, even if the hospital caught on fire.

I ain't got nuttin' to say to that.

He says you sure you feel like talkin' to me?

I nod.

He says I almost didn't come.

I nod again.

He says your lawyer here, Mr. Shainburg, is quite the salesman. The minute he told me he was representin' you, the only thing I could think to say was what for? I told him I'd been followin' your illustrious career, especially since your accident, and that while I appreciated that everybody deserves a lawyer in criminal matters he'd be wastin' his time. I told him I knew you when you were an overgrown, loudmouthed schoolyard punk, and you obviously had never changed. You know what he told me?

I shake my head.

He said Meely, for all of his rough edges, Junior is a different person these days. He risked his own life to save his friend. You know what I said?

I shake my head again.

He says I laughed my ass off at that.

I can feel myself startin' to hunch up like a kicked cat.

He says but Junior, I decided I'd come talk to you because, whether you did what they say you did or not, this *is* a hell of a story. And this is what I do—what I love to do. I'm a bluetick hound on a coon's track when it comes to stories. And thanks to your lawyer and those depositions he's let me see, I at least appreciate that our esteemed sheriff and his friend Rocko Marchante might've had a relationship that casts doubt on their version of events. Now, maybe you are the violent, miserable bastard of a two-bit crook that they say you are, but maybe, just maybe, they have their own motives for wantin' to stick it to you. So I'm all ears, Junior. Let's start, say, back at the Go-Go Bar and your gamblin' losses. And, of course, I want to know about your relationship with that Smurl guy. I mean, the sheriff, though some people think he's a few oysters short of a po'boy, is pretty damn clever to dredge that stuff up. Face it. It does give you two very good motives to do what they say you've done. And honestly, I'd like to hear that story because, what I know of it so far, it reminds me of somethin' you and your podnahs pulled on me all those years ago. I'm curious to know how you felt when you were on the other end of the stick.

He looks at me wit' that poker face of his and reaches into his jacket pocket and pulls out a pen and a notebook. He and Syd sit down in chairs Syd's pulled up to my bed.

He says well, Junior, I'm ready. Take your time. I'm in no rush. I got all day, in fact.

There ain't nuttin' about this I like. I look at Syd in a way that says this is total bullshit, podnah. And Syd glares at me in a way that says don't fuck this up, Junior. So I take a deep breath and start to tell my story. It starts to come out slow and then it starts to come out fast. A coupla hours later, I got it all tole.

Meely stops me now and then and axes me this or that. Then there ain't nuttin' more to say and everybody gets quiet for a while. Meely keeps scribblin' in his notebook and I wonder what the hell he could be writin'. Then he stops and looks at me. Then he says somethin' I don't expect.

He says Junior, I think you might be tellin' the truth, though my opinion mostly has nothin' to do with this interview. When we first started, I just had to give you a hard time because, face it, podnah, you *really were* a mean, miserable son of a bitch back then and caused my daddy and me a huge amount of grief. You changed our lives forever with your lies. Your uncle was worse than you were, if such things are possible. But I accept that was a long, long time ago. People can change, though I have to say that, what I know of honest change, it's a rare commodity—in fact, pretty close to a miracle. Still, I do believe it's possible under certain circumstances for people to redeem themselves. Even somebody like you, Junior. Even you.

I cain't think of what to say to that. He's talkin' Iris Mary stuff now.

I cain't think of what to say and I don't have to say nuttin' 'cause there's a knock on our door and suddenly Captain Mouton is standin' over me. He don't look happy.

He looks at Syd and Meely and says excuse me, gentlemen, for interruptin' but Raymond Marchante died two hours ago of a stroke in Canard General Hospital. Sheriff Geaux from Catahoula Parish called to say they were gonna file first-degree murder charges against Junior and Miss Parfait and try to get them transferred to Catahoula Parish as soon as possible.

The captain looks at me and says I think there's a good chance you're goin' home soon, Junior, though I wouldn't expect a parade.

I don't appreciate his smart-ass remark. But Syd pipes up and says thank you, Captain, for informing us. Now, if you don't mind, I need to talk about these developments with my client.

Captain Mouton nods and walks out of the room.

Syd turns to me with his hand on his bearded chin and says

hhm, well, an unexpected turn of events, Junior. Unwelcome, in a way.

I say Syd, in a way? In a *way*? If they send my ass to Canard General I can guarantee you that Go-Boy Geaux or one of his bad boys or one of Rocko Marchante's henchmen will find a way into the hospital and saw off some other parts. Like my head. Plus no tellin' what them bastids will do to Iris Mary if they get her in Go-Boy Geaux's jail.

Syd takes a deep breath and says well, maybe we can stall a transfer. You really aren't in any shape to travel. And with Marchante out of the picture, perhaps our good Sheriff Geaux will be content to let the wheels of justice grind on. Maybe he'd like to have a big showy capital murder trial to demonstrate what a brilliant and tough lawman he is. In that case, his interests would be in taking very good care of you and Iris Mary till the trial is over.

I say well, Syd, I'm glad one of us can be so calm about my life, or what's left of it.

Syd looks at me and then he looks at Meely. He says how fast do you write, Meely? I'm not trying to tell you what to do, but looking at this clinically, I'd say your story actually just got better.

And remember, son, dead men can't sue.

24

The day has turned to night and I ain't heard a peep from Syd. He went over to the jail wit' Meely to talk to Iris Mary. I'm dyin' to know how it went.

They done fed me—Styrofoam chicken and mashed potatoes that tasted like that paste we used to stick our papers together in school. The peas were wrinkled and cold and the bread was hard as blacktop, but I guess I cain't complain.

Nurse Hotard come in about a half hour ago to give me my pain medicine. Normally, that stuff makes me drowsy and I conk out right away. But I got rabbits runnin' 'round in my brain and butterflies in my stomach. There's somethin' perty doggone funny about Meely havin' my ass in his hands. And I don't mean ha-ha funny.

When Nurse Hotard come in, she said Junior, you have a very nice lawyer, that Mr. Shainburg. Now, this isn't any of my business, but he told me your side of the story and I have to say I found myself believing him. Captain Mouton tells a different tale, of course, though between us, I don't think he's as sure about this as he was. And not that it matters what I think, but I wanted to let you know.

She said oh, and your friend, Iris Mary, when she was here—there's just something about her, Junior. She seemed so, uh, so kind and down-to-earth.

I found myself sayin' thank you, Nurse Hotard. That's nice of you to say.

True. I'm startin' to *sound* like Iris Mary.

This is a small hospital, quiet most times and it's quiet now. Captain Mouton usually goes home at supper, leavin' one or two of his boys just out my door. Most nights I hear one of them fellas snorin'. Sometimes I get the wild hair just to roll out of bed on my belly and actually try to crawl out of here. But I wouldn't get far, and I'm in enough trouble already.

I lie in the dark wit' the lights out, just starin' up at the ceilin'. I'm starin' and starin' and wishin' I had my leg back and my fingers back and my money back and wonderin', even if I ever got those wishes, whether it would make a difference. If I got a chance to do it all over again could I do it wit'out messin' everything up like usual?

I realize this ain't gettin' me nowheres and that all I got in the world 'tween me and the Big Ditch is Syd and Iris Mary and a reporter who used to hate my guts and still might. Iris Mary would say I got Irene, too. And prob'ly God, though—serious—it's hard to think He's on Junior's side.

I'm finally startin' to drift off when I hear a noise—footsteps comin' quiet. It ain't like them nurses who walk in hard in the middle of the night and wake you up to give you this or do that.

I look toward my door and it opens.

The light's on out in the hall and I see two men standin' there—cops, and not the cops I know. I see 'em lookin' around and then they walk in.

One of them comes up to me and pulls out his gun. He puts it to my head and says how you feelin', Guidry?

I say perty good till you come in.

He says hah, you're the smart-ass everybody says you are. Anyway, don't worry about it, podnah, I ain't here to kill you. I'm just here 'cause Sheriff Geaux said Soileau, go get that asshole and bring him back to town. Plus, I wanted to see the man who would shoot his own podnah. Roddy Bergeron was good to you, bro! I know for a fact he kept you in whiskey and high-quality potted meat!

Soileau looks like a buzzard wit' a bad haircut. He puts his gun away. He says now, I know you kinda beat up, but me and my podnah here have borrowed one of them rollin' stretchers from just down the hall. There was only one nurse on duty down there and now she's busy—tryin' to get herself out of that locked closet. That deputy who should be at your door was down there at the nurses' station sleepin' on a cot. Now, that's the law for you! We gave him a li'l love tap to make sure he won't wake up too soon. So don't raise a fuss. We just gonna wheel you out and lay you down in the backseat of the patrol car and take you to Ville Canard. Now, if you raise a fuss, we might have to drop you off somewhere in between, if you know what I mean.

Soileau looks at his pal and they grin like *choupique*.

I know I'm dead—my luck's run out. I know the place they gonna dump me, too. 'Tween here and Ville Canard is a stretch of twisty two-lane built through the swamp. They got a bunch of board roads branchin' off the highway that go way back yonder, this way and that. You just drive to the end of one of them things and, wit' a concrete block or two, you can sink a man deep enough so that, after the gators and snappin' turtles and garfish are done, there ain't nuttin' left to find.

All the times I've fought in my life and now I cain't even raise a finger.

The second cop steps back into the hall and wheels in the gurney. They grab me hard and I moan and they say shhh, quiet, man, you might wake up the patients. They giggle like they think this is funny, too. I smell liquor on Soileau's breath. They pick me up and put me faceup on the cart. I see Soileau's 'bout doubled over wit' laughter.

When they get to the door, Soileau ain't laughin' no more.

There's three big-ass deputies standin' there wit' their pistols drawn.

The biggest one says what y'all boys think y'all doin'? This is St. Madeline Parish and this man is *our* prisoner. My name is Captain Mouton and I'm in charge of this investigation. Unless you can show me a warrant, I want y'all to get your hands off that cart.

Now, I gotta say, in my state I hardly know a friggin' thing. But one thing I do know—that man ain't Captain Mouton.

Soileau and his podnah look like cornered snakes that cain't decide what to do—bite or crawl off.

The biggest man—the one who ain't Captain Mouton—raises his gun about eye level wit' Soileau. He says let's see it, officer. Let's see that warrant. Otherwise, I wanna see you beatin' feet for the door. If you get out quick, you won't have to spend the night in our jail.

He looks back at his pals. He says I don't think they would like it, do you, boys?

One of the boys says oh, hell no, Captain. They definitely wouldn't like it. This very afternoon we locked up about twenty of them bad sumbitches that belong to the Harley-Gators, that motorcycle gang that practically burnt down Labadieville last year. Man, them boys find out they got a coupla cops in the cell with 'em and they'd take turns havin' a honeymoon. 'Course, I wouldn't tell them bad-asses these guys are cops, would you, Captain?

Soileau and his podnah raise their hands above their heads. The three big guys step away from the door and Go-Boy's goons walk out. The one who ain't Mouton says not so fast. Your guns— just unbuckle the holsters and let 'em slide down easy to the floor.

The gun belts go cloppin' to the floor. Soileau and his pal start to edge away and Soileau says somethin' about this is bullshit.

The big man pulls back the hammer of his gun and says podnah, you got ten seconds to make the door.

Soileau starts to raise his middle finger and the other two deputies raise their guns. The big man starts to count.

Soileau hauls ass, his podnah right behind him. I can hear them police shoes clickin' like ball bearin's on the tile floor.

The man who ain't Captain Mouton yells you got a half hour to make the parish line. If you ain't out, we'll run you out! I mean it!

I hear the door bangin' and a car startin' and the squeal of rubber. Them sumbitches are runnin' like mullet from a bull red.

The big man turns to me and says man, I hope they don't get a speedin' ticket! He laughs big as Hurricane Betsy when he says that.

I look up and say well, I know you ain't Mouton. You here to kill me, too?

He leans down and says, awmost in a whisper, no, Mr. Guidry. Your lawyer was worried about you. So were we, 'cause my boss had heard certain things. He thought we should come get you and take you with us till things cool down. By the way, Syd doesn't exactly know we've come. Mr. Marcelli thought it would be best if he didn't actually know.

He says isn't Syd a good goddam lawyer? He got my ex-wife off my ass like a surgeon removin' a wart. Of course, I had to give her a supertanker full of money but, lemme tell you, pal, it was worth every penny. Good damn riddance.

I got to think about all this for a second. All I can think to say is where we goin'?

He says aw, we got a nice place up on the river where we can all lay low for a while. I think you'll like it. Mr. Marcelli's even got you a nurse 'cause, face it, my pals and me—well, none of us are Florence Nightingale, if you know what I mean.

The boys all nod in agreement.

He says Mr. Guidry—oh, by the way, you mind if I call you Junior?

I say Junior's okay wit' me.

He says well, Junior, I have to warn you—that nurse is fine. Fine! Hell, I thought for minute about sawin' off my own damn arm if I thought I could get her to take tender-lovin' care of *me*.

I nod and say speakin' from experience, there's prob'ly easier ways to get some lovin' from a nurse.

The big man laughs. He says ha, ha! I think we're all gonna be pals—goombas, as we Italians say. Goombas! By the way, Junior, my name is Johnny. This is Monk and Larry. Anyway, we'll save the small talk for later. We better get the hell out of here.

I look up and nod. I say before we go, if you don't mind, would you look in that closet there and get my leg?

Johnny says your leg?

Yeah, my peg leg. They put it up at the top of that closet where I cain't reach it.

Larry or Monk—I've already got 'em mixed up—goes get my leg. He slings it over his shoulder like a baseball bat.

They wheel me down the hospital corridor and out into the cool night air. I see them boys shuckin' their cop hats and coats and tossin' them in one of them big metal garbage containers sittin' on the edge of the parkin' lot.

I get another surprise when we get to the getaway car. It ain't exactly a car. It's a big black hearse.

Them boys open the back and Johnny reaches in and passes out black suit jackets to everybody.

I say I hope I ain't gotta ride in the coffin.

Johnny smiles. He says not this time, goomba.

They grab the gurney and lift it and wheel me in the back. One of them sets the brake on the gurney and sits stooped over on a li'l bench next to me. He says you just rest, Junior. We got a ways to go.

I hear the front doors slammin' and the hearse purr to life. We go cruisin' off to God knows where.

25

I guess it's mornin'.

I wake up in a fog in a big four-poster bed and the sun's shinin' through a window that practically goes from the floor to the ceilin'. I look out and see I'm up high and eye level wit' a live oak so big and old that its branches stoop crooked to the ground.

I see the river. Wit' the sun shinin' on it, it looks like creamy chocolate milk. There's a big gray tugboat tryin' to chug a string of rusty barges up-current. I realize I ain't seen the Mississippi since I drove over the Huey P. Long Bridge on my way to New Awlins when I first hired Syd. I never liked drivin' over that narrow bridge.

I come in late last night, or maybe it was the night before, who knows. What I've seen of it, this hideout is somethin' else. It's a big house—a mansion, really—lookin' right over the levee at the river. I got no clue exactly where it is. Prob'ly somewhere between New Awlins and Baton Rouge. Seems like it took us a coupla hours or more to get here. I've only seen a few of the rooms. Some other fellas come out to meet the hearse and they all grabbed on to the gurney and then they rolled me up some big steps and clear around a big wooden porch, then put me in some kind of ole-timey elevator wit' accordion doors and took me up-stairs. They put me in a room wit' this bed wit' one of them metal hospital doo-jiggies on the side where they've hung my drip. The room has a mirror on the ceilin' and another clear across the wall.

That's how I first figgered out I'm in a whorehouse.

Then a coupla them girls come to look in on me and they shore wadn't dressed like nurses in them miniskirts they were wearin'. They didn't get too close but they looked perty good, what I could see of 'em. I heard 'em gigglin'.

Some other time I might've axed them girls to come over and see me. Who knows what might've happened? But I ain't in no shape for hanky-panky. No mood, neither. Funny how that is.

That nurse turned out to be every bit as fine as Johnny said she would be. She's friendly but she's all business, which is okay by me. Anyway, the second time she come to give me my medi-cine I axed her what her name was. She smiled perty and said Maria. Maria Marcelli. Caro is my uncle.

Later I tole Johnny, podnah, you coulda warned me the nurse was Caro Marcelli's niece. What if I'd made a pass at her?

He said no problem, buddy. We'd've just had to cut your dick off. Ha, ha, ha! Haw, haw, haw!

I guess it's good that I'm wore out as a broke-down marsh buggy and I ache like I spent the night sloggin' through *flottant*. Nurse Maria changed my bandages and said I'm doin' okay. She give me a li'l somethin' for the pain. Then I conked out.

Iris Mary was down there in my dreams. I think we mighta

been smoochin' or somethin'. I come to realizin' maybe I did wanna fool around—wit' Iris Mary.

This one room is about as big as my whole trailer and a hell of a lot nicer. The ceilin' must be twenty foot up and what the mirror don't cover is painted wit' angels and whatnots and there's a big shiny chandelier hangin' from a gold chain. That mirror on the ceilin' really bugs me 'cause I cain't help but see myself plain and it ain't a perty sight.

You could put four or five people in this bed it's so big. And I guess sometimes they do. Them mirrors might come in handy in that case—you wouldn't miss nuttin' at all.

I hear somebody cloppin' down the hall. There's wood floors everywhere here and everybody clops 'cept Nurse Maria, who wears soft white shoes. The door opens and a man walks right up to me. He holds out his hand and says Mr. Guidry, Caro Marcelli. I hope you're comfortable here.

I nod and reach up and give him a shake as best as I can. I say this is a hell of a lot better than the bottom of a swamp someplace.

He smiles.

The first thing I notice is that he's smaller than I expected, but he's got on a suit you ain't gonna find at the Bargain Store in Ville Canard. In fack, right away he looks like one of them men who will always wear his clothes better than you—you know the kind I mean. He looks about sixty. Silver hair combed back like a movie star. He looks like somebody done buffed and polished him. His skin is as pink as a baby pig's. Hell, he prob'ly does get buffed and polished every day, maybe by them girls that work here. I guess if I was the boss of the Mafia, I might look like that, too. He smells like he just come from a fancy barbershop.

He's got eyes like a hawk's.

He says I hope you've had a good sleep.

I nod. I say I ain't done nuttin' but sleep. How long I been here?

This is the second day. Sorry about the way we had to take you out of there. But we thought it was best. We have an informant in the Marchante operation and we heard about some nasty things some of his boys were planning for you.

I say that hearse was perty comfortable. I just ain't ready to ride in another one anytime soon. Live or dead.

He looks at me serious and says some of Rocko's boys are really sore about how you and your friend Miss Parfait roughed up their fearless leader. Now that he's dead, Marchante's gang won't be a gang much longer. Rocko was a snake and a liar but he knew how to keep his boys in line. Without him, they'll be at each other like cannibals. The one guy who could have taken over works for me, if you catch my meaning.

You mean the snitch?

He smiles and says that's right.

He says I guess your friend Miss Parfait is pretty handy with a statue.

I say it seems like she is.

He says Junior, don't you think it's downright miraculous? How she used a replica of the Blessed Virgin to save herself from Rocko the first time? And how she saved you later?

I think about this for a second. I say well, if you hit people hard enough wit' somethin' that hard and heavy, usually they fall.

He nods like I've said something serious. He says my mother, may she rest in peace, had one of those statues in her yard, too. She was a fine woman, Junior. Very religious. Most devout. She venerated the Holy Mother. Do you think your friend would part with it—the statue, I mean? I would pay for it. Handsomely.

I look up at the don. He seems to be blushin'.

He says now, I know this may amuse you, my friend, but I am mildly superstitious. I just have a feeling about that statue—that it may have certain, well, uh, protective qualities. You know, a man in my business can use all the advantages he can get.

I nod. I say you could ax Iris Mary. But it's sentimental to her. It belonged to her aunt, who was a nun and the last of her family. She give it to Iris Mary before she died.

He says I see. What a wonderful gift.

I say I hope you're not makin' her one of them offers we cain't refuse.

He laughs at that. He says oh, no. You've watched too many movies. I'm a businessman at heart, and besides, I have great respect for Miss Parfait. In a way, she's done us a real service. As have you, my friend.

He stops for a second and looks out the window. Then he says speaking of business, I heard you were a good patron of that place Marchante ran—what did Rocko call it?

The Hollywood Bayou Go-Go Bar?

That's it. I also heard you were cheated.

I was. Out of a ton of money. 'Course, that's what happens when you're stupid and drunk most of the time.

He nods. He says your self-awareness should serve you well in the future. As I'm sure you know, we had a stake in that place, though Marchante ran it. We gave him plenty of ways to make money—he didn't *have* to run a crooked blackjack game. Legitimate casinos make tons of money—tons—because the odds ultimately are with the house. It's all about volume and margin. We tried to invest in a couple of casinos over in Mississippi but certain persons in the law-enforcement community took exception to our plans and methods. A real pity. But Marchante was just greedy and he died owing us money. You know what they say, Junior. It's possible that lambs can lie down with lions—if the lambs cooperate. But sooner or later, pigs get slaughtered.

I don't think I want to talk to Caro Marcelli about people gettin' slaughtered.

I say so have you heard from Syd? Is half the law in Loosiana lookin' for me?

He says we've been in touch with Syd to let him know you weren't *really* kidnapped. He's down in Ville Canard snooping around on your case. Miss Parfait is still in jail in St. Madeline Parish, which is the best place for her for now. Sheriff Landrieu down there was very upset, to put it mildly, when he found out that Sheriff Geaux's cowboys had come to take you out of the hospital and roughed up one of his deputies. Poor Sheriff Landrieu is extremely perplexed as to what happened to you, since Sheriff Geaux's deputies denied they'd even been there at all. But they were stupid enough to march in with their uniforms on and the nurse they locked in the closet got a good look at the badges. She also turns out to be Sheriff Landrieu's cousin by marriage, so his grudge against Sheriff Geaux is now personal. Syd, being the very good lawyer that he is, is exploiting that as a way of making sure Sheriff Geaux's goons keep their hands off Iris Mary until he can get his master plan in play. Anyway, Marchante has gotten his just rewards, but Sheriff Geaux still needs to be taken down a notch or two. Such bigotry—calling my associates and me *dagos*!

He clucks his tongue. Anyway, I know Syd has a plan to unmask the sheriff for the bigot and criminal he really is.

Marcelli turns back to the window and there's a knock on the door and Johnny comes in. He says to Marcelli, boss, Syd Shainburg is on the phone wanting to talk to our pal Junior here.

Marcelli nods. He walks toward my bed and bends down and comes up wit' a phone that had been stashed down on a shelf on my bedside table. He says the phones in these rooms don't ring— we don't want to disturb our customers. But they receive calls. Here you go, Junior.

I take the phone and I hear Syd sayin' so how are they treating you, son?

I say it ain't a bad place, Syd. Where are you?

Oh, I'm camped out at a motel in your lovely hometown. By the way, Junior, parts of it are quite lovely and charming. I don't think I realized that when I first traveled down here on your personal-injury claim. I guess I could be something of an urban snob. But the man over at the Commercial Hotel on Main Street serves a very nice bowl of gumbo and is quite conversant in all manner of subjects with a sophistication I had not expected.

I say Syd, that's all good but you gotta tell me what the hell's goin' on.

He says at the moment, I'm talking from a pay phone in the lobby of the motel lest our friends in the sheriff's office here try to listen in. And believe me, they'd love to be listening in. Anyway, I've got good news, bad news, and strange news. Which do you want first?

Well, hhm, gimme the bad news first.

Okay. The honorable Go-Boy Geaux has produced an affidavit from your friend Smurl. It seems as though he's made some sort of miraculous recovery and has delivered a written statement. I doubt that it's real, Junior—I'd wager Smurl's still a wreck and they forged the whole thing. But the sheriff is using it to keep the Murder One charge against you.

I say okay, I figgered somethin' like that would happen. So what's the good news?

Junior, our pal Meely came through. Let me read you something in today's *Ville Canard Call*. The headline says MURDER CHARGES TO BE FILED IN CATAHOULA BAYOU INCIDENT BUT NEW QUESTIONS RAISED IN CASE. Now, bear with me, because there's a bit to get through. But I know you'll get a kick out of it.

Syd starts to read:

Was Raymond "Rocko" Marchante a hapless victim of a brutal crime, as local law-enforcement officials have portrayed him?

Or was he a victimizer—a ruthless, mob-connected lounge owner with a long history of sexual assault who bribed law-enforcement officials with money and underage prostitutes to keep a lucrative and rigged gambling operation running? In fact, did he victimize the people who are now accused of murdering him?

The prominent Catahoula Parish club owner died suddenly this week of a stroke that doctors said was related to injuries he received in what law-enforcement officers have described as a botched robbery attempt by a man with a grudge against him. But explosive depositions filed in an unrelated criminal case in a Mississippi federal court portray Marchante as a man with ties to a New Orleans crime syndicate who himself was being extorted by Catahoula Parish's top law-enforcement officer, Sheriff Ervil "Go-Boy" Geaux, to pay additional bribes to the sheriff to keep an apparently illegal gambling operation running. Called the Hollywood Bayou Go-Go Bar, the club is a popular and some would say notorious hangout for a rough-and-tumble crowd of oil-field workers, itinerant laborers, and drifters.

The Go-Go Bar was the object of a State Police raid three years ago; Marchante was arrested on charges of violating Louisiana gaming laws for what troopers called an ongoing illegal blackjack game and bookmaking operation in a back room there.

The club was briefly padlocked but reopened a short time later after the charges against Marchante were dropped following hearings brought by a Catahoula Parish prosecutor before a parish grand jury. Such proceedings are secret, and Lou Wicks, the district attorney at the time, said he was prohibited by law from discussing the grand jury's action. Wicks left office a year ago and is now in private practice; he serves as Sheriff Geaux's personal attorney. The grand jury's decision was openly criticized by State Police officials back then and set off a whirl of speculation in criminal court circles here that Marchante, a known friend and political supporter of Sheriff Geaux and a contributor to Wicks' political campaigns, had used such influence to escape the charges.

At the time, Sheriff Geaux, who hadn't been consulted by the State Police before the raid, went to the extraordinary length of calling a press conference to denounce what he called "evil and libelous rumors" about using his influence to get the criminal case against Marchante dropped.

The sheriff, in fact, gave a eulogy at Marchante's funeral and praised Marchante as "my good podnah" and "a religious man and generous civic leader who cared about the Boy Scouts and Girl Scouts and Little Leaguers—all the precious little children of the parish—and gave lots of his money to prove it." The sheriff also announced, at Marchante's funeral, his intentions to ask prosecutors to elevate the criminal charges to first-degree murder against two people arrested in the alleged robbery attempt of Marchante.

Syd stops to clear his throat. He says next comes some details about you and Iris Mary being arrested and your mysterious disappearance from the hospital. Now, you'll like this next part, Junior.

Even stranger, St. Madeline Parish Sheriff Maurice J. Landrieu called a press conference yesterday to complain that Sheriff Geaux had attempted to "interfere in the internal affairs of our parish" by sending deputies to the hospital to try to "hijack Guidry and take him back to Catahoula Parish, maybe with the idea of rough justice in mind." Sheriff Landrieu said the plot was foiled but declined to say how, and that he would ask the State Police to formally investigate the matter.

Sheriff Geaux, told of Sheriff Landrieu's statements, called them "horsebleep" and said if the Call *printed "Maurice Landrieu's stupidbleep comments, somebody over there is gonna get their bleep in a muskrat trap." Sheriff Geaux made these comments despite the fact that a* Call *reporter and editor made it clear to the sheriff that the interview was being tape-recorded.*

Syd stops again. He says getting a little testy, our sheriff is. Well, wait till you hear the rest of this.

Recently unsealed depositions in the unrelated mob case, filed in the 3rd Circuit U.S. District Court in Biloxi and obtained by this newspaper, portray the relationship of Sheriff Geaux and Marchante as one of mutual distrust and greed and also cast doubt on the sheriff's ability to impartially investigate the late club owner's alleged robbery-murder. The depositions were taken from an unnamed Federal Bureau of Investigation agent who placed a wiretap on Marchante's business and home telephones. In one recorded conversation, the date of which is unclear, Marchante responds angrily to a request from Sheriff Geaux to pay the sheriff $50,000 so that he could purchase a duck-hunting camp and lease in the Rice Bayou Swamp south of Ville Canard.

Syd says so isn't this marvelously entertaining? I'm skipping ahead again. The next part goes into the depositions—you know, the parts I read to you about Marchante calling the sheriff a greedy cocksucker and the sheriff making his improvident dago comment. Now, here's Sheriff Geaux at his finest again.

Shown copies of the depositions, Sheriff Geaux hotly denied he had ever made such statements to Marchante and then ordered a reporter out of his office, saying, "Your days in this parish are numbered if you print that bleep." Later, the sheriff's attorney, Wicks, phoned the Call *to complain of its "chickenbleep persecution and campaign of innuendo against Sheriff Geaux" and threatened to "personally kick the bleep" out of the reporter writing the story and "sue you and your bleeping newspaper out of existence."*

Sources close to the defendants in the Marchante criminal matter, however, say the depositions lend credence to statements by the accused, given to law-enforcement officials, that they were the victims, not the perpetrators, of the crime. Indeed, both Guidry and Miss Parfait have reportedly told investigators that Parfait, who was a live-in assistant to Marchante's aging mother, was twice sexually accosted by Marchante after Marchante learned that she had helped an alleged sexual-torture victim of Marchante's escape from his home.

Told of Guidry and Parfait's version of events, Sheriff Geaux called it a "steaming pile of dogbleep that only a moron would believe." The sheriff then phoned a reporter back to say that "if you call me one more time and ask me one more question about this bullbleep case, I'm going to send my deputies over there to drag you by the heels to jail."

Syd stops to catch his breath. He says as you can tell, Junior, our friend the sheriff is extremely vexed. And I have to say, this is far more than I expected of our journalist pal. Not only is it thorough and clear but it's pretty damn courageous stuff. Now, there's only a little more, but it's also interesting. Listen to this:

In other developments in the case, State Police apparently conducted a raid of the Marchante home on the day of Marchante's funeral. A State Police spokesman declined to confirm or deny that the raid had occurred or to say what officers might have been looking for or whether the raid was connected to the Guidry matter. But one person with knowledge of the incident said officers were looking for "ledgers or documents or photographs" that might shed light on Marchante's alleged ties to the New Orleans mob and his relationship to Sheriff Geaux. Though it is unclear what investigators found in that regard, they did uncover a note, written several days before, from Marchante's mother, identified as Elaine "Laney" Marchante. Apparently written after Marchante was hospitalized for the injuries allegedly caused by a fall, the note said she had "escaped the house with the help of the gardener" and was "leaving town because I fear that my son has turned into a monster and done terrible things."

Though investigators initially feared that Mrs. Marchante might have come to harm, they eventually tracked her down at her daughter-in-law's house in Waterford, Va., where she is said to be suffering from exhaustion and shock.

While Guidry had a previous arrest record for drunk driving and unpaid speeding tickets, Miss Parfait, until her encounter with Marchante, had apparently led an exemplary life. Her last known address was at a South Parish Catholic mission attached to St. Enid's Catholic Church and School, where she lived adjacent to an aunt, who was a nun and part of the mission's holy order. She moved

*away about a year ago to become Mrs. Marchante's live-in compan-
ion not long after her aunt died of cancer.*

Syd stops one more time. He says there's another passage here
about how some goons invaded the mission about the time Iris
Mary was fleeing Marchante's house and how some bayou men
came to chase them off and how the Mother Superior complained to the sheriff but, of course, to no avail. Now, here's your
eloquent sheriff and his lawyer again.

*Sheriff Geaux, reached one more time for comment, hung up on
a reporter. But Wicks, his attorney, telephoned the* Call *later and
said, "You guys are just making this up as you go along, aren't you?
Do you hear this? Ka-ching! That's the sound of my libel suit going
up a million dollars after every call."*

I hear Syd chuckle and then he says well, that's it, Junior.
Some piece, isn't it?

I say shuh, man, I can see Meely ain't changed. He just shot a
firecracker off up Go-Boy's butt. If I were him, I'd be haulin' ass
outta Catahoula Parish about now. Now, I know he had to take
his li'l dig at me about my arrest record and all, but at least he got
the truth out about Iris Mary. Plus, that girl's gonna be happy that
nuttin' bad's happened to Miz Laney. She's been worried sick
about the ole lady. Plus, I know all about them sumbitches in-
vadin' that convent down there. Roddy tole me hisself.

Syd says Junior, Meely wasn't taking a dig at you. He was
writing the truth. Face it, son, you've been leading a sloppy life—
damn sloppy—and some of it caught up with you. But the point
of justice isn't that you've made mistakes in the past. It's that
those mistakes have nothing to do with the current truth, which
is that you're an innocent man being framed.

I say Syd, I love it when you talk that way.

He says you may not love this so much. Remember when we started this conversation, I told you there was good news, bad news, and strange news?

Yeah, but, Syd, what the hell could be stranger than what you just read me?

Well, hold on to your prosthesis, son. So after the story comes out, I get a call from LaBauve. He asks me to meet him at a lawyer's office not far from the parish courthouse. He tells me to use a back entrance. Of course, given everything that's transpired, I don't think a thing of it.

When I walk in, Meely says Syd, I just wanted to tell you that I'm off the story.

Well, Junior, I was expecting anything but that.

LaBauve then tells me, look, don't worry. I've turned over all of my notes and sources to one of my colleagues who's real good. It's still a great story and I'm sure he'll do right by it.

I say Meely, are you serious? That was probably the best, most courageous piece of local reporting I've ever seen, even if it did favor my side. How can you step away?

Meely looks at me and says well, there's a little problem now.

I say what, surely the sheriff and that blowhard Lou Wicks haven't scared you off?

He says nah, no way. But I've become too close to the story.

I say what the hell does that mean?

He says it'll all soon become clear.

The next thing I know a door opens and a man in a suit walks up to me. He says sir, my name is Earl Dantin, the clerk for Judge Ashley Pettibone, judge emeritus for the 19th District Circuit Court of Catahoula Parish. This is a subpoena for you and your client Joseph Guidry to appear in Judge Pettibone's court tomorrow morning at a ten A.M. emergency hearing. If you don't produce Mr. Guidry, Mr. Shainburg, the judge has asked me to inform you that he will arrange lodgings for you in the parish jail. Furthermore, Judge Pettibone has ordered two state troopers to escort you during the rest of your stay in the parish. This is as much for the judge's interest in assuring your appearance as it is for your own well-being.

Well, Junior, I just looked at Meely and I realized I'd been set up. I was about to yell at him and call him unthinkable names when he stands and comes over to me and says sorry, Syd, but I didn't know what else to do. Ashley Pettibone might be the last truly honest judge in Catahoula Parish. Junior needs him, and, frankly, I need Junior to be there. That's all I can say for now. He then turned and walked out.

I hear Syd breathe deeply and I say Syd, what the hell?

Syd says well, Junior, this is indeed a strange kettle of fish. After LaBauve left, I went to see a local lawyer I'd met, to at least gain some intelligence regarding the judge in question. He told me Pettibone is totally aboveboard but, like our good friend Captain Mouton, something of a hard-ass. He said if you don't do as the judge has ordered, you *will* be in deep shit. So that's the deal, my friend. If I don't get you to court in the morning, I *am* going to be spending some leisure time in Go-Boy Geaux's jail.

I don't know what to say for a minute. The ole Cajuns have an expression for a mess like this—*un couillonage.*

I say Syd, unfortunately, I know Pettibone good and he knows me. He's the judge who handled my case long ago when I had that trouble wit' the LaBauves. True, he don't take shit from nobody. And he's prob'ly still got it in for me after all these years.

Well, Junior, we've got two choices. I can go to jail and you can hide out and get another lawyer and we'll see how this plays out. Or you can come to face the music—though I can't honestly fathom what the tune will be.

I ain't gotta think about this too long. Hell, wit'out Syd I'd be a gator chew toy by now.

I say Syd, I'm comin'. You just tell me how.

He says okay, son. Put Caro Marcelli on the phone for me. I think I can arrange proper transport.

26

They drive me down to Catahoula Parish in a station wagon this time—a Chevy Caprice, I think. One of them that has that fake wood paneling along the sides. It's Johnny, Nurse Maria, and three guys I ain't never seen before. One of them they call Roach is sittin' in the backseat next to me. Maria is on the other side. I gotta say Roach looks just like what they call him. He's got a pinched face and long nose and pimples like a teenager. Even though he's on the home team—I guess you could say he's my bodyguard—that guy gives me the *frissons* just lookin' at him. His eyes are cold and black as a wild mink's.

For the first time since I got shot and got my fingers took off, I realize I'm feelin' a bit better, though that ain't the same as feelin' good. I'm also fidgety as a mockin'bird on the nest wit' a possum scratchin' at the bottom of the tree. We drive along the river, passin' mansions like the one I stayed in, then tar-paper shacks with broke-down colored people sittin' on beat-up porches, then chemical plants belchin' stinky smoke into the air, then miles and miles of sugarcane fields. The sky's blue but thick wit' haze 'cause they're burnin' the cane for grindin'. Johnny's drivin' and gets off the river road and heads south down some lonesome two-lane highway snakin' through a cypress and willow swamp. There's nootras killed on the road about every hundred yards. I guess they got a million of them nootras in this particular swamp. They shore are stupid about cars.

I guess Johnny must know all the back roads around here— maybe that's part of a gangster's job. I got no clue where we are till we hit a T-junction and one sign says Ville Canard twenty-seven miles.

Soon enough, we're in the center of town and I see the court-house. Some people say it's perty wit' that court square and them ponds wit' them big orange fish in 'em and them big oaks that got planted long before the Civil War. But last time I was in the courthouse, the judge threw me in jail and took away my last good car. The time before that, the LaBauves and crusty-ass Judge Pettibone kicked my butt good. There ain't nuttin' particularly perty about the courthouse to me.

Johnny spies a parkin' spot and we pull into it and next I know I see Syd walkin' up to the car. What I see next don't make me happy—two big cops with them big cop hats, standin' in the shade of an oak, lookin' at us. Syd makes the car and says don't worry, Junior. They're my state troopers. He whispers you've got your bodyguards, I got mine.

I see Syd is smilin'. I'm glad one of us thinks there's somethin' funny goin' on here.

Syd looks over at Johnny and says thank you, Johnny. If you boys would get the wheelchair out of the back, we'll take Junior in through the back entrance.

I say to Syd, I can walk, really. I ain't feelin' all that bad. We'll just take it slow.

Syd says Junior, as your lawyer I'm advising you to take the chair. Given Judge Pettibone's reputation, it may afford us some small measure of sympathy.

I cain't argue wit' that.

Perty soon I'm in the chair and this is some parade I'm in. There's me, my Mafia podnahs, my cute nurse who's related to the Mafia, Syd, who's bein' paid by the Mafia, then them two big mounties protectin' us all. Mardi Gras ain't never been this strange.

They wheel me up a ramp and we go clackin' and cloppin' down the hall past a row of tall wooden doors that lead to the courtrooms. At the end of the hall, we come to a door that has a sign wit' Judge Pettibone's name on it in black wooden letters. Syd pushes the door open and Johnny and the boys wheel me down the middle aisle of the courtroom, wit' the nurse followin'. I look up ahead and see the place where the judge sits is empty. In the front row on the left, I spy Meely and a man I figger is his lawyer.

Johnny wheels me till I'm even wit' the right front row. Syd says stay in the chair, Junior, unless the judge asks you to do otherwise. I nod.

Syd and Johnny and the boys take a seat on the front bench. Nurse Maria stands behind me. She puts a hand on my shoulder. I kinda like that.

I look over at Meely and nod and he nods back and smiles. I don't know what I feel like but I know I don't feel like smilin' yet.

We sit there in fidgety quiet for a while when a door busts open and a man wit' a crewcut and a black suit walks in quick and says real loud, all rise for Judge Ashley Pettibone. The 19th District Circuit Court is now in session. Next, the judge walks in through the same door and walks up two steps to his seat.

He looks perty much the same to me, even though it was a coon's age since I seen him. He's still got that bald head and that red flush in his face. His hair, what's left of it, is grayer than I remember. He looks over the nose of his glasses out at the courtroom. He says Mr. Shainburg, if you're here, please introduce yourself to the court.

Syd rises, buttonin' his suit jacket, and walks toward a low wooden rail between us and the judge and says Your Honor, as the court has, uh, requested, I'm here with my client, Joseph Guidry. Mr. Guidry, the court is probably aware, was severely injured in the events that this court is also undoubtedly aware of, thus the need for the wheelchair today. And Your Honor, we acknowledge that Mr. Guidry is technically a fugitive from the law. However, we would like to have a chance to explain that disappearance, the need for it, and many other matters surrounding the criminal case against him. Mr. Guidry, in this case, is a man wrongly accused and—

The judge raises his right hand and says Mr. Shainburg, just hold on—save all the speeches until I'm ready for them. I appreciate you being here and getting your client here under these very peculiar circumstances. Even I am aware that our gathering here today is unorthodox, and, frankly, I'm not sure where to begin.

Then the judge peers around and says ah, I see young LaBauve is in court. All right, first things first. I want everyone except Mr. Shainburg, Mr. Guidry, and our friends in the State Police out of the courtroom. Mr. Guidry's nurse may stay if you think that's necessary, Mr. Shainburg.

Maria looks at Syd and Syd looks at the judge and says actually, Your Honor, I think we can excuse her for now. If Mr. Guidry begins to experience any difficulty, we can summon her.

I look at Maria and the poor girl looks relieved. Johnny and the boys look at Syd like they would be happy to argue wit' the judge if Syd wanted 'em to, but Syd walks over and says in a low voice to Johnny, you boys can go get some coffee. Just don't go too far. And if you see anybody with Catahoula Parish badges on their chests heading our way, you might want to tell the county mounties there. He points back to the state troopers.

Johnny nods, then everybody marches out. The courtroom doors swing open and I hear voices in the hall and then they swing slow and shut again and the voices fade away.

Then the judge looks out at Meely again and then at Syd and says okay, Mr. Shainburg, let me fill you in on why we're here. Our Mr. LaBauve here was a party to a case many years ago involving your client, Mr. Guidry, and his uncle. Young Mr. LaBauve had been charged with very serious crimes based upon what turned out to be fabrications told by your client and his aforementioned uncle. I presided over that case and justice was done only because a witness came forward at the last hour to corroborate LaBauve's contention that in fact Mr. Guidry and his uncle had been seeking revenge, not justice, against young LaBauve and his father, Logan LaBauve. By the time this reached my court, the senior LaBauve had fled the law and subsequently drowned. Of course, I've casually followed the career, if you can call it that, of Mr. Guidry, and it seemed evident to me that he was a man little changed, with no regard for decency or the law. However, I have read with some alarm the account penned by Mr. LaBauve here regarding the alleged robbery-murder of Raymond Marchante. His story has raised very startling and troubling issues for our community. Yesterday Mr. LaBauve came to see me with even more startling news. He told me that an eyewitness to the alleged robbery-murder of Mr. Marchante had materialized and that said witness indeed corroborated a great deal of what Mr. Guidry and his woman friend—what's her name, Earl?

The judge looks at the clerk and Earl says Parfait, Your Honor. Iris Mary Parfait.

Yes, right, Iris Mary Parfait. At any rate, according to Mr. LaBauve, the witness had seen and overheard things that made it clear to him that Miss Parfait was in fact a kidnap victim and that the alleged victims of this crime intended her grave bodily harm. Moreover, the witness could also in part corroborate Mr. Guidry's assertion that he had come to rescue Miss Parfait, not to rob Mr. Marchante. I said to young LaBauve, you are in the wrong place. Please go, and go quickly, with your witness to the sheriff or to the district attorney. But Mr. LaBauve said he came to me because the material witness was, in a way, a party to his old case involving Mr. Guidry and that he himself—the witness—had unresolved issues with the law here that might only properly be adjudicated in my courtroom. Normally I would not insert myself into these matters, but as the events of recent days seem to show, these are not normal times. So I heard young LaBauve out and now, more than I did before, I appreciate the sincerity of his intentions. Mr. LaBauve, is your witness now ready to come before this court?

I see Meely stand up and say yes, he is, Judge Pettibone. He is a man who, because of a history I hope you'll understand, is a bit wary of the courts and the police. He's asked to wait in the jury room until he's needed, so I'll get him now.

Meely stands and walks to a nearby door and opens it and motions to someone. A man, tall, dark, gray-haired, wearing a gray suit, steps out and walks wit' Meely toward the judge.

Meely says Your Honor, this is my father, Logan LaBauve.

27

I find myself suddenly tossed back in that field out on Cata-houla Bayou, my life drippin' away, and the man wit' the cap pulled down over his face standin' over me. *Of course* it was him!

But this cain't be Logan LaBauve, 'cause Logan LaBauve got drowned and ate by gators and is dead and buried in the church cemetery not too far from Momma's grave.

I gotta look up one more time to make shore it's all real. But I know it's real when he turns and walks slow toward me and bends down and says well, I'm glad to see you made it this far, Junior. You're one lucky dog.

He then turns and walks back toward the bench and is sworn in.

The judge looks at him and says Mr. LaBauve, are you here of your own free will?

Yes, Your Honor, I am.

And you are aware that being here could put you in some jeopardy regarding unresolved issues in your own case all those years ago?

Yes, sir. I'm not a man who knows a lot about the law, though I've run up against it a bit. But I've come back to get things straight, or as straight as they can be made. As you can see, I'm not gettin' any younger and I'd like to spend what years are left near my son.

The judge nods at this. He says well, I did pull the file on the case and it raises all kinds of perplexing issues, including who the poor man is that's buried in your grave, and the agony that perhaps his family has gone through not knowing where he is. But this is something we can talk about later. Now, your son is part of what some could interpret as a conspiracy to hide you from the law. But I've questioned Meely about this and have concluded that, technically, there was no perjury involved, at least in my courtroom. Basically, your son's emotional reaction to the fact that it *wasn't* you lying in that morgue was misinterpreted by certain people to mean that it *was* you, and your son was content to let that misinterpretation go unchallenged. Given the circumstances, I can at least understand his motives. That said, this court still maintains that justice will out, and that the proper way to have handled this would have been for Meely to have told the absolute truth and for you, Mr. LaBauve, to have surrendered yourself to the law and let justice take its course. Do I make myself clear?

I see the LaBauves noddin'. Then I see the judge look up and look over at me. He says Mr. Shainburg, could you wheel Mr. Guidry forward, please?

I get this lump in my throat. Oh, lawd.

Syd says yes, Your Honor, of course.

Syd pushes me forward and the judge stares down at me and says Mr. Guidry, for clarity's sake, I'd like to have you personally refresh my memory of those events all those years ago. Basically, as I recall, you involved your uncle, who was at the time a policeman for the old Ville Canard Police Department, in an effort to settle a score against young LaBauve here. Then you lied through your teeth to make it seem like you and your uncle were the victims of a crime, is that right?

I nod.

He says speak up, Mr. Guidry.

I say yes sir, that about covers it.

Okay, that's good to know. Now, there are a couple of unresolved issues that I must take seriously. One is the theft of a police shotgun. The other is the destruction of public property, notably a police car driven by your uncle and badly damaged by Logan LaBauve with his own gun that day. I believe, by the way, that your uncle has since passed away, is that right?

Yes sir, that's right.

Mr. Guidry, taking a not-too-liberal interpretation of those events, some people might argue that you, not Mr. LaBauve here, should pay for both the missing gun and that damage. And I *am* of the opinion that, whether we decide there is criminal liability here for Mr. LaBauve for fleeing, it's a debt to the parish that ought to be paid. What do you say to that?

I look at Syd and Syd says go on, you can answer.

Well, Your Honor, honestly I couldn't argue against it. But if you wanna know the truth, I'm busted. I got a nice chunk of money for my leg a few years ago but it's gone.

Gone? As I recall it was quite a wad of money, Mr. Guidry. Where on earth has it gone?

I blew it, Judge.

Blew it?

Yes sir. I drank and gambled a lot of it away and bought fancy cars and wrecked 'em. I, uh, chased women. I bought a lot of beer for people, a lot for people I didn't even know. Anyway, it's gone. Every nickel of it. I had me a trailer I coulda sold and give you the money. It wadn't worth much and I doubt it woulda covered a whole police car. But no matter, that got burnt down, as you might've heard. Some say I did it but I didn't. I had an ole truck, too, but, well, like you know, I wrecked that.

How do you pay your lawyer, Mr. Guidry?

I look back at Syd, who ain't got no expression on his face at all. I say I don't, sir. He's taken me on for free, I guess.

Mr. Shainburg, is that correct?

Syd looks at me and then looks at the judge. He says Your Honor, I acknowledge that Mr. Guidry is an indigent who can't afford my normal fees. But as you might know, Junior and I go back a long way, all the way to his civil suit.

The judge looks curious at Syd, like he knows more than he's lettin' on. Then he looks back at me.

How do you explain this behavior, Mr. Guidry? The court is interested in knowing.

You mean why I done all those stupid things and wasted all my money?

Yes, that's right.

I gotta think about this for a minute. Man, oh man, what kind of question is that?

I shrug my shoulders and say shuh, I wish I knew, Judge. Maybe I lost my mind along the way. I am, or was, a drunk—and I guess a mean drunk, just like my daddy is. I had a lot of chances and, one after another, I wasted 'em. Iris Mary would tell you that I wadn't good to myself so I couldn't be good to nobody else. She would say I've gone through life wit' my temper, not my head. She would say I always ran away from the messes I made stedda stayin' like a man and tryin' to clean 'em up. Maybe she's right, or maybe I'm just a bad seed, Your Honor. All of them things might be true.

The judge leans back and puts his hands behind his head. He closes his eyes for a minute, then looks over at me again. He says hhm, well, I at least appreciate your attempt at candor. Apparently, in your favor, Mr. Guidry, Miss Parfait has some kind things to say about you. She thinks you might not be the backsliding reprobate you have been painted to be. She apparently credits you with saving her life.

Yes sir.

Well, this is why we're here today, to sort out this mess. Okay, Mr. Guidry, the court considers it plausible that you are broke, and as you probably know, we don't have debtors' prison in America. The point for me was to make sure you acknowledged your potential liability. You or Logan LaBauve, or maybe both of you, will likely have to pay for this in some way. I haven't decided yet.

Yes sir.

I see Logan LaBauve raise his hand. He says Judge, excuse me. I'm not shore how these things are done but I can at least account for that gun. I put it away for safekeepin' in the event I ever got back this way. I'd be happy to give it back to the police.

The judge nods and says that's good to know and we can deal with that later. Now, I'd like Mr. LaBauve to tell us his story of that day out on Catahoula Bayou and how he came to be there. As a judge, I've witnessed many examples of irony but perhaps none more ironical than this. Would you please, Mr. LaBauve, tell us what you saw?

Logan LaBauve looks up at the judge and then glances over at me. He says yes sir, I'll tell you, but my son says there's one thing I should say before I begin.

What's that, Mr. LaBauve?

LaBauve turns to stare at me this time. Havin' seen a ghost already today, I figger he cain't say nuttin' that would surprise me more than that. But this just goes to show you what I know.

He looks back at the judge and says well, I axed Meely, after I read his story and I told him mine, to do some checking on Iris Mary Parfait. Now, Your Honor, I don't know Iris Mary, who's a few years younger than my boy, but as you may or may not know I originally come from the same neck of the woods that she comes from. My great-granddaddy was a full-blooded Humas Injun who lived in the Bayou Go-to-Hell salt marsh way back when this was French country. Anyway, me and Meely have dug around and figgered out that Iris Mary is our relation. Her grandmother was a LaBauve and my second or third cousin and—

I see Meely stand up and say Judge Pettibone, what my father is getting at is that he's here because he saw what he saw and came to me with his story because, even before he knew Iris Mary Parfait's name, he knew people would be in jeopardy if he didn't come forward. But when he found out her name and where she was from, he began to put things together. We just thought this is something the court shouldn't find out later.

The judge takes off his glasses and wipes them wit' his thumb, usin' the sleeve of his robe. He puts them back on and looks down and nods and finally says Mr. LaBauve, I appreciate you telling me this. It was absolutely the right thing to do. I just have to ask you, Logan, to make sure in your own mind that this won't influence what you tell me here today. Are you sure what you're about to say is the truth and only the truth?

Logan LaBauve looks up at the judge and says Your Honor, except for the day of that ruckus, I've never really laid eyes on Iris Mary Parfait, though if this mess all gets straightened out, I shore would like to meet her for real. Now, the truth is, I'm a man who's told a fib or two in his day, but I like to think I'm done with fibbin'. I'm gettin' too doggone old to lie about anything and I'd like to believe I'd tell what I saw, even if it went against Iris Mary. But there's one thing I can tell you for shore.

What's that, Mr. LaBauve?

Logan LaBauve turns and points his long finger at me. He says I'd never lic for the likes of Junior Guidry.

28

I've been thinkin' about that for months now, what Logan LaBauve said that day—that he would never lie for the likes of Junior Guidry. Even back then I awmost said hey, podnah, I wouldn't want you to lie for me. But I held my tongue, which was the right thing to do. I'm a lot better at doin' that these days.

Anyway, I wadn't plannin' to say it bad. The point is, I *didn't* want him to lie for me. I've kept thinkin' about what he said— that he was gettin' too ole to lie. Maybe it's possible that a man one day—even the likes of Junior Guidry—gets tired of lyin'. To everybody else, and 'specially to himself.

I gotta hand it to the ole man—he saved my butt. Turns out he'd been livin' down in Florda all these years and just wanted to come home for good. He'd had a perty adventurous life down there. Been in a bad-ass hurricane and all kinds of stuff. He'd snuck back several times to see his boy, and turns out Meely had gone down to Florda lots of times to see him.

So he'd come home, awright. He tole the judge he'd walked clear from Florda and it took him two whole months to do it.

He was walkin' through that finger of swamp on the way to see the ole LaBauve house, which has long ago fallen down, when he came upon Iris Mary and the bad guys. He said he was way across the slough, out of sight, wit'out a gun and no way to get across to help wit'out swimmin' over there, which woulda prob'ly got him killed, either by them outlaws or snakes or gators. He said he was about to yell out, not that it would have done any good, when I drove up. He tole the judge how Roddy and Smurl got the drop on me, how later I rammed Rocko's car wit' my truck, how me and Roddy traded shots, how Iris Mary put a whuppin' on the back of Smurl's noggin about the time he was gonna blow me away. He said after he saw Iris Mary bandage me up and run off for help, he realized the only way over that slough was across a footbridge a mile back up the swamp. So he practically run all the way there and all the way back. That's when he come and fixed my bandage and give me that water. He said he done it even though he knew, when he saw me close up, it was me he was helpin' and he was still sore about that business long ago 'cause it had kept him away from his boy. He tole the judge he wonders if he coulda done more but that he was still fearful of the law and hadn't decided to give himself up yet.

After he said all that, the judge tole them state troopers that he was puttin' me under their protection and that they needed to find me some comfortable place outside of Catahoula Parish. He got Earl to get Sheriff Landrieu on the phone and they made some kinda deal to get Iris Mary sprung so the troopers could guard her, too. We both ended up in a fancy hospital surrounded by pine trees way up someplace over by Shreveport. Turned out it was basically a crazy house for rich people. One ole boy come up to me one day and swore he'd caught a bass some time ago and put it in a tank and it had turned into the face of Jesus and had swum up his nose and now was in his head and he saw everything Jesus ever saw. Otherwise he seemed like a perty good ole boy, 'cept, bein' from North Loosiana, he didn't know how to play *bourre*. Too bad.

Iris Mary and me were in rooms side by side. We were only there for ten days when we got sprung for good. Turns out that the podnah that Meely turned his story over to wrote another big damn piece in the paper and quicker than a bass takes a shiner the feds got involved and they come down and carried Go-Boy Geaux off in handcuffs. They said that sumbitch was bellowin' like a bull bein' dragged to the packin' company and threatenin' to kill Judge Pettibone, me, Meely, and about half the people in town. Next anybody knew, he tried to hang himself in the fed jailhouse up in New Awlins. Syd says when they raided Rocko's house, they didn't find any Polaroids of Rocko. But they did find some of the sheriff.

And one of those girls was a boy.

Syd says nobody's goin' to jail in this case 'cause ain't one of 'em fit to stand trial. It turns out that they shore in the hell did forge that statement from Wiley. Not only is that sumbitch not got a tongue but he's got the palsy so bad that he shimmies like *flottant* under a marsh buggy.

When Iris Mary and me got put in the hospital together, she come runnin' in to see me and she kissed me like she meant it. And I kissed her back the same way 'cause I doggone did mean it. And I didn't waste no time. About the second day, I axed Iris Mary to marry me.

See, I thought I'd thought about everything, and I thought the likes of Junior Guidry was done wit' bein' stupid. But what's the first thing Iris Mary axes me?

She says Joseph, there is something I desperately need to know. You know about my relatives. I remember when we first met you called me lily white. Well, you know, I am far from that. The LaBauves are my nearest kin now. They are what you used to call *sabine*—a term they despise and I despise. But Joseph, think about it. If we have children, so many things are possible. They could look like you or they could be like me—albino. And what if they took after my grandfather? Could you handle that?

And you know what I did?

I looked down for just a second.

Well, it wadn't just a second.

I looked down and shuffled my feet instead of lookin' at Iris Mary. And she tousled my head and said thanks for being honest, and walked away. And I yelled after her, no, Iris Mary, no, don't go, please! It wadn't that! It wadn't—

But she was gone and she wouldn't see me, even though we had a week more in the hospital.

I went to live wit' my sister Irene and Iris Mary went back to her li'l apartment at the convent down Bayou Go-to-Hell.

And I went to bed for two weeks and could hardly get up and Irene kept sayin' what's wrong, Junior, I know it's not your fingers. And so I tole her the story, every bit of it, and she said what, you're givin' up so easy? Go talk to the girl, but first figger out what you gonna say to her.

What could I say to her that would make a difference, Irene?

Well, it depends, Junior. She axed you a good question. Maybe

you now have a good answer. I mean, *does* it matter to you?
Does it?

I said no, it don't. And the one other thing I know is that
wit'out Iris Mary, nuttin' matters to me. Nuttin' could be worse
than losin' her.

Irene said well, as a girl, I have to say that's a pretty good answer. I wish I knew a man who would come and say that to me.
Go see her, Junior.

What if she won't see me?

Junior Guidry! Go find your woman. What you got to lose?

I said everything.

She said go find your woman, Junior. Now! If you lay around
here and mope much longer you *will* lose everything.

I got up off my ass and cleaned myself up and got me a ride to
that convent on the bus that runs down there once a week from
the courthouse square. I found Iris Mary outside on a bench and
she didn't see me comin' up, which is prob'ly best. I had brought
some straw flowers from the Bargain Store in town 'cause I didn't
have money for real roses. She looked up and saw me comin' and
smiled and the next thing I know I was down on my good knee
wit' my head in her lap, cryin' like a baby.

I couldn't figger out that deal at all. I didn't even cry at
Momma's funeral. Then I stopped myself from cryin' and I said
look, I come from nuttin' and if I lose you, I go back to nuttin'.
Oh, I'm not gonna fall back into the bottle—I'm done wit' that.
But I know I will never be happy wit'out you, Iris Mary. You're my
chance. You talk about redemption. Well, here I am. I wanna save
myself but I cain't do it alone. You can help save me. You can help
save me from myself. You tole me not to run from my feelin's. You

tole me not to run away from the people I love or the people who love me. So here I am.

This time I see it's Iris Mary who's cryin'.

I say one other thing. I don't care what kinda kids we have as long as they healthy. Honest, I think it would be best if they looked like you and had your sweet disposition and your good sense. But they'll be what they'll be, and, no matter what, I got plans to be a real daddy for a change.

And Iris Mary looked down at me and said you mean all that, Joseph?

And I said I mean all that and more.

And you know what's the best thing about that?

I did mean it. I meant all that and more.

29

Iris Mary and me got married on the fourteenth of June. She found an Episcopal preacher in Ville Canard who was friends wit' some of the nuns down her bayou to marry us since we couldn't get married in the Cat'lic Church 'cause of my divorces. She said if any two people needed the good luck to be married under God, it was us.

I myself thought a justice of the peace woulda been okay but I wadn't gonna argue wit' Iris Mary about that one. In fack, ole Junior here ain't plannin' to argue wit' Iris Mary about much.

Though I knew it pro'bly wouldn't do no good, I did ax Father Giroir on Catahoula Bayou if he would perform the ceremony 'cause I knew it woulda pleased Momma if we got married in the bayou church. He said he was sorry but he couldn't do it. I didn't say nuttin' then, but I got mad about it later and was gonna go back and give him a piece of my mind but Iris Mary said Joseph, he's only following the rules. She said life's too short to worry

about such things. She said last time I checked, the Episco-
palians and the Catholics have the same God.

The ceremony was short and sweet. Logan LaBauve give her
away. She had to put the ring on my right ring finger, since I don't
have a left one.

Irene clapped her hands and said Junior, the third time's the
charm!

We had a small reception at Elmore's. Some of them nuns
come. Iris Mary even invited Father Giroir and doggone if he
didn't show up.

Typical Iris Mary. She wants everybody to get along and be
part of everything.

Meely come, too, and he give us a gumbo pot for a present.
The ole man brought me a cowboy hat made out of gator skin
which he said he made himself down in Florda. And doggone if it
didn't fit just right and look sharp.

Iris Mary made me keep it on my head the whole time even
though it was hot as hell. She said it would be what she called a
good gesture. I'd never heard that word before but I got what she
meant.

Daddy come wit' Irene. I wadn't gonna invite him but Iris
Mary suggested it would be the right thing to do. And I guess,
thinkin' about it, it was.

We didn't have liquor, though we bought beer—Pearl and
Dixie—for people who wanted it. I drank *pop rouge* myself. Iris
Mary drank root beer. But Daddy musta brought his own whiskey,
though he wadn't drunk at the end—least not fallin'-down drunk
like usual. He was lit up but otherwise okay.

Even Daddy seems to like Iris Mary. And Daddy, him, he don't
like nobody.

We invited my brothers and Lolly-Lee. Everybody's scattered all over creation and none of 'em could come, though my brother Paul, the college man, called to congratulate me. Iris Mary said well, Joseph, that's *something*. Sometimes with a family that's had a hard time of it, you've got to be patient.

We had a fiddle player. Wadn't the same as havin' a whole zydeco band but he played and sung "Jolie Blonde." Me and Iris Mary danced okay, though you might be surprised how havin' all your fingers to hold on helps when you're dancin', especially when you missin' a leg. Iris Mary nuzzled my cheek and said cher, you dance so smooth I believe a mule could follow you.

I knew that wadn't true but I didn't mind that she said it.

Sometime toward the end of the reception, a well-dressed man come up and tapped Iris Mary on the back when she was talkin' to Daddy. Next I know I hear her say oh, you shouldn't have, and the man sayin' oh, no, I insist.

I go over there to see and doggone if it ain't Caro Marcelli. He'd pinned five one-hundred-dollar bills to Iris Mary's dress. He said it's an Italian tradition, Miss Parfait, and then introduced himself as a good friend of Syd. He winked at me.

Syd come, too, and brought his wife and kids. Good-lookin', every one of them. He taught me a nice Jew word, *mazel-tov*, which I think means good luck. I've since said it a few times to other people and I don't care that they look at me funny. I like it.

Iris Mary and me decided we didn't have no honeymoon money. We decided the five hundred dollars Caro Marcelli pinned to her dress should be put aside. But Irene moved out of her house for the night and put clean sheets on her featherbed and filled up her bedroom wit' flowers and left some shrimp and *an-*

douille gumbo on the stove and a note on the kitchen table sayin',
You lovebirds have fun!

We ate our supper and then Iris Mary said you've got to take
your wife to bed properly, Joseph.

I said what you mean?

I want to be carried over the threshold.

You mean you want me to pick you up and carry you to bed?

That's right.

I said well, that might be a problem, seein' as I got only one
good hand and one good leg.

She said well, like you keep telling me, I don't make a sack of
oysters. And you're not weak, cher. You just have some parts missing.

I said what if I drop you?

You won't.

Iris Mary got up from the table and come sat in my lap. She
tousled my hair and kissed me on the cheek and then we had a
real kiss, our first real one, if you know what I mean. She whispered in my ear, oh, Joseph. Oh, cher.

She kissed like a schoolgirl, which I guess I didn't mind.

I could tell right away there was one thing about ole Joseph
that wadn't missin'. I said let's go to bed, girl.

She said aren't you glad we waited?

I said no, not really. I've wanted you bad for quite a while now.
But I'm glad tonight's the night, 'cause if we'da waited much
longer I might have exploded. Then you'd be sorry, wouldn't you?

Iris Mary giggled and kissed me. She said I'd be the sorriest
woman in all the world.

Iris Mary stood up and then I did and then I cradled her back
and got my wooden one under her legs and picked her up. She

grabbed me around the neck and off we went. She giggled. I was so afraid I'd fall or drop her that I couldn't see nuttin' funny about.

I walked liked Frankenstein but I didn't fall on my ass.

I put Iris Mary down on the bed gentle. She pulled me down on top of her and kissed me again and then said I'll be right back. She got up and went into Irene's bathroom and come out wearin' somethin' like you'd see them girls wearin' in *Playboy* magazine. I realized right then and there how me bein' drunk when I first met Iris Mary musta messed up my eyes.

That girl was hot!

She said Joseph, may I help you out of your clothes?

I couldn't even say nuttin' 'cept do I leave my leg on or off?

She said I'm going to let you keep your appliances but nothing else. I want you naked as an oyster at low tide.

I said this all might take some doin' 'cause I cain't move like I used to.

Iris Mary bent down and kissed me and said hush, cher. You don't have to do anything for a while.

Low tide come quick. I was a happy oyster. Iris Mary got naked herself and then straddled me.

She said do you know what Irene told me about men?

I looked at Iris Mary. I couldn't imagine what was comin' next.

She said Irene says a man wants his wife to be an angel in the parlor and a slut in the bedroom.

Irene tole you that?

She did. So I want to try a little something, cher. Something that I believe you said should involve two hands. If you don't mind.

I couldn't say nuttin' to that.

Iris Mary said I've bought some oil. Edible oil.

She unstraddled me and scooched over to Irene's night table and come out with a green tube.

She wriggled back over and straddled me again and put some of that oil in her hands and then started rubbin' me up and down. Then she leaned forward and held her right hand up to me.

She said smell. It's cantaloupe.

I smelled and it shore was.

She said I *love* cantaloupe.

Then she bent forward again and whispered in my ear, you know, even though Father Giroir wouldn't marry us, I did go talk to him about our wedding night. I still consider myself a good Catholic. And Father said people married under God are allowed to please each other in many, many ways so long as, when the moment of bliss comes, a man satisfies himself inside his wife.

Iris Mary said—no kiddin'—so I'm going to do that thing with two hands, Joseph, and then I want you to satisfy yourself inside me. Okay?

What could I say to that?

Shuh, if I coulda figgered out how to send the Pope some flowers, I woulda sent him ten dozen roses!

We didn't sleep that night, hardly a bit. We fell asleep when Irene's ole rooster crowed in the dawn. Before I went to sleep, I said I love you, Iris Mary. I said thank God I found you.

And you know what Iris Mary told me? She said maybe God sent *you* to me, Joseph.

Iris Mary says the strangest things sometime.

We'd been stayin' temporarily wit' Irene but we moved into a li'l shotgun rent house in a part of Ville Canard called Shady Park. It ain't much of a house, size-wise, but it's a quiet neighborhood wit' oak trees linin' the streets. The first thing Iris Mary did was to put that statue in the yard and the first thing I said is cher, you want me to repaint the ole girl? She's lookin' a bit rugged.

Iris Mary said that would be nice, Joseph.

I'm a perty good painter and I shined her up good—blue and white like she was before. I figgered wit' that bad girl in the yard, we didn't need no watchdog. Word had got out about the statue and all them li'l ole ladies in the neighborhood come by, clackin' their rosaries and leavin' flowers. So many of them ladies have rubbed her on her noggin' that the paint's already wore off.

Though Iris Mary and me are country folk, we moved to town 'cause she has bad memories of Bayou Go-to-Hell and I couldn't live down Catahoula Bayou no more. Roddy's family was all busted up about the shootin' and I was afraid I'd keep runnin' into them and it would be bad for all of us.

We was podnahs long ago, me and Roddy. I don't know where he went wrong. Or maybe I do. Maybe he was like me—always a bit wrong or always goin' off in the wrong direction. Maybe he was just unlucky. Maybe he never met a ghost or angel to save his sorry ass.

Still, I know it's a shame. I liked Roddy's daddy and momma. Long time ago, I knew 'em well. Momma and Roddy's momma were friends.

I had no idea how we was s'posed to make the rent on our house but Iris Mary said I have some money that will last us for a while. Till you get on your feet.

I laughed at that. I said you mean till I get on my foot.

She said don't you go feeling sorry for yourself. You're alive, which is lucky, and we've got each other, which is lucky, too.

I couldn't argue wit' neither of them things.

After a while, Iris Mary made me write a letter to Berta and Lolly-Lee. Actually, she tole me what to say, but I wrote it in my own hand. It said I was sorry for the things I done and sorry for not bein' much of a daddy or husband. It said I would like to try to do better in the daddy department.

We got back a letter from Berta sayin' it's a little late, Junior. Why should I show this letter to my daughter?

This pissed me off real good. I said to hell wit' her, what's a man gotta do?

Iris Mary said write another letter, Joseph. And another one after that if you have to. The fact that she answered at all is a good sign.

Iris Mary don't cut me much slack.

I wrote back and said okay, all them things are true. You got me there. I'm remarried and have got sober and I want to do right even though I know everything cain't be put right. Actually, Iris Mary perty much wrote that one, too. But I'da never sent it unless I thought it was okay.

We ain't heard nuttin' back yet.

Iris Mary says patience is a virtue, Joseph.

By this time, I'd figgered out what that meant.

She makes me go see Daddy. She makes me call Irene. She and Irene have become good friends. They talk that woman talk. I don't wanna be anywhere near 'em when they talk that stuff 'cause they laugh and giggle and about half the time I think it might be about me. In fack, I'm shore it *is* about me. I don't know whether to be pissed off or *honte*.

Irene comes to see me and every time she comes she says well, Joseph, look at you, ain't you somethin'?

I say what does that mean?

She pinches my cheek and says you got color in your face. You look happy! Happy!

I say since when you call me Joseph?

She says I'm like Iris Mary. I never liked Junior.

Daddy ain't really changed. He prob'ly won't. Most times when I go see him, he's too drunk to talk or he wants to argue. I don't argue wit' Daddy no more. We brought him over one time for supper 'cause Iris Mary said Joseph, he's the only daddy you've got. He come in and was okay at first. He talked to Iris Mary, though he didn't have much to say to me. He never does. But he'd brought some bottle wit' him that he'd hid and he kept slippin' outside and was facedown in the gumbo before seven o'clock. Iris Mary took the gumbo away and went and got a blanket and put it over him right there at the table. We finished our supper. He slept there all night, snorin' away.

I woulda pitched the sumbitch out in the yard myself. But I didn't say nuttin'. Sometimes I think Iris Mary is too soft.

Sometimes I think I'm gettin' that way myself.

She says your daddy is sick, not mean.

I'm not so shore about the last part.

Once day Iris Mary said do you still dream of Armentau?

I said not much.

She said do you know where he is?

I said I have no idea. Last I heard he was livin' in that flop-house where I lived for a bit.

She said we should go try to find him.

What the hell for?

You should talk to him, Joseph.

About what?

About the accident. You should find out what he really thinks. What he remembers.

I 'bout lost it that time. I said Iris Mary, Armentau's a shithead, like I tole you. The farther I stay from him the better. You can ax me to do anything but don't ax me to go see Armentau.

She looked at me and said okay, there's no reason to be crude, and I know it's upsetting so I won't ask you again. But I want you to think about it.

Once again, I'm thinkin' about it even though I don't want to. What the hell would I say to Armentau, anyway?

One day Iris Mary come in and said I went to see Mr. Deshotel today.

You mean Nonc Deshotel?

That's right.

About what?

About what happened with Miss Annadelle that day.

I said Iris Mary, I appreciate what you're tryin' to do, but it'll never get made right with Nonc. He hates my guts.

She said don't be so sure. Here's something you ought to know. Mr. Deshotel and I had a long talk and his aunt happened to be there. Oh, he's still really mad at you, but I can tell you one thing I know for sure—he misses your work.

He tole you that?

No, but Miss Annadelle did. She said he's been through about six dispatchers since he lost you. She said not one of them has come close to being as good as you were.

So?

So she said she'd try to have another word with her nephew.

Of course, you'd have to go and apologize. And they might not pay you what you used to make.

I said you shouldn't have done any of this wit'out tellin' me, Iris Mary. It ain't your fight.

She said there is no *fight,* Joseph. What happened was an unfortunate accident, even Mr. Deshotel knows that now. He reads the papers. He knows all about Wiley Smurl. And I know you miss your job. I know it was something you were good at. We all need something like that in our lives.

I said well, it would be nice if we could make the rent, too, and I could help support my beautiful wife.

She said anyway, if it was a fight, I'd take your side. People who love each other look after each other.

You mean cover each other's asses?

She smiled and said yes, that's one way of putting it.

A few days later, Nonc called and said goddam it, Junior, against my better judgment I've listened to my aunt. I understand you might have somethin' you wanna say to me.

I said I do. I started to say I was sorry but Nonc interrupted me. He said no, not over the phone. You get your sorry ass over here tomorrow mornin' and we can talk. I ain't makin' no promises about nuttin'. I wanna see the man your wife was talkin' about. I'm not sure I believe he actually exists.

I said okay.

He said okay?

I said yes sir, Mr. Deshotel, I'll come by.

He said that's better, Junior, or Joseph, or whatever the hell your name is these days. Ten o'clock and don't be late.

I said yes sir.

He said you bring your wife, too. My aunt would like to talk to her about a business proposition of her own. She's not as spry as she used to be and she lives in a big house alone and is thinkin' she needs some help a few days a week. I understand Iris Mary used to look after people.

Yes sir, she did.

Okay. I'll see you both tomorrow.

30

I've gone back to work for Nonc Deshotel at Gros Bec Drilling.
I make eight dollars an hour, half of what I used to make. But I
didn't lose a step when it come to dispatchin'. I can still talk that
Awl Patch b.s. wit' the best of them. Nonc don't talk to me much
'cause Nonc's a man who's decided he's gonna forgive me nice
and slow. But Miz Annadelle says he's happy as gumbo wit' my
work.

One Saturday mornin' when Iris Mary was away at Miz Annadelle's, I heard a knock on the door. I got up from the kitchen
table, where I was havin' my coffee, and opened the door. It was
Logan LaBauve. He was carryin' a big paper bag.

He said hello, Junior, do you mind if I come in for a minute?
I've got somethin' I need to talk about.

I hadn't seen the ole man since the weddin', though he'd come
to see Iris Mary a few times while I was at work. But I guess I was
gettin' used to surprises in my life.

I said shore, come on in.

He come into the kitchen and I said can I pour you a cup of coffee?

He said that would be nice. I turned my back to get his coffee and when I turned around he had dumped a pile of paper on the table.

I noticed perty quick it was money.

He said that's a hunderd thousand dollars there in piles of hunderd-dollar bills. I took it out that fella Rocko's car the day of the shootout. You'd sprung his trunk open when you rammed his car and it was in there. I guess I've heard since that it was his bounty for Iris Mary.

I didn't know what to say to that.

He said that's more money than I've ever seen, for shore. That's a heck of a lot of money.

I found my voice and I said it shore is.

He said well, at first I thought about turnin' the money in to my boy. But I didn't wanna do nuttin' too sudden. I love my boy but he's a bit of a straight arrow, if you know what I mean.

I nodded at that.

He'da wanted me to turn it over to the law. But you know what would happen then, Junior. It would get stole.

I nodded at that, too.

He said anyway, it's a hell of a lotta money. So I decided I might keep some of it but I thought I should share it with my relations.

You mean Meely?

Oh, I'll find a way to get some to Meely. But I want to give some of it to Iris Mary.

You do? Well, you should give it to her, then.

He said Junior, what I know of Iris Mary, I think she's a lot like my boy. If I come to give it to her, she'd wanna call the law to see about it.

I said that's true. I know Iris Mary well enough to know that's prob'ly what she would do.

He said so I thought I'd come and give it to you to hold for her. Not all of it. I'm gonna keep half. I got my eye on some property down Catahoula Bayou. Our ole farm is for sale and about twenty acres around it. Now that the judge has dropped them charges against me, I thought I'd become a gentleman farmer. Maybe grow me some cane and raise some gators in a pond in the back. I've even got me a lady friend over on the west side of the swamp. I might start dancin' again, and what I remember of it, dancin' takes a bit of money.

I said if the truth be told, you prob'ly could keep all of it and who would say you didn't deserve it?

He said well, like I said, it's a lot of money—a lot more than I need. And, like I also said, Iris Mary is family. Plus, I heard that that ole boy cheated you perty bad.

I said that he did.

He said I know the judge made you pay for that police car I shot up.

I said he did. We givin' twenty dollars a month. At least he let me pay what it cost back then, not what it would cost now. I owe about four grand.

He said then this should help you out. If I were you I wouldn't tell Iris Mary, 'cause she'll just get on you to give it back.

I said she shore would.

He said well, okay, that's why I come.

He then counted out fifty thousand and put it back in the paper sack. He left the rest on the table.

He drunk his coffee in quiet and went. He shook my hand before he left.

He said oh, and one other thing. Don't let me down on this, Junior. Me and my boy have come to be awful fond of Iris Mary.

I said yeah, she has a way of growin' on people.

I counted out five thousand into a paper sack and then I went got me a burlap bag on the back porch and I put the rest of the money in there and hid it way under our bed. Then I took the five thousand and walked over to the edge of Ville Canard Square where Hank Crochet runs a used car lot. I'd bought my ole banged-up Plymit from Hank when I was rich. I'd planned to get it fixed up all new.

I said Hank, I got five grand and I need somethin' reliable, preferably a truck.

He said Junior, I ain't seen you in a coon's age, podnah. You doin' all right?

I said never better.

He said I read all about you in the papers. Man, that was some shit, huh?

I said yeah, it was.

He said I think I got just the truck you lookin' for.

It was a cherry-red Chevy, about five years old, wit' forty thousand miles on it and one of them camper deals on the back. I knew Iris Mary liked red. I said Hank, if you can make it come out to five thousand, tax, tag, and everything, we got a deal.

He said you still got a license, Junior?

I said I think so but don't worry about that. I ain't drinkin' no more and I'm gonna get all that stuff straightened out.

He said okay, you come back in about two hours.

I picked up my truck and drove back home and got my money sack out from under the bed. I put it on the seat next to me in the truck and I drove out on the Catahoula Swamp Road. When I got to that flophouse where I knew Armentau used to live, I pulled into the parkin' lot. I went in and there was Ridley Grabert, the grumpy ole bastid who was runnin' the place when I stayed there.

He said doggone, Junior, what the hell you doin' here, son? I thought you'd died.

I held up my stumpy hand and picked up my stump of a leg a bit to show him. I said I'm gettin' whittled down slowly but I ain't dead yet, Ridley.

I said where's Armentau?

He said Billy Armentau? That skinny li'l guy with the tattoos all over his arms?

I said yeah, him.

He said Junior, you won't believe it. That bastid had an overdose in my place about six months ago and I thought shore he'd killed his own sorry ass 'cause the ambulance guys who picked him up give up on him 'fore they got him out of here. He was always drunk or stoned or some goddam thing. They'd already pulled the sheet over his head in the hospital, then guess what? That sumbitch threw the sheet off and started hollerin' for Jesus. Scared the hell out of them nurses. Anyway, he come out of it and wouldn't you know, he went straight. Last I heard, he'd moved out to Gibson Bayou and joined some church on the bayouside out there. You know, one of them churches that's got white people and colored and all kinds of weird shit all mixed up together. I hear they hold poisonous snakes and beg them snakes to bite 'em. I'm serious, Junior.

I thanked Ridley and drove off.

Gibson Bayou ain't a big place. It's a spur offa Catahoula Bayou and winds mostly through swamp. Catahoula Bayou got some rich and poor. Gibson Bayou got mostly poor. I drove out there, though I took it slow 'cause it's a bumpy, narrow road. I spied the one church that was on the bayouside, a li'l two-bit cypress shack leanin' toward the bayou wit' a steeple on top. It was a church about like my trailer was a mansion. There was ten or twelve cars in a jumbled-up clamshell parkin' lot. I bounced the truck in there and got out and went to the door. I carried my sack of money wit' me.

I listened.

People were singin'.

I opened the door a bit and there was doggone Armentau. He was at the front. He had his right hand up and his eyes closed and he was singin' his ass off—somethin' about God or whatever.

Armentau, if you ax me, wadn't singin' worth a damn. He had on a black suit wit' a white shirt and a skinny black tie. It's the kind of suit people get buried in.

I pushed through the doors and said, loud as I could, 'scuse me, Billy Armentau? That you, Billy?

Man, Armentau opened his eyes and the few people who were there turned around and I could see that ole Billy knew me like a *bec croche* knows a hungry alligator.

He said Junior Guidry, this is a house of God, and I don't want no trouble.

I said well, I'm here to give you somethin' I owe you.

He said well, I ain't gonna fight you, Junior. I'm done wit' that. I am a man of the Lord.

I said well, that's good, Armentau. That will make it a lot easier for me. It doggone will.

I walked up to the front carryin' my sack and when I got close to Armentau, one of them people in the front row, an ole boy bigger'n me, stepped in front of me. But Armentau held up his hands even higher and said no, my brother, the Lord's will be done. Let us turn the other cheek.

I walked right up to Armentau, then dumped the money, all of it, out on the floor.

I said excuse me, but it's true, like Iris Mary said, that you helped pull my sorry butt up on the rig that day. If you hadn't, I woulda fell off and the sharks woulda eat me just like they ate my leg. Now, I cain't give you all this money, 'cause I got a wife now and a daughter I owe ten thousand dollars to, but I'm gonna give you some of it.

I got down on my knees in the pile of money and I started countin' out the stacks and throwin' them up on the li'l rise that Armentau was standin' on. When I got to five thousand, I figgered that was plenty. I scooped the rest back into my bag and I stood up and said there you go, buddy. Now, don't you go spendin' this all in one place.

Shuh, the look on Armentau's face was better than any look I coulda got if I'd just whacked him wit' a cane knife.

He said why are you doin' this, Junior? What's the trick?

I said I'm just payin' my debts is all. Now, don't expect me to come up there and hug you, 'cause, even though you sober and have got God, you're still butt-ugly. You shore the hell are.

Then I gathered up my sack and slung it over my shoulder and walked outta there like Santa Claus.

You coulda heard a gnat sneeze in that church.

I drove home and went inside and made me some fresh coffee and poured the money out on the table. I sat there all afternoon thinkin' and drinkin' my coffee till I heard Iris Mary come in the house. It was about dark then and she come in the kitchen and said hey, cher, what are you doing sitting here in the dark? And what's that truck doing in our driveway?

I said I'm thinkin'. And that truck's ours.

She turned on the light and said thinking about what?

Then she saw all that money on the table. She said Joseph, what—?

I put up my hand and I said no, cher, I didn't rob a bank. Sit down, 'cause I got a lot to tell you.

Then I tole her everything—about Logan LaBauve comin' over, about me buyin' the truck, about me goin' to track down Armentau, about Armentau bein' a Holy Roller and all, and about me givin' him the five thousand dollars. I said I'm not shore, Iris Mary, that any of what I've done is right but I know it would have been wrong not to tell you about it.

Then Iris Mary got up from the table and walked around me and rummaged through the money like she was lookin' for somethin'. Then she came over and sat on my lap and took my head in her hands and kissed me on the forehead and said I guess we'll need a bank account. I guess we might be able to send our children to college.

I looked up at Iris Mary 'cause that's not exactly what I expected to hear. I said you're not tellin' me you're knocked up, are you?

She said no, I'm not. But, Joseph, the night is young.

I gotta say one thing—that Iris Mary has a way of gettin' ole Junior's britches stirred up.

I said so we're gonna keep the money? I'll give it back if you want me to.

Iris Mary put her arms around my neck and snuggled in and didn't say nuttin' for a good while. Then she said well, Papa Logan was right. Had he given the money to me, I would have turned it in—that's just how I am. But he didn't, and now I couldn't do that without causing lots of problems, mostly for him. After everything he's been through, I think he deserves some peace in his life. And he *is* my relation.

I couldn't argue wit' that and I couldn't think what else to say. So I said you know, Iris Mary, we pro'bly got enough money now to buy a double-wide outright.

She looked at me and had this grin on her face and shook her head and I knew one thing for shore—we wadn't never gonna live in a trailer.

Never.

I said Iris Mary, let's me and you go for a drive in our new truck. To celebrate.

She said okay, where to?

I said anywhere.

Perty soon we were on the New Awlins highway and I realized there *was* somethin' I wanted to see.

We cruised on up to the wide shell parkin' lot of the Holly-wood Bayou Go-Go Bar. I pulled in and saw that big ole neon sign where I knew it would be—lyin' all twisted and broke on the ground. I looked past the sign and saw for a fack that what I'd read in the paper the other day was true. Some ole boys had

driven up in some four-wheel-drive pickup and lassoed that sign
and pulled it to the ground. Later that same night, the bar had
burnt clean to the ground.

The story was written by my podnah Meely LaBauve. It said
the police were lookin' for a gang of big sumbitches who were last
seen haulin' ass way down Bayou Go-to-Hell.

Somebody even said they saw a nun in the car.

Glossary of Cajun Terms

andouille (ohn-doo-EE) — a spicy Cajun pork sausage.

bec croche (beck-CROSH) — an ibis.

boude'd (boo-DAID) — pouty; upset.

boudin (boo-DEHN) — a spicy sausage, often stuffed with pork, rice, and onions; one variety is called "blood sausage."

Cajuns — the modern-day descendants of eighteenth-century French-speaking exiles who were expelled to Louisiana by the British from Canada's Acadia Province during the French and Indian War; more broadly, South Louisiana residents of various ethnic backgrounds who have adopted Cajun speech, customs, and food as their own.

chaque'd (cha-KADE) — drunk or high.

chenier (shin-YERE) — a small, tree-covered island rising from the marsh.

cher — in French, "dear." The Cajuns pronounce this *shah* (short *a*, as in "at") and often use it in hybrid sentences such as, "Mais, cher, how you doin'?"

choupique (SHOO-pick) — also spelled *tchoupique;* alternately a mud fish, bowfin, or grunion. Also a cypress trout.

cochon (co-SHOHN) — a pig.

cochon de lait (co-SHOHN duh lay) — a suckling pig; also a social gathering centered on the roasting of a suckling pig.

coonass — a derogatory term for Cajun.

couillonade (coo-yohn-NOD) — rigamarole.

cou-rouge (coo-ROUGE) — a redneck; literally, "red neck."

crapuleux (crap-uh-LOH) — worthless.

dosgris (DOH-gree) — a small duck ubiquitous in the marshes of South Louisiana.

ehn — the Cajun equivalent of "huh," as in "So, podnah, how you doin', ehn?"

étouffée (ay-too-FAY) — a stew of brown gravy, typically made with crawfish and shrimp.

flottant (flo-TOHN) — in French, "floating" or "buoyant"; in Cajun, a floating marsh.

frissons (free-ZOHNS) — chills; goose bumps.

gaspergou (GAS-per-goo) — alternatively, *casse-burgau;* a freshwater drum named for the cracking sound it makes when it feeds on shellfish.

goggle-eye — a freshwater perch.

gris-gris (gree-gree) — a hex; a curse or spell.

gros-bec (GROW-beck) — a heron.

honte (haunt) — embarrassed.

jambalaya (jam-buh-LY-uh) — a Cajun rice dish similar to paella, often made with shrimp.

"Jolie Blonde" — title of a traditional Cajun ballad.

Laissez les bon temps rouler — "Let the good times roll."

loup garou (loop-ga-ROO) — the Cajun equivalent of the werewolf.

nootra-rat — properly, the nutria, a South American rodent. Introduced accidentally into South Louisiana in the 1950s, it chased the muskrat from much of its native habitat and is now considered a nuisance.

po'boy — the Cajun version of a submarine sandwich, often made with fried shrimp or oysters.

podnah — the Cajun pronunciation of "partner."

pop rouge — strawberry soda.

poule d'eau (POOL-doo) — a coot; literally, a water chicken.

roseaus (ROW-zows) — a thickly clustered, canelike reed found along bayou banks.

sabine (sah-BEAN) — a word of Spanish origin meaning literally "river" but used typically as a pejorative to describe people of mixed American Indian descent.

sac-à-lait (SOCK-oh-lay) — a panfish, specifically a crappie.

sauce piquante (sauce pee-KOHNT) — a spicy Cajun tomato stew, usually made with rabbit, turtle, or chicken.

stingeree (STING-uh-ree) — the Cajun pronunciation of "stingray."

traiteur (thray-TURE) — a healer; in some usages, a witch.

trier (three-AY) — in French, "to pick"; among Cajuns, a fishing term meaning to separate shrimp from trash fish after pulling in the trawl.

zydeco (ZY-dee-co) — a mix of Cajun/Creole music and blues, sung in Louisiana French, in which the accordion is typically the lead instrument.

The author acknowledges as the primary source for these definitions *A Dictionary of the Cajun Language* by the late Reverend Jules O. Daigle, published by Edwards Brothers, Ann Arbor, Michigan, in 1984.

A Guide to Pronunciation

of Cajun Names

Ardoin (ARE-dwehn)
Armentau (AR-men-taw)
Authement (OH-tuh-mohn)
Bergeron (BEAR-zher-rohn)
Bonvillain (BON-vee-lehn)
Boudreaux (BOO-drow)
Cancienne (KAHN-see-ehn)
Chauvin (SHOW-vehn)
Crochet (CROW-shay)
Daigle (deg: alternatively, DAY-gull)
Deshotel (DEZ-o-tel)
Eschete (ESH-tay)
Gaudet (GO-day)
Gautreaux (GO-troh)
Geaux (go)
Giroir (ZHIH-wah)
Grabert (GRAH-bear)
Guidry (GID-dree)
Landrieu (LAN-drew)
LaBauve (le-BOVE)
Mouton (MOO-tohn)
Prosperie (PROS-puh-ree)
Parfait (PAR-fay)
Plauche (PLOH-shay)
Sevin (SAY-vehn)
Soileau (SWAH-low)
Trahan (TRAH-hahn)
Verret (vuh-RETT)

ABOUT THE AUTHOR

KEN WELLS grew up on the banks of Bayou Black, deep in Louisiana's Cajun belt. He got his first newspaper job as a nineteen-year-old college dropout, covering car wrecks and gator sightings for *The Courier,* the Houma, Louisiana, weekly newspaper, while still helping out in his family's snake-collecting business. A career journalist, he was a finalist for the Pulitzer Prize in 1982 and currently is a senior writer and features editor for Page One of *The Wall Street Journal.* He lives with his family on the outskirts of Manhattan. *Junior's Leg* is his second novel.

Visit Ken Wells and Cajun country at:
www.bayoubro.com.

A NOTE ON THE TYPE

This book was set in Fairfield, the first typeface from the hand of the distinguished American artist and engraver Rudolph Ruzicka (1883–1978). In its structure Fairfield displays the sober and sane qualities of the master craftsman whose talent has long been dedicated to clarity. It is this trait that accounts for the trim grace and vigor, the spirited design and sensitive balance, of this original typeface.

Rudolph Ruzicka was born in Bohemia and came to America in 1894. He set up his own shop, devoted to wood engraving and printing, in New York in 1913 after a varied career working as a wood engraver, in photoengraving and banknote printing plants, and as an art director and freelance artist. He designed and illustrated many books, and was the creator of a considerable list of individual prints—wood engravings, line engravings on copper, and aquatints.